The Star Hunters:
Chasing Shadows

K. N. Salustro

DEDICATION

For Mom, Dad, and Jacki, who taught me
how to dream, and to follow even the crazy
ones. For Dakota, who lent his personality and
signature stares to the arkins. And for Ben,
who never let me give up.

CONTENTS

PROLOGUE: HUNT

The leaves rustled softly as Lissa shifted. The roughness of the tree bark pushed through her clothes and the cold night air bit down to her skin, but boredom gnawed at her more than anything else.

Waiting is the worst part.

She pulled her enerpulse pistol out of its holster and examined the weapon. The metal was sleek and dark, not a single mar nicked into the clean surfaces. No chances of a misfire. Lissa pressed the pistol between her knees and cupped her hand over the energy capsule holder. She unlocked the cover and slipped it back. The power source gave off a faint glow, and her black glove gobbled up the soft white light.

The rhyme surfaced automatically: *White-hot, killing shot.*

Lissa slid the cover closed. The lock clicked and she placed the pistol back in its holster. The weapon rested against her hip with an easy familiarity. When Lissa shifted again, pulling her legs close to her body, the pistol shifted with her. Its momentum felt anxious. Hungry, almost. Lissa did not like that feeling. She distracted herself by knuckling her thighs, working the stiffness and the cold out of her muscles. She should have dressed warmer, should have worn an outer layer over the hunting outfit, but that would have called for thicker, heavier

1

clothes prone to catching on the branches. Better to suffer the chill than a fatal snag. As Lissa looked out beyond the tree leaves, she was glad that the air was not quite cold enough to coat the world with frost, but the night was still treacherous.

The full moon hung high in the sky and stained the world silver-gray. The sparse trees stood tall and still, their leaves bleached white. Shadows clung to the tree trunks and the underside of the thickest bunches of leaves, waiting out the midnight hour. Beyond the last lonely trees, the distant shuttles gleamed the color of old bones. The windows of most of the shuttles gaped wide and dark, but there was one vessel with a healthy interior glow. The live shuttle waited for the signal to cast off and head for the starships docked just beyond the atmosphere. That signal wouldn't come until one last passenger had boarded. Lissa waited for that passenger, too.

She stretched her arms and looked wistfully at the shadows beneath the trees. She was in a good sniping position, but the place was unsafe. She had time for one shot, and then she needed to move. The instant she left the shelter of the leaves, she would be caught in the open and the dark hunting clothes would not help her under the glare of the moon. But for that, there was Blade.

Lissa glanced at the branch below hers, at a black patch darker than the surrounding night. The blackness slowly resolved itself as Blade, the arkin that had been with Lissa for years. The arkin lay stretched out along a thick branch, her back legs dangling off the limb. Her front claws were hooked into the bark, and her chin rested on her foreleg. Her wings were folded neatly along her back, but her tail flicked restlessly and the stiff tufts of fur at its tip scraped against the tree bark. The arkin's tail made little more than a faint *hsssp* every time it touched the tree, but the sound was enough to set Lissa on edge. She preferred silence.

"Easy now," Lissa whispered. "Just a little longer."

Blade sighed once, very softly, and her tail fell still.

One quick shot, Lissa thought.

It was always one quick shot. That was how Lissa worked:

clean and fast. She never lingered, never wasted time or let first chances go by. She usually aimed for the head, but the heart or some other soft spot worked just as well when the target did not present itself cleanly. She did not like to draw things out any longer than she had to. The quicker she took down the target, the quicker she got off-planet, collected the bounty, and paid the medical bills.

She was behind in payments. Most of the recent high-paying assassination bounties had surfaced in dangerous territories, either within easy reach of the Star Federation or deep in Anti-Neo-Andromedan strongholds. This bounty was at the very limit of her comfort zone, and the proximity to the Star Federation space station made the target especially dangerous. Taking out an officer was risky enough, but to do it on Earth via long-distance sniping was to slap the Monitors across the face. One quick signal to the station and by dawn the planet would be swarming with Star Fed ships.

With dry amusement, Lissa thought of the target profile broadcasted by the contractor. *Target's smuggling activity,* the profile had said, *interferes with private operations. Vague connection to S.F., bribery suspected. Terminate on sight.*

Lissa translated that as "Kill the problem, reap the reward. If you're smart, investigate the Star Fed connection before acting." Some data sifting revealed that the target was a smuggler of steadily increasing renown. His Star Fed connection was that he was bribing a low-ranking officer, trading goods for a blind eye and a reasonably clear smuggling territory near Earth. More sifting, and Lissa discovered that all of that was the backstory for an undercover Star Federation officer in the field. He had claimed the records of a recently deceased smuggler as an identity boost.

Lissa suspected the contractor had left that detail out in hopes of attracting a sloppy hunter. There was no better way to avoid paying off a bounty than to set the Star Feds on an unskilled hunter. But there always was the chance that someone like Lissa would pick up the trail, and the last thing any contractor wanted was a revenge hunt. Most contractors only broke the scheduled exchange if they knew for certain that the winning hunter no longer roamed the stars. The smart ones never broke exchanges at all.

The way this bounty was set up, the contractor would be waiting at the rendezvous well ahead of schedule with the payment in full, but Lissa had almost withdrawn from the hunt anyway.

She usually passed on the Star Federation contracts. They were few and far between and always offered high bounties, but the last thing Lissa wanted was a captain or a fleet commander honing in on her. This time, however, she was desperate enough to pick up the trail.

Desperate, but not reckless.

She had mapped out the locations of the shuttle area's securities and had practiced the escape flight with Blade until their muscles could flawlessly relive the memory of the motions. There was a ship waiting to take them off-planet as soon as the hunt was over, and Lissa was confident that they'd be able to outrun the Star Feds. Earth was close to the main Star Federation station, but just far enough to give the escaping ship a small crack to slip through. Full evasion would depend on the skill of the transport ship captain, but his reputation as a smuggler preceded him. He'd know how to hide her. Lissa just needed to survive the initial rush of Star Feds and she'd be free and clear, but she never let herself forget that she was holding tight to threadbare luck. One wrong move and everything would unravel.

She couldn't afford to lose this bounty. Aven's life depended on a successful hunt. His treatment had already tapped into the reserve funds and once those dried up, the doctor would be pulled out, and Aven would have a couple of weeks left. Maybe three or four, if he was lucky. Or unlucky, depending on how the disease played out.

He needs you, a voice whispered across the years, *more than you need him. Take care of him.* Lissa was trying, but that had been difficult enough without the virus.

Lissa stretched again and pushed the thought away. She

would have more money and Aven would have more time. His doctor—a man who had fought the medical board for the resources and the chance to save Aven's life, and who had only won after Lissa assured him and the board that she would cover the treatment's cost herself—had promised a breakthrough within the next few months. He said that he felt he was getting close. Lissa wanted to believe him, but knew better. Still, she felt a faint flicker of hope. Although that might not have been rooted entirely in Aven's progress.

Most of her money went towards his treatment, but the remainder was spent on supplies, temporary shelter, and charters between planets. She travelled more than she really needed to. She could have set up a more permanent base and stayed close to Aven, but she never felt at peace if she was still for too long. Sometimes guilt pricked at her, and she wondered if Aven begrudged her long absences. He had to be lonely, but if he was, he tried very hard not to let her see. She doubted that he hid the loneliness for her sake. His pride had always been a bigger stake, sometimes to the point where she felt suffocated by his shadow, but that was not why she travelled.

And she wasn't travelling. She was running. Running as fast as she could, but the money had run faster and now it was almost gone.

Almost there, she thought. *One quick shot.*

Even when Aven had been healthy and strong, their lives had come down to one quick shot. One quick shot had kept them alive once Aven had learned how to stomach taking a life. He had proven to be a very quick learner, and so the Shadow was born.

The Shadow had roamed the galaxy for several sidereal years now, hunting high-bounty targets and always staying just ahead of the Star Feds. One quick shot brought in the much-needed funds for travel, food, and temporary shelter. Eventually, one quick shot bought them *Lightwave*, a small, fast, beautiful starship. When the virus took hold in Aven's lungs, one quick shot funded the treatment after the money from the sale of *Lightwave* had run out.

Five long sidereal years of one quick shots and medical payments and charters to planet after planet after planet had slipped by, and now another payment was due, and now there would be another quick shot. Then there would be the trip to Phan, and the short reunion. Lissa hadn't seen Aven in months, and guilt pricked at her again, although the feeling was growing weaker all the time. Aven did not seem keen on putting the medical funds to good use.

"Physically," the doctor had said, "he's started to improve. Mentally, he is failing, and that will undo everything."

Years of illness had gnawed away at Aven, and he was losing the desire to hold on. Lissa couldn't believe he was giving up now, after all they had been through, but in spite of her pleas and reassurances and occasional bursts of rage, Aven had decided that now was as good a time as any to slip over the line. Part of her wanted to let Aven go, but the rest clung to him. He was her only surviving family member, was all that was left of a life so far away that it felt like someone else's. She wanted to hold on to that past life, but Aven did not care enough to keep a firm grip, and she hated him a little for that. Maybe that was why she had let so much time seep in between hunts.

Take care of him.

Lissa frowned and stretched again, working the cold out of her arms. She reminded herself that the other high-bounty targets had all been in very dangerous territories. Pursuing them would have been suicide. Tonight's hunt was risky but easy, and would be over soon. The target was in sight.

Lissa moved into her sniping position. It was awkward on the tree branch, but she crouched low and quickly found her balance. She drew her enerpulse pistol and sighted along the barrel. She watched her target's vehicle—a bulky but sturdy mess of metal and engine—draw closer, a faint whine growing louder as the craft sped forward. The vehicle slowed as it reached the docking area, and approached the live shuttle at a low, cautious glide. The target's craft paused a short distance from the waiting shuttle, and the shuttle's doors slid open to let the captain emerge. The captain stood in the spilled light from the shuttle's interior and made an annoyed gesture at the target's vehicle, which quickly touched down.

Lissa's grip on her pistol tightened as the vehicle opened its doors and a lone figure emerged. Lissa hesitated just long enough to confirm the target's identity. Then she rolled her shoulders a little to compensate for the distance.

One quick shot—

CHAPTER 1: NAMES

Orion's hard gaze was something Lance was only half-aware of as he sat in his private quarters of the Star Federation space station, staring through the thick pane of unbreakable glass that made up an entire wall of his quarters. The other three walls were dull gray, unornamented and cold. A large cot stood in the corner of the room, a mess of tangled blankets on top. There was a padded mat in another corner where Orion slept. Save for the large hover chair that Lance sat in, there was nothing else in the room. The place even smelled sterile, but Lance had grown used to that. With the exception of Orion's bed, Lance had never needed anything other than what the Star Federation provided. His clothes were stored in a small closet built into one of the walls and so well hidden that the seam of the cabinet was invisible. Lance had no other possessions. Born and raised on the Star Federation station, he was used to this kind of life. There had been a time when he had hated living like this, but those days were long over now. He also spent so little time in his quarters that the state of his room did not matter. And when he did stay on the station for extended times, he was content with the cot, the chair, and the view of the stars.

Lance often sat staring out at space, losing himself in his

thoughts. Every so often, a starship would streak across the field but Lance would only give them passing glances if he looked at them at all. Today, Lance looked in the direction of Earth. He would be headed there soon, and after uncovering an unsettling clue in the Coleman murder case, he was not looking forward to the journey. He had been staring towards Earth for the better part of an hour now, growing more and more uneasy as the time slunk away.

Stand and Protect.

Tail twitching in irritation, Orion whined and tapped Lance's leg with a paw.

"Knock it off," Lance said without breaking his level stare at the stars. "You're not that bored."

Orion groaned loudly, but walked away and stretched before lying down and closing his eyes.

Lance looked out into space for a moment longer, then sat back and lifted his datapad. He studied the three displayed images. Two of them were dark and blurry, and it was impossible to see any definite details. The third, however, showed the bounty hunter commonly called the Starcat bright and clear. She crouched on the edge of a building, poised to leap, and looked back over her shoulder, surprise and rage boiling in her eyes. She had survived the jump and evaded capture, but the damage had been done. The Star Federation knew her face.

The Starcat had the habit of stalking her prey for days before moving in for the final strike. She enjoyed forcing her targets into fits of paranoia, and loved toying with their fear. She wasn't the only bounty hunter that mixed work with play, but her physical characteristics made her unique and proved that the name "Starcat" was not solely based on her behavior. Her body was humanoid, but her face was distinctly feline, complete with a set of long white whiskers and a catlike nose. She also boasted a wicked set of fangs and clawed hands and feet that served as her weapon of choice over energy-pulse firearms; many of her targets were found with deep slashes in their bodies, and missing limbs were not uncommon. She only used an enerpulse pistol or rifle when she couldn't get close enough to use her claws. That rarely happened.

"What do you think," Lance said as he turned the datapad, showing Orion the Starcat's picture. "Cross her off the list?"

The arkin looked at the picture, snorted, and pulled the corner of his mouth back into a half snarl. His yellow eyes flashed, hard and bright against the slash of black fur across his brow.

"I thought so."

The Starcat was a very skilled assassin, but she had slipped up and her latest target had escaped. The target, a human male badly shaken by his time as prey, had delivered to the Star Federation a scrap of hair torn off the Starcat in a struggle. With the Starcat fully identified and traceable, Commander Keraun had lunged after her trail. Lance had contacted Keraun just a few short hours ago, and learned that Keraun's squad had found fresh leads and was beginning to close in. The Starcat was nowhere near Earth and Captain Coleman's murder site.

Lance looked away from the Starcat and focused on one of the dark, blurry images. A few vague details separated one fuzzy picture from the other, but Lance had studied both so closely that he could tell them apart at a quick glance.

The first image showed a glimpse of the Phantom, one of the deadliest bounty hunters to ever roam the galaxy. The hunter lived up to his name. After he struck, he evaporated into the unknown and was not seen again until his next target had been chosen. The Star Federation had picked out a few dark, blurred images of him from security feeds, but all this really showed was the hunter's lack of fear and his ruthlessness. He liked to get close to his targets and confront them directly before taking them out, and he never seemed to go after live bounties. Not from what the Star Federation could tell, at least. Every Phantom target that the Star Federation knew of was deceased.

Aside from the behavior brand, the Star Federation knew

only two facts about the Phantom: the hunter was male, and he traveled with a large arkin. The species of the Phantom's traveling companion had been known for the past few sidereal years, but despite their best efforts, field soldiers and Intelligence members alike had failed to learn any additional information about the Phantom's arkin. Thanks to Orion, Lance had been put on the squad that performed the field investigation, but even with his knowledge and Orion's help, all that the squad had learned was that the Phantom's arkin was just as elusive as the hunter himself. Orion was able to pick up on the scent of the Phantom's arkin at each hit site, but the trails always went cold and there wasn't even a scrap of fur waiting at the end. Sometimes there were paw prints and claw marks, but these revealed nothing other than the animal's impressive size.

Looking at his datapad now, Lance knew that he would not discover anything new about the Phantom. He wasn't upset about that. He would not need more information about that particular hunter. Not today.

The final image on the datapad offered even less information about the featured bounty hunter. Unlike the Starcat, the Shadow left no trail to follow. Unlike the Phantom, the Shadow kept well away from all targets. Glimpsed or not by survivors or security devices, he or she immediately slipped away after each hit. Nothing was known about the hunter, no physical description or trademark other than keeping a disturbingly impressive gap between him or herself and the target. The Shadow never wasted time, never wasted chances, and never wasted shots. The hunter's sniping abilities were legendary, rivaled perhaps only by the Phantom. The Phantom had the most hits, but the Shadow held the record for the greatest distance.

The Shadow was one of the newer hunters on the top of the Star Federation's list of Alpha Class criminals. Lance had not thought that the hunter was bold enough to go after a Star Federation soldier just yet, let alone a captain, but the Shadow had never conformed to what were considered to be the traditional rules of the bounty hunting game. The Shadow had gone after high-bounty targets from the very start of his or her career, attracting a lot of attention before gaining experience. But the hunter also let long periods of inactivity slip in between jobs. Five sidereal years ago, there had been a shift in the Shadow's pattern, and the strikes became somewhat less common and pulled within a shorter radius, but there were still surprisingly long lapses between targets, which meant only one thing: the Shadow hunted for money and nothing else.

Most bounty hunters paralleled the Starcat and the Phantom, taking time to torment their targets and trademark their hits. But not the Shadow. That hunter was in the game strictly on business. Lance knew that if he could get one small clue about that business, he would have the chance to come closer than anyone ever had to capturing the Shadow. But that was too much to hope for.

Lance sighed tiredly and lowered the datapad. "Maybe we'll learn a bit more today."

Orion blinked at him.

"Coleman was an idiot," Lance said, "and I have no idea how the hell he secured his rank with all those shady stories tied to him, but let's make sure he didn't die for nothing, yeah?"

Orion growled softly in agreement. And with that, Lance's communicator came alive.

Lance accepted the transmission, and a holographic projector in the little machine displayed the head and upper torso of a member of the Intelligence Unit. No matter how many times he spoke with one of the many Yukarian members of the Intelligence Unit, Lance was always unprepared for the large, glittering black eyes that fixed on him. A pair of long antennae sprouted from the Yukarian's angular skull just above the eyes and matched the bluish-grey skin of the rest of the Intelligence member's face, although age had stained the tips of this Yukarian's antennae a deep blue.

"I apologize for the delay, Commander Ashburn," the Yukarian said, his voice a deep rasp. "There were a few files that needed my attention, and then Captain Backélo wished to speak with me. I hope you are not too inconvenienced?"

Lance stiffened at Backélo's name. "What did the captain discuss with you?"

"Captain Backélo requested to see any new data that had come in. He said that he wanted to know exactly what was important enough to warrant the attention of all captains serving under you, Commander Ashburn. I'm afraid he was very persistent, but as per your instructions, I refused to give any information and told him that you would explain everything in the mission briefing." The Yukarian's antennae twitched. "He did not seem pleased."

"I don't suppose he mentioned having his crew together?"

"He did not, Commander."

"Wonderful," Lance said, wondering how Backélo could have found the time to prod around the Intelligence Unit.

Backélo was one of the five captains accompanying Lance to Earth and, like the other four officers, was supposed to be preparing for the voyage. He needed to assemble a squadron and see to the initial preparations of his assigned ship before reporting to the briefing room. Enough time had been allotted to the captains for that, but just barely. Lance himself had managed to finish his own tasks a little earlier than he had thought he would, and he had decided to review the evidence from the Intelligence Unit. He wasn't surprised by the delayed response from the Yukarian, but the news about Backélo angered him.

If Backélo holds me up, I'll have him patrolling the trade routes.

It was one of the harsher punishments. Patrollers kept a lookout for bold pirate fleets that sabotaged radars and made runs on merchant starships, but for the most part, the task was slow, monotonous, and draining. Trade route patrollers often limped back to the Star Federation space station physically and mentally exhausted, even when they worked in teams and undertook the task in shifts.

Backélo will work alone if he's not at the briefing.

"What did you wish to discuss, Commander?" the

Yukarian asked, bringing Lance out of his cloud of anger.

"I need confirmation on something," Lance said. His voice was tinged with heat, but he brought himself under control. "Bring up the shuttle dock security footage from Earth. Watch very closely after the camera swings around."

As the Yukarian brought the recording up, Lance activated his own copy of the recording on his datapad. A hologram projection came up and displayed the last few moments of Captain Coleman's life. For what felt like the hundredth time, Lance watched Coleman's transport vehicle as it came to a halt and hovered in front of the shuttle. The shuttle doors opened and Lance watched as the shuttle captain stepped out.

"Let's go," the shuttle captain growled, waving at Coleman's vehicle. "We've waited long enough for you."

Coleman's transport touched down. The door opened, and the Star Federation officer stepped out alone. He stood looking at the shuttle captain, his skin bleached white and his copper-colored hair turned a bizarre shade of red by the moonlight. Coleman wore heavy traveler's clothes and carried a pack slung over his shoulder. He was ragged and dirty, but he stood tall and his shoulders were squared. He looked relieved to be boarding the shuttle. He took a step forward, and disappeared in a flash of white. The light was there for only an instant, and then Coleman was falling to the ground, half of the side of his skull exposed and blackened, and the edges of his remaining skin scorched. The camera abruptly whipped around and focused on a few sparse trees that bordered the shuttle docking area. Lance heard the shuttle captain's startled and then horrified cries, but the trees remained the focus for the remainder of the security footage.

"I don't see what you're talking about, Commander," the Yukarian said after the recording had ended.

"It's subtle," Lance said, "very subtle, but it's there. Watch the shadows around the base of the tree on the far left of the recording just after the camera switches."

The Yukarian's head turned as he replayed the footage. After a while, he opened his mouth to say something, but froze and let the words die. "I see it, Commander." The Yukarian's antennae twitched. "How did you think to look there?"

"Call it a combination of desperation and a lot of luck. Also known as intuition."

The Yukarian did not laugh. "The shadow is too large to be that of an Earth bird," he said. "Perhaps I can determine the actual shape." The Yukarian worked in silence, and made a clicking noise when he had finished. "This does not look like anything to me, but does the shape have any meaning for you, Commander?"

Lance's communicator beeped, and a second hologram flickered into sight. It showed the shadow from the security footage, but from what the Yukarian had calculated to be an aerial view. Lance studied the shape. "It's what I thought it would be," he said.

"How so?"

"It has wings, and a body large enough to support a passenger. Check the infrared levels for the source."

The Yukarian's antennae twitched. "You do not seem to need me, Commander."

"I said I wanted confirmation," Lance said. "Please confirm or refute."

The Yukarian studied him for a moment, then turned and began to work again. Lance adjusted his own hologram and displayed the infrared levels. There were a few bright blotches throughout the image, most likely birds or bats, but there was one on the far left that was a little bigger and brighter than the others. It had been dismissed as nothing more than a bird a little closer to the camera, but Lance had seen the shape of the shadow it cast. His projected aerial view of the shadow had been considerably rougher than the Yukarian's, but it was close enough.

"Based on the height from the ground," the Yukarian said, "and the angle of the light, I have a few rough figures for the size of the source."

Lance's communicator beeped and displayed an image of the source in infrared framed by numerical calculations. Lance read the data, and then nodded. His own results had not been far off.

"The data suggests a large creature," the Yukarian continued. "Winged, it would seem, just as you said. But there are a number of creatures that could fit these proportions, if they are accurate."

"They're accurate," Lance said. He stood up and moved to Orion's side. He wrapped his arm around Orion's neck and pulled the arkin into the communicator's range. "This is the species." Orion blinked at the Yukarian, then yanked his head free. "What we need now is the individual. Which bounty hunters travel with an arkin?"

The Yukarian reached up and ran a three-fingered hand along one of his antennae. "Most notably, the Phantom. He is the only one on the Alpha Class list, however. There are a few assassins in the lower tiers that travel with arkins, but I doubt any would have pursued a Star Federation officer, and certainly not with this degree of finesse."

"Very true," Lance said. "Which makes the Phantom our bounty hunter. Or it would, if that was the Phantom's arkin."

The Yukarian's antennae twitched violently. "We have no data on the Phantom's arkin, Commander Ashburn. How can you—"

Lance cut across him. "I've seen the paw prints left by the Phantom's arkin. That beast is very heavy, and very powerful. The data from the security footage cannot match that arkin. The arkin we're dealing with now is smaller and lighter, but a lot quicker. Unless the Phantom is terribly underweight, this beast would never be able to carry him."

The Yukarian traced his antennae with a finger again. "But what more does that reveal? You have determined the Phantom is not the one who assassinated Coleman, but there are no other Alpha Class criminals who travel with arkins." He paused thoughtfully. "I suppose a lesser hunter could have taken the assignment, but..."

"But none of them would have gone after a captain as their first Star Federation target," Lance finished. "Even if they had not broken though Coleman's backstory, the Star Federation connection should have warded them off. So it must have been a reputable hunter. And," he glanced at the infrared display, "after seeing how well this hunter's managed to keep hidden, and how far away they were when they took the shot, we know for certain that the hunter has a lot of experience and skill. That makes me think of the Shadow."

The Yukarian's antennae twitched again. "The Shadow does not travel with an arkin, Commander."

"Not that we know of, but we know very, very little of the Shadow. Traveling with an arkin would explain a few things about the hunter, especially how he or she is able to escape so quickly after each hit."

"There are other explanations for that, Commander."

Lance's temper flared. "If you have them, by all means, share them. I would love to know that I'm not sending my soldiers chasing after one of the deadliest and most unpredictable bounty hunters in the galaxy, but it looks like I'm doing exactly that. And there's no use in denying it, because when they have to come up against the hunter, they might survive a few seconds longer if they're warned than if they charge in blind."

The Yukarian looked unblinkingly at him for a long time. "I confirm the identity of the hunter as the Shadow, Commander Ashburn," was all he said when he finally broke the silence. Then he broke the transmission.

The hologram flickered and faded, and Lance threw the communicator across the room. It hit the far wall and rebounded with a *click* before falling to the floor.

Lance dropped to the floor next to Orion. He leaned against the arkin and put his hand on the beast's head. The arkin's gray fur was thick beneath his fingers, soft but tough. He rubbed Orion just behind the ears, and the arkin slitted his eyes in pleasure.

"I need a break," Lance said. Orion grunted, and Lance lightly tugged one of the arkin's ears. They both knew that was not going to happen.

After a few more minutes on the floor, Lance pushed himself to his feet. Orion rose with him, and they crossed the room. Just before they stepped through the door, Lance bent down and picked up his communicator. It was undamaged. That did not make him feel any better.

CHAPTER 2: REDEMPTION

Jason had just finished choosing his squadron and overseeing the initial preparations of his assigned starship when Commander Ashburn's message about the change in the mission briefing came through. Ashburn said he had reason to speak to all of his captains, not just the ones accompanying him to Earth. He left it at that.

The commander sounded urgent but calm, and Jason found that he was far from worried despite all the warning signals. Nothing but Alpha activity could warrant the attention of all of a fleet commander's captains, but Jason could not bring himself to worry. He was looking forward to the mission.

Jason had recently returned from the Andromeda Reach, an outer arm of the Milky Way that had once been home to some of the richest planets in the galaxy, but became a haven for renegades after the Andromedan War. Fear of a full-scale intergalactic invasion had chased the merchants and most of the civilians out of the region, and the Reach had decayed. Fifty sidereal years of silence from beyond the fringes of the Milky Way failed to calm any fears, and the Reach became prime territory for smugglers, pirates, black marketeers, and drug lords. The Star Federation had begun patrolling the Andromeda Reach in recent years, but barely a dent had been made in the area. There was still too much fear of an Andromedan attack to garner any support for a widespread cleanup of the Reach.

The Andromedan War had been several years in the past when Jason was born, but he grew up with the failed Andromedan army and the gallantry of the young Star Federation as staples in his history lessons.

The last of three children born to wealthy spice merchants, Jason had been put through piloting school and his talent had caught the eye of a Star Federation recruiter. Jason and so many space-born humans like him had eagerly joined the Star Federation in order to keep their galaxy safe from future attacks, but as intergalactic peace dragged out, intragalactic struggles began anew and the Star Federation became the police force of the Milky Way. The Reach, however, remained as a reminder of what lurked across the void between galaxies, and the Star Federation eventually decided that the Andromeda Reach needed to become a symbol of security rather than one of fear. Jason was one of the officers who had volunteered to begin the "renovations," as the Star Federation soldiers often referred to the raids on the renegades.

Jason had just returned from a month-long stay in the Reach, leading hunts for pirates and smugglers. His company had consisted of seasoned soldiers at first, but a lot of them had been replaced by cadets fresh out of training near the end of the renovation. Renegades were often dangerous for merchant or civilian starships running the trading routes, but those same renegades fled from Star Federation crafts. The exceptions either perished or limped away from the dogfights. The Star Federation kept its ships outfitted with advanced weapons and thrust drives, giving the pilots all the advantages they could ever want or need in a dogfight.

Out in the Andromeda Reach, Jason's personal agenda had been interrupted by an assignment to take a few cadets on a first-mission run. It was a simple task, and Jason had been given the assignment simply because there was no other field training available for the new soldiers. There had been a lull across the galaxy, and the areas that usually held easy targets for untried cadets had fallen quiet. Commander Ashburn had finally sent the cadets to the Reach, and asked Jason to take them through their first real mission.

And then Ashburn gave me the worst cadet in the universe.

The cadet in question had proven unfit for the field, had been terror-stricken at the thought of seeing battle. How he had managed to pass the Star Federation's examinations was a mystery.

Someone needs to check that test, Jason thought. *Or court-martial whoever let that kid join the ranks.*

Family history tying the cadet to an esteemed admiral would keep the latter from ever coming to fruition, but there was no excuse for what had happened on the mission.

The cadets had been stealthily transported to the Andromeda Reach, and Jason had met them at a Star Federation outpost planet. From there, they took a large ship into the Reach and began scanning. On the main ship's tracker, they picked up on several renegade crafts lurking on the outskirts of an asteroid field and the small, individually operated fleet of fighter starships was released. The main ship sent out a signal to sabotage the trackers of the renegade ships, and the fighters moved in. Jason led the strike, bringing the cadets in a silent glide through the field. The targets had been unaware of their stalkers until one fighter prematurely opened fire.

Jason had watched the guilty ship closely, looking for signs of unease. To his surprise, his least favorite cadet had kept the ship on a steady course, never once allowing the vessel to break formation or even shudder. Thinking that his initial judgment of the cadet had been wrong, Jason called the fleet into action. He finished his order just as the cadet's grip on the controls slipped and the fighter dove at an asteroid.

Startled but calm, the cadet tried to bring the ship back on course. A hand accidentally brushed the sensitive weapons controls, and the asteroid perished in a burst of dust. That was the cadet's explanation, at least. Jason's version of the story was summed up by two words: fucking moron.

The speed at which the renegade vessels disappeared was truly amazing. For one tense moment, their ships hovered among the asteroids. And the next, the renegades sent their ships sprinting through the field and were lost.

Jason could not lead a follow-up hunt. Sending untrained cadets after renegades in a wild pursuit through an asteroid field would be sending them to their death. He was guaranteed to lose a few cadets at the very least; if the asteroids did not prove deadly, then any lurking enemy ships would. With that knowledge resting heavily on his mind, Jason let the renegades go.

He looked for another group of renegades, hoping to make up for the failed run. He found none. Word that the Star Federation was on the hunt had spread, and the Andromeda Reach suddenly became a very quiet place. A few brave trade ships were the only crafts Jason's squad regularly encountered. Out of boredom, Jason continued to take the cadets out in the fighters and train them in basic maneuvers and formations. There was only one tense moment when a small cloud of renegade starships appeared and went after the cadets during a practice run. Jason led the counterstrikes and showed the young soldiers how he had earned his reputation as a pilot. He had never been on the losing side of a dogfight in his entire career.

Even with that reputation behind him, however, Jason's training mission had been a complete failure and his return to the space station had been a shameful one. No one outright mocked him, but Jason sensed a shift in the way soldiers around the station looked at him, even the lower ranking ones. Ashburn had said nothing about the failed mission, and had simply contacted him a few days later with orders to get a squad together for a new mission.

Jason had felt a prick of annoyance at Ashburn's decision to ignore the failure. He would have preferred to have the problem acknowledged so he could have the chance to redeem himself, but this next mission would give him the opportunity to do just that. As he moved through the space station to the lifts that would bring him up to the deck of the briefing room, Jason's stride was eager and confident.

The lift ride was stretched by a few stops, and Jason grudged each of them as soldiers filed in and out of the transport, but the doors finally slid open for him and he leapt out. He was halfway down the long hall when he heard another set of lift doors open behind him. He glanced back, recognized the captain emerging, and walked off as fast as he could without breaking into a run. He had almost reached the briefing room door when Captain Backélo's voice rang out, smooth and cold. "Hey, Stony! Hold up!"

Jason groaned, but stopped and turned to meet the oncoming soldier.

A native of the planet Rhyut and a member of one of the bizarre human-hybrid races left over from Earth's early and highly experimental First-Contact era, Backélo stood almost a full head taller than Jason's six feet. His skin was a pale cream color while his eyes and hair were blacker than a moonless night. The strands of his hair were thicker than human hair, more like lengths of coated wire than hair, and today he wore it tied at the base of his neck in a low ponytail that hung halfway down his back in a thick cord. With his hair drawn back from his face, his odd, elongated eyes were exaggerated, and the slitted blue pupils had a shifty look to them.

Jason could have disliked Backélo based on his sneaking, devious eyes alone, but the crowning glories were the cocky grin that often stretched across the Rhyutan's taught, bony face as well as his enjoyment for dragging others into endless, one-sided discussions. Backélo's grin was particularly sly today. Jason could think of no reason for that, but he was content to remain ignorant.

I'm going to regret not walking into that room when I had the chance.

Jason was surprised by the levelness of his own voice when he said, "Hello, Captain Backélo." He usually did not try to hide his disdain for the Rhyutan. Backélo never seemed to care, however, and was happy to talk at Jason if no one else was available, and sometimes even when several others were around.

He likes torture, Jason thought. *That's the only explanation. He knows I'd rather slam my head against the wall than listen to him.*

"So, Stony," the Rhyutan began, "did you hear what happened?" Backélo continued on without pausing for breath. "A bounty hunter struck again. Went after one of our own this time. Ashburn just can't control them, which really isn't surprising. Bounty hunters respect only what they fear, and Ashburn's nothing to fear."

Jason grunted absently. *I could have pretended I didn't hear him and just walked through the door. Wouldn't have been that difficult.*

Backélo abruptly changed tactics. "So, Stony, I heard you were in the Andromeda Reach for a while."

Immediately, the indifference fell away, replaced by a cold guard as Jason focused on the Rhyutan.

Backélo's grin widened. "You were hunting renegades, weren't you? Catch any?"

"No," Jason replied flatly. "Had a cadet in the fleet wh—"

"Blaming your subordinates, Stony?" Backélo's eyes glinted, and the bizarre blue pupils narrowed to even smaller slits. "Not exactly a valiant way to cover up your own screw ups, is it?"

A voice cut in before Jason could answer. In a way, the interruption was a saving grace. Jason did not know how much longer he could stand listening to Backélo before he silenced the Rhyutan with a fist. Jason probably would have become a celebrated hero for that, but very few of the higher-ranking officers would have seen him in that light. Ashburn was not one of those few. The knowledge did not stop a spike of hatred for the newcomer, but the feeling faded almost immediately.

"That's never stopped you," the new voice said coolly.

Jason glanced over his shoulder and his anger melted away as he recognized Erica. She stood close to Jason's side, just beyond his shoulder, but she stepped around him and said, "Whose fault was it this time that you missed catching your drug dealer, Captain Backélo?" She was two heads shorter than the Rhyutan, but her eyes were calm and fearless as she stared up at him. "What's that, the sixth time he's gotten away from you? Or are you still saying it's just the third?"

Backélo looked back at her with obvious rage. He clenched his fists and flexed his muscles, tensed as though ready to hit her. Jason shifted, and the Rhyutan felt Jason's cold stare. He kept his eyes locked on Erica, however, and held her gaze for a moment longer. Then he gave her a smile that was more like a snarl, whipped around and skulked past Jason into the briefing room. The door snapped shut behind him.

Erica let her breath out in a disbelieving whisper. She looked at Jason and he felt a small charge of excitement. He hadn't seen her in a while, not since before his mission in the Andromeda Reach, and he realized he had not fully remembered what she looked like. She was paler than he had thought she was, and fatigue pulled at her eyes, but she was still beautiful. Her hair shone bright yellow under the light, and her eyes were muddy brown, but there was a softness to them that Jason had always liked. Her skin was smooth, but a few lines were taking hold around her mouth. Jason didn't care, though, and she didn't seem to think he was any worse for wear either. When he pulled her to him and lowered his head, she returned his kiss.

"Nice to see you too," she said when he finally released her.

Jason smiled at her. "Thanks for scaring Backélo off, but I could have handled him."

"Without words, you mean," Erica said, and she lightly punched him in the shoulder. "Sorry, but we can't have any fighting among soldiers, Captain Stone. If you want to hit someone, get back in the field."

"I might get to do that soon enough. Ashburn's sending me out to Earth."

"I've got the Earth run, too," Erica said. She smiled, but it faded quickly. "Do you have any idea what happened? I tried to find out but the higher officers have orders from the admirals themselves to keep it closed. No one lower than a fleet commander has any idea what happened, which can only mean one thing, of course."

"That we're dealing with an Alpha, yeah."

By Erica's gaze, Jason knew that he'd hit an answer, but not the one she was thinking of. She looked at him for a long, silent moment. "It also means they don't want the news getting out."

"Right. And aside from the fact that they think we're going to run and tell the entire galaxy, that tells us what?"

Erica looked away thoughtfully. "It could be almost anything, but if they're only trusting the high ranks, it's bad."

"We've dealt with bad, but either way, we should get in there. Don't want to piss Ashburn off by walking in late."

Erica reached up and kissed him again. "All right." Then she led the way into the briefing room.

The room buzzed with a dozen different conversations, most in the Galactic Unified Voice, but there were a few spoken in languages outside of Galunvo. Jason's trained ear picked up on a few snatches of the conversations, but the voices drowned each other out and what he heard was a confused mess of rumors and theories. He quickly gave up trying to figure out the direction of any single discussion and he and Erica slipped side-by-side into their seats. Erica was immediately pulled into a conversation with the captain on her other side, leaving Jason free. He glanced around the room, decided to keep himself out of the discussions, and surveyed the other captains.

The gathered officers were a wild mix of races. Those with skin ranged in color from red to blue and everything in between. Those with scales or fur were just as diverse. Some of the captains had patterns on their bodies: stripes, spots, whorls, zigzags, blotches, and one with what looked like flames to Jason, although they were pale turquoise in color. Some of the captains had horns, some extra limbs, some special breathing devices. The only common elements were the dark gray Star Federation uniforms emblazoned with the small red-and-gold captain insignias.

Jason rolled his gaze over each captain. They were all engrossed in their discussions and no one returned his glance. Even the hologram projections of the captains currently absent from the space station were deep in conversation with their neighbors. All of them were offering their own theories on what had happened.

Jason drummed his fingers on the tabletop, wondering where Ashburn was and how much longer the commander would keep them waiting. All of the captains were assembled.

Almost all, Jason realized as his gaze hit an empty seat. *Coleman's late. As usual.*

Coleman often walked into briefings late. He never seemed to have a solid excuse for it, just that he was always busy with something vague. Ashburn was not one to take disrespect lightly, and Coleman was a regular patroller of the trade routes. The captain did not seem to care, though, and Jason often wondered if he secretly preferred the patrols to the more dangerous fieldwork. Several captains had thrown around the idea that he had struck a deal with one of the larger and more successful pirate crews, getting a cut of their prize for turning a blind eye on their strikes. The theory wasn't all that farfetched, and it did explain Coleman's steady increase in wealth. Everyone knew that he must have been getting the funds for his new real estate ventures somewhere other than his Star Federation salary. Whether Ashburn saw any truth to those rumors or not, he had finally sent Coleman out on a real assignment, the captain's first in nearly a full sidereal year.

Bastard will probably skip the briefing altogether. Jason sat back in his seat. *Bet his excuse is he got into a wrestling match with an Ametrian.*

Before Jason could imagine how Coleman would fair in that matchup, the briefing room door opened and the room fell silent. Jason rose with the rest of the captains and saluted Commander Ashburn as he took his place at the head of the table. His gray arkin Orion stood next to him and regarded the captains with hard, bright yellow eyes.

Ashburn returned their salute and the captains sat again. He looked around the room, and Jason saw his eyes pause at Coleman's empty seat before moving on.

Trade routes again, Jason thought as he studied the commander's expression. *Definitely.*

Ashburn finished surveying the captains, but instead of speaking he looked down at his datapad. He stared at the thin machine for a long time.

Jason had never seen Ashburn do this before. Usually, the man was calm and confident, obviously secure in his rank. Grudgingly, Jason admitted to himself that Ashburn was a natural-born leader, and he'd been bred for command. Both of his parents had been Star Federation officers, and Ashburn had grown up with the promise of a military career secured in his future. When he was sixteen years old, he had bolted from the station and disappeared without a trace, but just shy of two years later, he had returned with Orion in tow and a burning desire to begin training as a Star Federation soldier. But that did not change the fact that Ashburn was rebellious, radical, and only twenty-eight years old—four years younger than Jason.

Jason had needed to fight for recognition throughout his life. As the youngest of three siblings, his older brother and sister had constantly overshadowed him. Whatever the Stone siblings did, they did together, and Daniel and Ranae had excelled at almost everything. Almost. Daniel had come home one day with the wild desire to undergo fighter starship pilot training. All three siblings had been enrolled in separate classes, but Jason had outperformed both of the older Stones and advanced well ahead of them. Triumphing over Daniel and Ranae had been sweet, but Jason had discovered that he loved piloting all the way through to his core, and he had embraced his calling while his brother and sister found their own. Daniel eventually went on to take over the Stone family's merchant business, Ranae settled on a wealthy planet and started an architectural firm with her partner Tomás Ramirez, and the Star Federation extended an enthusiastic invitation to Jason. By the time Jason graduated into the ranks, he had lost contact with the forever-busy Daniel. Ranae kept in touch, however, and by the time Jason was wearing a cadet's uniform, she had designed three major buildings in the planet's capital, married Tomás, and been pregnant with their first child. Hers was a happiness that was forbidden to Star Federation soldiers, but Ranae had told Jason that she was proud of him. Somehow, that had been enough, and Jason had jumped eagerly into his career. Then Ashburn had come along.

Back when Jason had been a lieutenant, Ashburn had been under his command after emerging from training as a nineteen-year-old cadet. Orion had accompanied him through training, and Ashburn had been granted permission to keep the beast with him at all times. He was not the first Star Federation soldier to keep an arkin, but Jason had been wary of Orion all the same. Jason had, however, recognized Ashburn's skills as a soldier and trusted him to keep Orion under control.

Of course, even then, Jason had also known that Ashburn was the type to only follow the orders he wanted to. And unfortunately for Jason, Ashburn had happened to disagree with almost every order he was given, but still managed to make all the right moves at all the right moments. What Jason called luck, his superiors had called bravery, initiative, and intelligence. Ashburn had been promoted to lieutenant by the end of his first year in the Star Federation. He and Jason had remained equals for the next couple of years, and they had worked alongside each other under Captain Moranth. Jason had not enjoyed working with Ashburn and often thought that he was reckless and relied on his arkin too much, but Jason had to admit that he would have done the same with Orion at his side.

The arkin was a large and powerful feline beast that boasted unbelievably keen senses of sight, hearing, and smell. His body was lithe and hard muscle rippled beneath his gray coat. He moved fast when running and even faster while in flight; the set of wings just behind his forelegs were large and strong, capable of supporting Ashburn's weight for hours at a time. Wicked claws tipped his four paws and his fangs were sturdy and sharp.

Orion was made all the more impressive by his battle scars: a slash across his left foreleg and an enerpulse burn on his left flank near his back leg. The burn was an old injury that predated Ashburn's Star Federation days, however, and the fur had grown back long ago, although it remained darker and rougher than the rest of his coat. Orion had undeniably helped keep Ashburn alive in the field, and Jason often tried to convince himself that the arkin was the reason why Ashburn had been chosen to fill Captain Moranth's rank when that officer had been promoted.

But there was more to it than just Orion. Even on his own, Ashburn was a very valuable soldier. He was strong, smart, and knew when to send his squads in and when to pull them back out. He was reckless when operating alone, but as a leader, he was levelheaded and never sent soldiers on suicide runs. He always left the most dangerous work for himself. Jason had initially thought that Ashburn was glory-hungry, maybe looking to immortalize his name, but after serving under Captain and later Fleet Commander Ashburn, Jason knew that that was not the case at all. Ashburn cared about his subordinates. And his subordinates cared about him, although in a few soldiers' cases, Jason thought it was less his reputation and more his blond hair, green eyes, and broad shoulders. Stress lines had appeared at the corners of the commander's eyes and mouth, dark against his light skin, but they were faint and he still looked young. Jason often felt the urge to trip him, just to shatter the perfection for a moment.

If I had to spend a year patrolling the trade routes, it would be worth it, Jason thought. He fought the urge to smile, but the grin died as Ashburn suddenly spoke.

"You all are here because of an incident that happened on Earth earlier today." The commander began to work with his datapad, but he did not look up. "The Earth Monitors have managed to keep it quiet, but we are taking no chances. We have kept this secret because we do not want a mass panic in the area, and we do not want word getting out that the Star Federation is sending a small fleet to Earth with the sole purpose of finding and capturing or killing the one responsible." Ashburn raised his eyes. "No matter what, you are ordered to keep silent about this mission. Those making the Earth run, inform your subordinates when you are closing in on your target, and *only* your target. Word cannot get out. One small leak, and the target will escape in the chaos. We may never have a chance like this again."

There was an uneasy ripple across the room, but resolve hardened as Star Federation experience kicked in and the captains leaned a little closer to Ashburn.

"We were lucky the target chose to act on Earth, and that the Monitors were able to contact us almost immediately after the strike. They have been watching all starships around Earth, and we have a total of five crafts targeted. Those of you who are accompanying me, we leave to intercept as soon as the station crews have finished outfitting our ships."

Ashburn activated his datapad and slid it across the table. It skidded to a halt near the middle, almost directly in front of Jason. A large, spherical hologram flickered into focus, showing a bulky transport vehicle speeding forward over moonlit ground.

"This," Ashburn said, "is the security footage we received from a shuttle dock on Earth. The camera was positioned just over the shuttle door."

The bulky vehicle slowed as it approached the camera and glided to a halt. There was a soft *whoosh* as the shuttle doors beneath the camera opened and the captain stepped out. "Let's go," the shuttle captain growled, waving at the transport.

The vehicle touched down and its doors opened. Several onlookers shifted in their seats as Captain Coleman stepped out of the craft. Coleman looked tired and ragged in the moonlight, but relieved as he started forward. Then there was a flash of white, and Coleman fell to the ground, half his head eaten by the enerpulse shot. The shuttle captain's cries drowned out the sharp intake of breath in the briefing room.

31

But no one had the chance to wince as the camera quickly whipped around and focused on a sparse line of trees in the general direction the shot had come from. The footage abruptly changed into infrared levels and a box appeared around a bright orange splotch in one of the trees.

"And that," said Ashburn, "is the Shadow."

CHAPTER 3: SPRINT

The five starships leaving the Star Federation space dock thrummed with restrained power. The *Argonaught* models were massive, but they were sleek and predatory, their curved hulls the signature rich, dark gray of the Star Federation. The insignias blazed in black and gold on the ships' sides gleamed proudly in the light from the space station: wing emblems poised at the top of a beat and encircled by a ring. "Stand and Protect"—the words of the Star Federation—was inscribed in the Written Unified Voice under the insignia.

The ships themselves looked ready to snap out of the docks and take off on a hunting flight, but the soft touch of their captains sent the *Argonaughts* gliding easily away from the station. With power humming through the ships' engines and the forward thrusters glowing blue with energy, the crafts anticipated the jump. The five ships cleared the Star Federation dock, hung suspended for a moment in nothingness, then received the signal from their captains. The engines brightened eagerly, and the ships shot forward and were lost among the distant stars.

Lance sat in the control room of the lead starship *Argonaught IV* with Orion at his side, and waited. All around him, soldiers sat at the wide array of controls and calmly worked as the starship surged to top speed. The ship ripped across the galaxy faster than light, and her four companions followed suit. It wasn't long before the first target appeared on the fleet's trackers, and Lance sent Captain Urganna's ship after it. The second target appeared a few minutes after she had gone, and Captain Rashad was put on its trail. Backélo took the third, and Anderson went after the fourth. Lance's ship sped on towards Earth, tore past the solar system, and drove after the fifth and final target. The Star Federation ship had just picked up on the smaller craft when Urganna's transmission came through.

"We captured a small smuggling craft," she said. "The crew surrendered the cargo without a fight, and the captain let us search the entire ship without any trouble. We found nothing else."

Lance told Urganna to stand by for further orders. She didn't have to wait long; Rashad ran into trouble with his target, and he requested reinforcements. Lance sent Urganna to assist him, and together they brought the target under control with minimal casualties. The ship was another smuggler, but the cargo was alive and crammed below the main deck. Lance had the two captains transport the slavers and the rescued captives back to the Star Federation space station.

Backélo captured his target with no trouble, and Anderson had similar luck. They both reported smuggled cargo: spices ranging from mildly hallucinogenic to flat-out deadly on one craft, and an assortment of weapons on the other. Nothing else was hidden aboard the ships.

"Exchange coordinates, set up a rendezvous, and place all of the smuggled cargo and the captives onboard Captain Backélo's ship," Lance ordered in his transmission back to the two captains. "When the transfer is finished, Captain Backélo will continue to Earth and speak with the Monitors about any and all new developments. Report back to me before acting further, Captain Backélo.

"Captain Anderson, you will follow us, acting as reinforcements. Contact us when you've finished the exchange, and we'll send our coordinates." Lance ended the transmission and glanced at the tracking screen again.

He was surprised by the target's speed. The Star Federation ship was closing, but the intercept point was still several hours off. Lance wondered how much longer the captain of the target craft would keep the ship sprinting. The smaller ship had already skipped over several ports and looked to be making a run for the Andromeda Reach. If the captain maintained the current faster-than-light speed, the ship's energy cells would drain long before the ship reached Phan, the first port in the sector. Lance watched the ship on the tracker for a while, and his gaze slowly darkened as he realized he had been wrong. The curve was subtle, but definitely there.

It's not heading for the Reach. It's turning.

Lance moved to the helm. Captain Stone was seated there, piloting the ship himself. He handled the large craft expertly, his touch on the controls light and quick. Stone loved piloting, and seized every chance to take command of a ship. He handled the single-pilot fighters and the massive transport ships with equal skill, although Lance knew that Stone preferred the fighters.

He just might get to fly his favorite today, Lance thought, and he tapped the captain on the shoulder.

Stone looked up at his touch. His dark eyes took on a glint of annoyance as they focused on Lance. "Sir?"

Lance ignored the flintiness of the gaze and kept his tone level. "I'd like a word, Captain. Please follow me." Lance turned without waiting for an answer. He walked to the control room door and slipped through without looking back. He heard Orion's claws clicking on the hard floor as the arkin followed him out. The door snapped shut behind them.

The gray walls and floor and the bright lights overhead offered the illusion of motionlessness as Lance and the arkin wandered down the hall. The *Argonaught's* halls were wide, perfect for a squadron of soldiers to move through, and clear of anything that would inhibit motion. The walls were smooth, doors to other rooms were widely spaced, and what might have been corners on another starship were broad curves on this one. Star Federation ships were bred all the way through for attacking, not defending.

Plenty of room to run, he thought. *No room to hide.*

The openness was meant to be more of a blessing than a curse. In dogfights, the wide halls let soldiers sprint to their stations without strangling the flow of bodies. If the fight took place onboard the ship, the design was still meant to be an advantage. Star Federation soldiers were not trained to hide. They were trained to fight, and they worked best in numbers and on the offense. Lance hoped that if they captured their target, and if a fight broke out, and if that fight migrated to the Star Federation ship, there would never be a need to fall back.

Lance heard the door to the control room yawn open again. He slowed his pace to let Stone catch up. The captain fell into step with Lance and looked at him expectantly, but said nothing.

Lance hesitated, searching for the best voice for his fears. He realized there wasn't one, and settled for blunt. "We're walking into a trap."

Stone was not surprised. "I had been wondering," he said slowly, "if you had noticed the change in the target's course, Commander."

"It's the Viaz, isn't it?"

"That's my guess, sir."

The Viaz was the desert of the galaxy. The sector held roughly one hundred and sixty planets. Three of those could sustain life, but barely, and what lived there was tough, rugged, and dangerous. The closest life supporter was Ametria, a huge chunk of rock with sparse vegetation and massive, deadly creatures. Few starships had ever dared a venture to the planet, and even fewer had returned. The survivors had the sense to keep clear of the atmosphere.

The other two inhabited planets were on the far side of the Viaz, too far for any starship to make in a single trip from Earth. Not even a Star Federation ship could have made that journey, let alone a craft the target's size. The power supplies would run dry long before the ship hit the Viaz's halfway point.

"They must have someone waiting for them, sir," Stone said. "Maybe a larger ship ready to transport them across the Viaz. They know we can't follow."

"No," Lance said, "we can't follow. But they should know we wouldn't have to. We're fast enough to catch them long before they reach the outskirts." Lance crossed his arms and leaned against the wall. He glared at the ceiling. "Something's wrong. Very, very wrong."

Stone said nothing.

"I think the best thing to do is keep after the target," Lance said after a pause. "Keep up the pressure of the chase and see what they do. But we'll let up a bit as we approach the intercept point."

"They'll know we suspect something," the captain said.

"That might make them hold off on springing whatever they've set, and we can scrape through this." He was very aware of the enerpulse pistol holster slung across his hips. The weight of the weapon was far from comforting. "We just need to keep them at arm's length until Captain Anderson is on her way with reinforcements. Then we can move in and hold them until her ship arrives."

Stone fixed a hard gaze on Lance, but said nothing.

He'd rather make a move as soon as we're in striking distance, Lance thought. *Run in before they have time to look over their shoulders. Any other ship, any other target, and I'd do just that. But not today.*

Lance dismissed Stone and watched him head back for the control room. Before the captain disappeared, Lance called out, "Captain Stone?"

Stone paused and half-turned back to Lance. "Sir?"

"It's time to tell the soldiers. They need to be ready for this."

The captain's gaze softened. "Yes, sir. Should I do it?"

"No, I'll do it myself in a few minutes. Just be ready for some damage control after I make the announcement. There are a few cadets that I'm worried about. We can't let them scare themselves into shock."

Stone nodded. He saluted Lance sharply, then stepped down the hall and disappeared around the curve. His footsteps receded quickly and Lance heard the distant sound of the control room door.

Lance sighed once, deeply, and looked at Orion. The arkin stared back with level yellow eyes.

"This is going to be tricky," Lance said. "No room for mistakes."

Orion grunted and half unfurled his wings. He shook them a little and then pulled them back in against his body. He flattened his ears against his skull, pawed the ground, and grunted again.

Lance leaned heavily against the wall. "I've never understood your taste in adventures."

CHAPTER 4: ALPHA

Ashburn had overestimated the damage control Jason had needed to perform, but the reaction of a certain lieutenant to the announcement of the target's identity set both officers on edge. Jason snapped the soldier back into place, but the lieutenant's excitement quickly returned and he kept whispering to his neighbors at the control panel about how much he was looking forward to having a shot at an Alpha. Ashburn told Jason to keep an eye on him, make sure he didn't do anything stupid, and for once, Jason accepted the order without any secret resistance.

The Shadow had secured their place in the Alpha Class a long time ago thanks to the carnage left at several early hit sites. High profile bounties rarely left themselves vulnerable, and the Shadow's early targets had put up enough guards to rival the size of a standard Star Federation squadron. The early hunts had left the targets and most of their guard dead or dying, and the sheer force of numbers was enough to put the Shadow on the Alpha list. As the hunts went on, the hits became cleaner and sparser, and more guards were left alive. Some of the higher officers had hoped that the Shadow had been a burst of death that would fade quickly, but the cold fact remained: the hunter was getting better. Fewer bodies meant fewer shots needed to take out the target, and with the Shadow's current hunting streak, Jason knew that a squadron of Star Federation soldiers would not stand much of a chance. Once the commanding officers were picked off, the hunter could take the lower ranks out at leisure. Soldiers like the overeager lieutenant would make mistakes, lining themselves up for execution. And if they weren't already dead, Jason knew that he and Ashburn would only be able to watch.

Erica's transmission offered some comfort. She said that she'd completed the exchange with Backélo and was ready to trace their route. After Ashburn relayed the ship's current coordinates and the projected intercept point, Erica confirmed the position, and then said that she would be standing by should there be anything else to discuss. Jason took the cue and excused himself from the control room, telling Ashburn that he wanted to check the fighters. Ashburn let him go, but not before fixing him with a searching stare.

"I wouldn't be surprised if Ashburn knows," Jason told Erica over the private transmission a few minutes later. He stood in the empty fighter bay, in front of one of the wicked hellhound models. The fighter was dark and angular, all glassy planes and severe edges. Jason pressed his hand against the cold metal of the nose, feeling the seam where the nose would split and reveal the barrel of the pulse cannon. The energy blast from a hellhound was intense, and could throw the craft violently off course without a skilled pilot. Jason loved the hellhounds, but for once, he wasn't looking forward to making them bark. "We haven't broadcasted it, but we haven't been too subtle about it, either."

"He doesn't know," Erica said flatly. "If he did, one of us would have been transferred to new command by now."

"Mm." He ran his fingers over the nose of the hellhound. "You didn't see the look he gave me."

"Jason, if he suspected *anything*, he'd have put Backélo's ship on reinforcements, not mine. You know how the high officers try to stamp these things out. Wasted effort, I say. It's not like these things mean anything."

He froze, eyes narrowed. "They stamp these *things* out, Ric, because they know that these *things* happen, and that they do mean something. They just don't want us doing anything stupid for each other because of them."

Silence.

Then, softly, "Look, I didn't mean... You know I didn't mean that."

Jason said nothing.

After another pause, Erica said, "What's Ashburn's plan for your target ship?"

"Stick with her. Fall back a bit once we approach the intercept point. See what she does."

Erica rolled a disgusted noise over her tongue. "That's it?"

"That's what Ashburn wants to do."

"And what do you want to do, Jason?"

He hesitated, dropping his hand from the nose of the hellhound. The empty cockpit stared at him, blank and dark and cold. He turned away. "I don't know, Ric."

"How do you not know?" she exploded. "You should be charging in, snapping up the target, and turning around before they have time to look over their shoulder!"

"Yeah, maybe." Jason felt the quiet of the fighter bay press against him. He suddenly wanted to be back in the bright control room with the hum of the ship and the voices of the soldiers in his ears. "Ashburn feels that something's off. He's... nervous. I think."

Erica snorted. "That's a hell of a commander we have."

"I'm nervous too, Ric," he said quietly, and cut the transmission line. He looked over his shoulder at the empty cockpit of the hellhound. The glass screen gleamed like a blind eye in the dim light of the fighter bay. "And that's what scares me."

CHAPTER 5: SHIFT

There was something they were not telling her. Lissa read it in the stiffness of the crew, in their lingering gazes. The voyage had started out fine, but something had happened two hours in. Getting away from Earth had been her priority, so she'd left the crew and the captain to their business and let the sudden shift play out, but she had also made a point of keeping her back to the walls and watching the crew closely.

She wanted to put the weight of the crew's anxiety on the Star Federation. She had told the captain to be ready for a pursuit when she had chartered the trip. The captain had asked for a higher upfront payment, but he'd been boarded by the Star Federation before and had assured her that his crew would know how to hide her. He and his crew had shown no interest in what she would be doing before she came aboard.

But something happened that had stretched the crewmembers' nerves close to the breaking point. Lissa doubted that prowling Star Feds could do that. Veteran smugglers knew how to keep calm under pressure, and this was not a crew of amateurs. No matter how much she wished otherwise, she had to release the Star Feds from all responsibility. Something else was at work. Something she knew she'd have to fight her way out of.

She spent some time walking up and down the length of her small cabin, running through the list of the Shadow's recent hits and trying to figure out whose death could have warranted a hunt for a bounty hunter. She could name plenty of individuals and organizations that would have been grateful for the chance to squeeze the Shadow's throat, but none would have known where to start looking for the hunter. Someone else, then. Someone unknown. Or maybe...

No. She'd been very careful, always checking her own trail and keeping an eye out for some telltale sign. Nothing had surfaced yet. She was still safe from them, at least for now.

"Right." She looked over at Blade, who had claimed the narrow wall cot during Lissa's pacing. "Time to visit the captain."

The arkin snorted, leapt down from the bunk and followed Lissa out into the hall. They found the control room easily enough, but Lissa hesitated before opening the door. She felt naked in the traveler's clothes. Her hunting outfit was stored in the vacuum cube tightly secured to her belt, but she'd kept the close-fitting, soft-soled boots and the thin gloves of her hunting outfit. The traveler's clothes were looser and considerably brighter than what she wore on hunts. Fading into the shadows in the new outfit could never happen, and she often found herself gripping the hem of the light jacket, ready to rip the cloth out of the way and draw her hidden pistol at the smallest snag. Worst of all, her face was uncovered. Lissa doubted that anyone would have questioned her if she'd worn the hunting mask—the crew must have seen stranger things on their runs across the galaxy—but keeping covered would have announced that her identity was sacred to her. Better to pretend that she wasn't afraid to be seen, and so she pointedly ignored the stares of the crewmembers in the control room as she opened the door and stepped inside.

The captain stood at the helm, his back to Lissa and a narrow aisle of hostile glares between them. Lissa started towards him, never once making eye contact with the crew, but she was only halfway to the captain when a growl from Blade warned her. She spun around, snapping the barrel of her pistol into alignment with the advancing crewmember's face. The man had a weapon drawn, but had barely raised it past the level of his hip by the time Lissa's pistol was staring him dead in the eye. He froze, and the room fell into silence. The captain took a long moment to acknowledge the change in air.

"Whichever of you was stupid enough to point a pistol at her," the captain said without turning, "stand down."

The crewmember slowly replaced his weapon and sank back into his seat.

Lissa lowered her own pistol, but kept it in her hand.

The captain looked over his shoulder at her. "I suppose you'd like to know how the journey's going."

"For a start." Lissa moved towards the helm, letting Blade linger a moment to flash her fangs at the crewman that had challenged them. He recoiled in his seat.

"We could be doing better." The captain stepped aside and let Lissa see the tracking screen. A very large ship had nosed its way on to the edge of the tracker. "We didn't expect the Star Feds to be on us this soon, but we have enough power to hold the gap for a while longer."

Lissa shook her head. "Better to save the cells and submit to the search."

The captain looked steadily at Lissa. "Better to have not let a bounty hunter on board in the first place."

So he knew that much. Lissa kept her face neutral as she leaned against the control panel, raised her pistol and rested the barrel on her shoulder. "Just do what you can to get me to Phan. Let the Star Feds come aboard if you have to, but keep a steady course and don't blow the power out." She smiled at him, but her eyes were hard. "Work with me, Captain, or I'll get to port on my own."

The captain's gaze flicked to his crew for a moment. He sighed once, very heavily, and opened his mouth, but a sudden transmission over the ship's main communicator drowned out whatever he was about to say.

"You're moving too slow."

The smile dropped off Lissa's face at the sound of the voice. Cold, cutting, and familiar. Fear snaked up her spine. *It can't be them.* Her mind raced through the last few months, searching for the point where she'd slipped up. *No, it's someone else. It must be.*

The captain turned to the ship's communicator. "We can't hit top speed. We'll burn through the cells and black out on the return."

"Losing our cargo to the Star Federation is not an option."

"You made that very clear earlier."

Earlier? The rage flared, but Lissa pushed it down.

"Good, but the point still stands, Captain. You're too slow. Your ship has more than enough power to outrun the Star Federation and arrive at the meeting point. As you are unwilling to push your ship anywhere near top speed, however, we feel that your services are no longer required, and control of your ship has passed to new hands."

The ship lurched suddenly, throwing Lissa and the captain off balance and tossing a few crewmembers out of their seats. There was a sudden scramble as the still-seated part of the crew whipped back to the controls and tried to block the hacker. They were too late. The ship lurched again, settled, and began to gather speed steadily.

"We will see you at the meeting point, Captain. And we expect our cargo to be undamaged."

The transmission went dead.

"Get control back!" the captain barked. "Get our speed down and turn—" He grew very still as the barrel of Lissa's pistol rested against the back of his skull. The crew gradually shifted its focus as the silence pressed down.

"Who did you deal with?" Lissa said quietly.

The captain said nothing.

"Tell me." Lissa pushed the barrel of the enerpulse pistol harder against the captain's head.

Softly, the captain said, "No names. They approached me right after you chartered the ship."

"How many of them?"

"Two."

"What did they look like?"

"I couldn't see them. No one could. They covered their faces, kept out of the light, all those tricks."

"What was the deal?"

"They offered a lot of money for a simple smuggling job and said the cargo would be aboard by the time we were ready to leave. I told them that sounded a bit vague, but they assured me it would come. Didn't take much to figure out they were talking about live cargo that would deliver itself. Namely, you."

"And you agreed."

"Yes. But at the time, I didn't know who you were. None of us did."

Lissa shifted, but kept the pistol in place. "And now? Who am I now?"

The captain tensed. "You are the Shadow."

Lissa hit a pressure point on the captain's back, sent him sprawling across the floor. She leapt after him, knocking him flat as he twisted around and tried to draw his pistol. She kneeled on his shoulders and pinned him with all her weight. That wasn't enough, and he began to struggle. He fell still when she pressed her pistol against his forehead. The crew began to rise, but Blade froze them all with a snarl and a deep growl.

Lissa stared down at the captain, directly into his eyes. He was human, copper-skinned and dark-haired, with brown eyes and high cheekbones. His face was narrow, lean, strong, and defiantly calm as he stared up at Lissa. She looked back at him with hot rage, but felt the tight grip of fear around her heart.

"Who's looking for the Shadow?"

The captain swallowed. "I don't know."

Lissa pushed down on the pistol, forcing the captain's head against the floor. "Do not lie to me."

"I don't have a name," the captain insisted. He kept his dark eyes trained on Lissa's. "Just a message."

Lissa let up on the pressure a bit.

"They wanted me to tell you this just as we reached the

rendezvous and were about to hand you over. Probably hoped you would kill me and save them the trouble."

The pressure increased again.

"They said, 'The seventh star burns brightest.'"

Lissa went numb.

A heavy silence punctured by Blade's growls played out, but no one moved.

Lissa very, very slowly became aware of her body again. Heat had leeched out of her completely, and she realized that she was shaking. She did not know how her hand had kept its grip on her pistol, but there was no room for relief as she came back into herself and focused on the captain. Rage surged through her, and she saw her own reflection in the captain's dark eyes harden into a murderous mask.

"Bonus for the girl," the captain whispered.

She stopped herself from pulling the trigger, but only just barely.

"That was the funny thing," the captain continued. "They knew that a hunter had chartered my ship, but they made it sound like I would be delivering a man to them. They told me not to expect a young woman, but to keep an eye out for her. And then they described you almost perfectly."

Lissa felt the rage ebb. Relief swept in. *They don't know. They still think it's Aven.* She almost relaxed, but she forced herself to hold firm and keep the captain down. Her gaze hardened again as she searched his face. "And now? Who are they expecting you to deliver now?"

"The bounty hunter." The captain looked at her steadily. "But not the girl."

Lissa studied the captain for a long, silent moment. Then she sat back and lifted the barrel of the pistol off his forehead. An angry red circle marked where the weapon had bit into his skin. "Turn on me again," she said as she lightly tapped the center of the mark with her finger, "and I'll aim right here." She stood up and stepped away from the captain.

He pushed himself into a sitting position, and was helped the rest of the way up by one of the crew. They both took a step away from Lissa, but the fear in the captain's eyes was aimed elsewhere now. "These people... How fast do they have you running?"

Lissa's eyes narrowed, but she felt the change in the room. The crew tensed, leaned towards her. Some were still frantically trying to regain control over the ship, but even they paused and looked at her. They waited to learn just how terrified they should be.

She looked back at the captain. "They call themselves the Seventh Sun. They're..." She glanced around the control room, at the tense faces of the crew. They had seen her face, but none of them had recognized what she was. She felt her heartbeat rise, threatening to spin out of control. She took a breath to steady herself. She had to make them see the danger hanging around them, had to convince them to throw their lives into the hands of the Star Federation. But maybe revealing the origins of the Seventh Sun wouldn't be enough, maybe too much time had passed since the war. "They're a Neo-Andromedan group."

Then again, maybe not.

Lissa had meant to tell them more, to tell them that if they were ever given the choice between rotting away with their loved ones on a Star Federation prison planet or being captured by the Seventh Sun, they should run willingly into the arms of the Star Feds. She'd meant to tell them that even if they made it to the Star Feds, they'd never truly be safe. To tell them that the Seventh Sun would always be behind them, watching and waiting, but the crew erupted.

There were shrieks of terror and outrage, cries of "Nandros!" and "The sub-human scum is back!" and a long list of profanity in languages that Lissa did not fully understand. Two of the youngest human crewmembers—no older than sixteen by the looks of them—began sobbing, one of which spat out "I don't want to turn into one of them!" in between tears. Lissa had not heard that wild myth before, and a disbelieving scowl almost swept across her face, but she reined herself in when the ship's first officer, a stocky flat-faced human, jumped up and declared his readiness to rip the first Nandro he saw clean in half, then beat the rest of the Nandros to death with the legs of the first one. The calmest member of the crew was a Yukarian female, but she sat rigid in her seat with cold hatred pulsing across her face.

Blade had flinched away from the crew at the first outburst. She padded back to Lissa and stood with her shoulder pressed against Lissa's leg. Lissa let her hand drop to the arkin's head, thinking that in all their years together, this was the first time they had both been caught by total surprise. Lissa had hoped for some sort of reaction, but the strength of what she'd awoken drove her back a step.

Looking at the crew, Lissa realized that she really should have expected this. Most of the crew was human, and then there was the lone Yukarian. Both of those races harbored a special hatred of Neo-Andromedans and, in the case of the humans, their behavior wasn't totally unjustified. That was what made them all the more terrifying.

There was a voice low in her ear. "You're lucky."

Lissa looked away from the crew and met the captain's eyes. Steady brown eyes. Human eyes.

"You can't tell from a distance, but if you get close, you can see it, if you know what to look for. It's in the eyes. In Nandros, the eyes are metallic, almost. Yours are softer, but it's there. The hardness. Silver, not gray."

Lissa said nothing.

"Usually there are stripes, flecks, something weird that screams, 'These are not human eyes.'" The captain frowned at her for a long moment. "You're very lucky."

Then he stepped forward and his voice snapped out like a whip, bringing the crew back under control. He sent his first officer out to warn and rally the rest of the crew, then began to set up a blanket defense team against the Seventh Sun's hacker. When he called Lissa over to the counterhack team and told her to teach them how to outrun the Nandros, his crew looked at her expectantly. They looked her in the eye, but none of them knew what they were looking at. One glance at the captain, and Lissa knew that there would never be a need to tell the crew the truth if she kept them safe.

If.

CHAPTER 6: CHASE

The trackers showed the target ship gathering momentum. Lance stood in the control room, watching as the speed gap between the ships dwindled and winked down to nothing. The distance between the vessels became fixed.

"At this rate," Captain Stone said, "they'll black out at Ametria."

"That has to be a contact point," Lance said. "They'd have let us get closer if they had a trap. Made sure we were hooked on the bait." He leaned on the control panel between two soldiers. "How are we on power?"

"Still over fifty percent capacity," an ensign answered.

"Just enough for a sprint to the Viaz," Lance said. "Maybe we can keep a decent speed for a ways after but we'll never make it back to port." He frowned and tapped his finger on the control panel. "Contact Captain Anderson."

Anderson's acknowledgement weaved into the control room a minute later.

Lance greeted her. "Status, Captain."

"We're following you at top speed, Commander. We'll hit the last coordinates you gave us in three minutes."

"Reduce speed to seventy percent max velocity once you hit the location, Captain Anderson."

There was a pause.

"I don't understand, Commander."

"The target is making a run for it," Lance said. "We may need a tow by the time this is over."

"Yes, sir."

Lance had a cadet send Anderson their latest coordinates, then he cut the transmission line. He frowned at the trackers again.

"We'll catch them," Stone said. "They'll have to slow down if they don't want to black out."

Lance nodded. "But can we get to them before whoever else is out there?"

Speech died in the room as the soldiers worked at the controls. Stone had relinquished the helm, and he and Lance stood side-by-side, watching the trackers. The target ship maintained speed, the distance gap never changed, and no telltale blip appeared on the far side of the trackers. Whoever or whatever the target was running towards, there was still a long way to go.

The two ships sped on, barreling towards Ametria. When the planet came in range of the trackers, there was still no sign of another ship.

"I don't like this," Stone muttered.

"No," Lance said. "Something's wrong." He thought for a long, hard moment. "All right, that's it. Turn us around, we're letting it go."

The transmission burst through the *Argonaught's* communicator on the tail of Lance's last syllable. The target ship was warning them.

CHAPTER 7: BREACH

"Engines," Lissa said.

The Yukarian crewmember—Myrikanj was her name—shifted the focus of her counterattack to the system Lissa had named. The crewmembers around her kept up a broad attack on the Sun hacker, hoping to spread his or her attention too thin and let Myrikanj break through. The Yukarian added push wherever Lissa told her to. So far, they had come up against an impenetrable wall, but Lissa was trying a new tactic with Myrikanj.

"Navigation."

The Yukarian shifted.

"Lights. Communication. Engines again."

Myrikanj kept up with Lissa's orders, jumping from system to system with surprising speed. Her blue hands flew over the controls, and her antennae trembled with concentration. Lissa and the captain stood over her shoulder, watching her maneuver through the hacker's defenses and hit a wall every time. Lissa sent her in a new direction whenever she became stuck.

"What else do we have? No, stay away from ventilation. We don't want that going down by mistake. Try tracking. Now the outer airlocks. Engines once more."

Myrikanj continued the onslaught for hours, although Lissa gave her free reign after the first few minutes. The Yukarian knew the ship far better than Lissa did, and Myrikanj began to dig into parts of the ship's computer that Lissa did not know existed. The blanket defense crew was rotated every so often, and Myrikanj plowed straight through three shifts before she asked for a break. She spent thirty minutes in a bizarre meditation state that involved a soft but reverberating chant, then returned to the controls and launched back into the war. The blanket crew switched once more before Myrikanj found a weakness in the Seventh Sun's defense, and she broke through.

The crewmembers not on the hacking line began to cheer Myrikanj on, and even the captain became infected with their elation. One look at Lissa, however, and he sobered immediately.

"She shouldn't have been able to do that," Lissa said.

Myrikanj kept up the attack alongside the other hackers, but the rest of the crew quieted down at the captain's sharp command.

"She hit a gap that wasn't there before, in a spot the Sun's kept a firm grip on the entire time." Lissa glared at the systems display as the battle raged on. "What are they so focused on that they let that slip?" Her eyes fell on the tracking screen. The system itself was out of their control, but the trackers still showed the pursuing Star Federation ship.

The captain followed Lissa's gaze. "Oh, damn." He snapped his attention to the hacking line. "Go after communication! Forget everything else, just get that back up."

"The engines would be a better idea," Myrikanj offered.

"Not if they take the Star Feds."

Lissa gazed transfixed at the trackers, hoping that she was as lucky as the captain had said she was, that she looked human enough to fool the Star Feds. That would depend entirely on who was on the Star Fed ship, but she allowed herself the hope. "When you get the Star Feds," Lissa said to the captain, "tell them to take us onboard, if they can."

Slipping through the Seventh Sun's wall must have thrown their hacker off, and Myrikanj pressed the advantage. She and the defense crew managed to take hold of the ship's communications, and the captain sent a transmission to the Star Federation ship. The broadcast hit a wall, one that Myrikanj quickly breached. The Seventh Sun moved to block the Star Federation terminal. Their hacker managed to throw up a basic defense, but Myrikanj moved in and blasted through before the Sun's wall was fortified.

"Captain Montag of starship *Resolution*, sending warning of hacking attack. *Resolution* has been breached, all systems under attack. Requesting assistance from Star Federation starship. Transfer crew of *Resolution* to other ship if possible. Repeat, beware of hacking attack. *Resolution* requesting assistance from Star Federation starship. Transfer crew to—"

Myrikanj and the blanket defense crew were ejected from the system, and communications went under lockdown.

"Well," Montag said after a steady pause, "that's that. Think the Star Feds can keep control?"

Lissa looked back at the trackers and said nothing. Whether they did or did not, she'd face her enemies soon.

Out of the corner of her eye, she saw that Montag was considering her. "If they can snag us," he said, "we'll have to show you, but we won't tell them who you are."

She met his gaze, then looked at the crew. The flat-faced first officer was back in the control room, and he caught her eye as she glanced around. "We'll tell them you're one of our navigators," he offered with a smile. Then he grimaced. "Let's just hope we're not dealing with Keraun or we're all fucked. Nandros are bad enough as it is, we don't need a psychopath, too."

Lissa nodded her thanks and agreement, but then her gaze snagged on Myrikanj. The Yukarian barely glanced up from the controls, but the fleeting stare was piercingly cold.

Myrikanj knew.

CHAPTER 8: ALLIES

Ametria loomed ahead of the ships, huge, dark, and ruthless. The red light from the planet's dying sun soaked the rocky surface and threw deep shadows into the canyons. The soldiers had regained power over the fighter bay and a few superficial systems in the control room, and they had put the hellish planet on display. Thick lines of shade snaking over blood-colored rock flooded the screen. The *Resolution* glided straight towards the Ametrian surface, her engines flickering as her power cells died.

The *Argonaught IV* had maintained control over speed despite the hack. The warning transmission from the target ship had arrived in time for the soldiers to throw up defenses around a few systems. The trackers still showed no sign of the hostile ship, even after the counterhack team checked the system and declared it untouched.

Lance paced the control room, watching over the shoulders of the soldiers as they fought the hacker. The counterhack team had slowed the *Argonaught IV* and kept distance between the Star Federation ship and the *Resolution*, but they had lost navigation earlier and *Argonaught IV* was on a collision course with the smaller ship. They did have the fighter bay, however. Lance could send out a fleet of fighters and blast the *Resolution* out of the way, but he wasn't desperate enough to give the order just yet.

Captain Stone was of a different mindset. "We either ram them or shoot them out of our way," he had said earlier, quietly but defiantly, and still loud enough for a few of the soldiers to overhear. "We can't take control back if we have to deal with damages. For all we know, the hacker could be ready to rip our shields off and shove the *Resolution* down our throats."

"They warned us, Captain Stone," Lance had replied. He didn't keep his own voice down. "I will not destroy those that saved us when they could have let the ambush carry through."

"And if they're part of the ambush?" Stone shot back, loudly this time. "They want to come aboard. Why not just give them open access to the arsenal and lock ourselves in the prison block? It would save them and their hacker—"

"I said I would not blast them out of existence," Lance said calmly, but his rage had reached a boiling point. "Not that I would bring them aboard. We can't ignore the possibility that the *Resolution* may be in as much danger as we are, but if the worst should happen and you don't believe that you and your soldiers can handle a small band of renegades, then by all means, Captain, blast the *Resolution* into oblivion."

Stone bit down on whatever else he had wanted to say.

Neither Lance nor Jason Stone had forgotten that the Shadow was onboard the *Resolution*, but as the ships sped towards Ametria and the power began to flicker and die on the smaller ship, the possibility of an ambush from the crew of the *Resolution* faded. When Lance gave the order to concentrate all counterhack efforts on bringing the carrier bay under control, Stone only offered a half-challenging glance. When the *Resolution* was finally pulled in to the *Argonaught's* carrier and secured at a holding dock, the smaller ship's lights were completely dead and her engines sputtered dimly. The *Resolution's* crew spilled out of the airlock the instant the bay had been re-pressurized, and was greeted by a squadron of Star Federation soldiers, all with firearms at the ready. Caution had outweighed concern, and Lance took no chances.

Ventilation on the *Resolution* must have been on the verge of failing; most of the crew wore breathing masks and emergency ventilation packs. They eyed the weapons trained on them as they emerged from the ship, slowly removed their respirators, raised their hands above their heads, and spread out, giving the Star Federation soldiers a clear view of all of them. Lance wondered how many times the *Resolution* had been boarded in the past. This had become a routine for the crew.

The *Resolution's* captain—Montag, Lance recalled from the warning transmission—stepped forward after his entire crew had exited the ship and lined up for inspection. As Lance moved to meet him, he took note of the passengers of the *Resolution*: they were a mostly human crew with a few other species thrown in. Twelve of them were male including Montag, nine female, two androgynous, and one—

Orion surged forward before Lance could stop him. In the scramble to regain control over the carrier and bring the *Resolution* aboard, Lance had forgotten to expect an arkin on the other craft. He had also forgotten how long it had been since Orion had seen another arkin, and the gray bounded forward eagerly.

The black arkin made it clear that it had no interest in greeting Orion, and it bared its fangs and growled. Orion skidded to a halt, considered the black for a moment, then curled his own lips back into a snarl. The woman that stood next to the black arkin slowly reached down and touched its tensed back. The black looked up at her, then back at Orion. It snorted once, then dropped its snarl and sat down. It kept its bright amber eyes fixed on Orion, but offered no more challenges.

Orion considered the black arkin for a long moment, then stepped forward cautiously. He halted a pace away from the black arkin, stretched his neck a little, and sniffed. His tail flicked once, then he snorted, turned away, and padded back to the line of Star Federation soldiers.

Lance considered the woman that had calmed the black

arkin. She was thin and of medium height, small-breasted and athletic, probably quicker than she was strong. She stood with her shoulders squared, but like the rest of the crew of the *Resolution*, her head was tilted submissively down to the floor. Lance had only a distorted view of her face, but he could see enough from the rest of her.

Her hair was as black as the fur of her arkin, and was drawn back into a tight braid with not a strand hanging loose against her golden brown skin. She wore a set of nondescript traveler's clothes, but her boots and gloves were considerably darker than the rest of her outfit. She wore a jacket over her clothes that came to about mid-thigh on her, but with arms held overhead, the jacket had pulled back to reveal an enerpulse pistol. Lance thought that, had her arms been lowered, the jacket would have hid the weapon completely. He realized that no one else from the *Resolution* had tried to conceal their firearms, and as he looked closer, he realized that some were unarmed.

Lance wondered if Montag had taken the Shadow and her arkin aboard willingly, or if he had no idea to whom his back was turned as he looked at Lance and said, "Well, I guess those two won't be friends any time soon."

"I'd say that's about right," Lance replied as Orion slipped past. He turned with the arkin's movement and made a sharp gesture to three soldiers, who lowered their pistols and snapped to attention. "Weapons sweep," he barked, and the three soldiers moved forward and began searching for and removing weapons from Montag's crew. The Shadow handed over her pistol without hesitating, and let a soldier search her for a concealed weapon. The soldier lingered over the thick leather belt she wore, and the pouches and objects that studded its surface were given some inspection, but he cleared her of dangerous items and moved to the next person.

Lance turned back to Montag. "Welcome aboard the Star Federation starship *Argonaught IV*. Your warning may have saved all our lives, Captain Montag."

"And you saved ours just now," Montag returned, eying

the insignia over Lance's heart before adding, "Commander." Montag let his gaze slide over the Star Federation soldiers as they disarmed his crew. "I don't blame you for your caution," he said, "but I can promise you that we all want to come out of this alive. We're not stupid enough to turn on you."

"Of course not," Lance said, "but I also can't let your crew wander the ship freely."

Montag's gaze hardened, but he said nothing.

"They will have to be confined on the prison dock," Lance continued. "We'll release them once we're in a better position than a headlong rush for Ametria, provided we can count on their full cooperation."

Still nothing.

"But since we may need assistance from you, you and three of your crew will join us in the control room."

Montag hesitated, then nodded his assent.

It was more than Montag could have hoped for, Lance knew, but he had a special interest in the renegade captain's selection. Montag's decision would reveal his intentions.

Lance eyed the crew of the *Resolution* again, and his gaze caught on the Shadow. If Montag meant to trigger a secondary ambush, he would need the hunter to remain free. Star Federation soldiers could handle four renegades. An Alpha Class bounty hunter was another matter entirely, but if he chose the Shadow, Montag and his entire crew would spend the rest of the journey in the prison hold, no matter when or where the voyage ended.

Montag called the short, thin Yukarian forward. He introduced her as Myrikanj, the one who had broken through the communications barrier. Next he picked out a stocky, flat-faced human male, his first officer. Montag gave Lance a hard look and said that the officer was to remain with his crew, but outside of the prison block with permission to act as a go-between for Montag and his crew. Lance agreed, but assigned a Star Federation escort to keep an eye on Montag's man. Lance understood Montag's mistrust, but he wasn't about to give one of the *Resolution*'s crew total freedom. Montag agreed to the conditions, and his final choice came without any hesitation.

"I suppose she technically counts as two, but she and the arkin are inseparable," he said.

The Shadow and her arkin moved forward, and Lance was about to give the order to take down the renegade crew when Montag spoke again.

"She's the one who really saved us."

Lance frowned, the command half-formed on his tongue.

Montag's tone was reserved but admiring, full of wariness but also gratitude. "She knew what we were up against. What we *are* up against."

Lance let the order fall off his lips. "And what is that, exactly?"

Montag hesitated, picking his words carefully. Lance didn't need a response from him, however.

As the Shadow stepped forward, she finally raised her head and locked eyes with Lance. Bright, clear, silver eyes. None of the usual telltale markings in the irises, but still unmistakable, and Lance felt his heart stumble over its next beat.

The Shadow was Neo-Andromedan.

CHAPTER 9: BARGAIN

There was an involuntary sharp breath, a widening of the eyes. Sudden tension in the posture. All of the customary signals. The fleet commander knew.

So far, not so lucky.

Lissa expected the order to ring out, expected ten Star Federation soldiers to leap at her and pin her to the ground. Blade would maybe get three of them if she moved fast enough, but she would be shot, probably killed. Montag could feign ignorance, deny that he knew what she was, and the brilliant Myrikanj would take her cue from him. The rest of Montag's crew would be so outraged that the Star Feds could never accuse them of hiding a Neo-Andromedan. Then she would spend the rest of the journey in the prison block under heavy guard until the Seventh Sun overtook the ship and came for her. Unless the commander killed her first. He was human, after all.

The attack never came. A few of the soldiers watching Lissa and Blade shifted their grips on their weapons, but they remained eerily still. Lissa counted twenty-seven humans among the ranks, more than half of all the soldiers assembled. One of the senior officers—a tall, broad-shouldered human with close-cropped dark hair, darker eyes, and deep brown skin—frowned as Lissa and Blade drew closer. He glanced from them to the commander, and his anxiety changed to anger as she and the arkin advanced and the silence played out.

Maybe Montag has it right, after all.

When Lissa reached the commander, he extended his hand to her. She recognized the human custom, and pressed her own hand into his, feeling the strength of his grip. She made a point of matching him.

"Fleet Commander Lance Ashburn," he introduced himself as he released her hand. "My first officer, Captain Stone." He gestured to the tall, dark, angry human.

Captain Stone's gaze hardened into a full-on glare, but Lissa returned his stare coolly. She wondered how long it would take the rest of the soldiers to fix her with a look like that. They must have figured out by now that she was a bounty hunter, probably one off their Alpha Class list. They would have sent a smaller ship if they were expecting someone less dangerous. Still, she'd managed to catch them off-guard. They hadn't been expecting a Neo-Andromedan. No one ever expected them. Not since the war, and from the look of things, it had been too long for even the Star Federation to keep the memory fresh in all of their soldiers. The seniors, though…

Lissa considered Ashburn again. Fit, lean, straight in the spine and straighter in the nose, square-jawed, with a prominent chin and somewhat less prominent cheekbones beneath pale olive skin. Blond-brown hair and green eyes. Definitely handsome, probably intelligent. One of the Star Federation's golden soldiers. She'd have to be careful around him, but she could work with a mute Star Fed. There would be an opening eventually. Waiting for it would be the worst part.

Captain Stone, on the other hand, would be a problem. If he had been the commanding officer, Lissa would have been in the prison hold by now. But he wasn't, and she was free for the moment, and he did not look pleased about it. He was a little taller than Ashburn, narrower in the face but broader in the chest. Also handsome, but made a little less so by the unbending glare. Quick to anger, but more than capable of holding his emotions in check. Disciplined, then. A good soldier. Someone who would prefer to play by the Star Fed's rules, but might be persuaded to break from them with the right motivation. She'd have to watch for that, see if she could figure him out a bit more.

"My name is Lissa," she said to Ashburn. She nodded a greeting to Stone. He glowered at her in return, but still said nothing.

"Lis-suh," the commander said, his Galunvo accent putting a small drawl on the last syllable.

She nodded again.

"Captain Montag says you know what we're dealing with," Ashburn said. He either ignored Stone's hostility, or was totally unaware of it. Lissa did not know which to hope for.

"I know a bit about them," Lissa said. "Not a lot, but enough to give us a chance."

"She knows more than she lets on," Myrikanj put in. Montag shot her a sharp look, and Lissa saw Ashburn take note of the glance. "She was the one who came up with the counterhack strategy that let me break through the wall around communications," the Yukarian continued. "She *knows* these people."

Well played, Myri.

In three sentences, Myrikanj had set Lissa up as a potential inside operator. The more Lissa revealed about the Seventh Sun, the guiltier she would seem. She couldn't explain her history with them. That would demand too many secrets, too many truths.

Montag looked at Myrikanj with nothing short of horror, then turned to Ashburn and started to stumble out an explanation. The commander brushed the fumbled words aside.

"We wouldn't be talking now if she didn't," Ashburn said. He switched his gaze to Lissa. "I'll tell you straight, because I want straight answers out of you. We know who you are. We know what you've done, where you're coming from and, with a few questions put to the right people, we can drag where you're going out of the shadows. Work with us now, and I can promise leniency later. Leniency, not freedom. That is the offer." He extended his hand once again. "Take it, or learn to love the cell we give you."

Lissa spent a few stunned, silent moments processing what the commander had said. He'd given her the extra tip, told her that the Star Feds knew that they were dealing with the Shadow. There were too many crimes to balance Lissa's freedom with a ship full of lives, but Ashburn had promised leniency later.

When is later?

Not when—or if—they broke free of the Seventh Sun and rushed back into Star Federation space. There would be an army waiting to bring the Shadow to justice. The best Lissa could hope for would be life sentencing on one of the prison planets. Then again, maybe that actually was the leniency Ashburn meant. He had to know that the reward would never balance what she would be giving up.

Why offer me anything, then? Why deal with a hunter? With a Neo-Andromedan? What are they planning?

Lissa's gaze fell on Captain Stone. His mouth hung open in total surprise, but outrage began to crawl out of his eyes and over his face. Lissa suddenly realized what Ashburn was offering, and she grabbed his hand and shook it much more violently than she had meant to.

"Deal," she said before Stone could find his voice. Montag looked at her incredulously, and Myrikanj's antennae trembled in surprised outrage.

"Good," Ashburn said. Then he turned away and ordered Stone to escort Montag's crew to the prison hold. The captain frowned hard at his senior officer, but accepted the order without further challenge and picked out several soldiers to form the escort. Montag's first officer went with them when they led the renegade crew out of the carrier bay.

Ashburn set a small squad led by a lieutenant to search and guard the *Resolution*, then led Lissa, Montag, and Myrikanj to the control room. A long column of Star Federation soldiers fanned out behind them.

Lissa studied the design of the ship as they wound their way through its halls. Broad, bright, curving halls with no corners or crevices. There were doors to rooms here and there, but they flowed with the sweep of the halls and there were no dips or protrusions to mar the arcs of the ship's interior. These halls were made for running through as an army. For charging. They made retreat dangerous, and there was no place to hide. If the Seventh Sun managed to get their agents aboard, they would decimate the Star Feds. She'd have to warn Ashburn about that, but not until the Sun had come knocking on the ship's hull. That knowledge could give her the opening she needed.

A soft growl from Blade brought Lissa's attention to the arkins. After their initial tense greeting, they had been fairly calm, although the ever-watchful Blade had pinned Ashburn's gray arkin with a hostile stare and had looked nowhere else.

The gray arkin had divided its attention between Ashburn, Montag, Montag's crew, Lissa and Blade. It was comfortable among the Star Feds and didn't seem to care what the soldiers did, but it kept a close watch on Lissa as she and Ashburn interacted. Protective, loyal, closely bonded to Ashburn. Lissa wondered if maybe one of the gray's battle scars told the story of Ashburn's history with it, but that wasn't something she expected or needed to learn. But Lissa had the feeling that Ashburn and his arkin were very rarely separate from each other.

Blade, on the other hand, and although fiercely loyal to Lissa, had always been a bit more independent. Whenever she and Lissa grounded themselves on a planet, the arkin would usually go off for one or two days, hunting and exploring the terrain. The first few times Blade had disappeared, Lissa had been afraid to travel for fear of losing the arkin forever. There had been a few uncomfortable brushes with danger, though, and Lissa had been forced to move.

Once, she'd encountered a group of Anti-Neo-Andromedans that had appeared on the second day of one of

Blade's hunts. They hadn't recognized Lissa for what she was, but past experiences had trained her to run rather than risk, and she'd fled the city. She spent four days traveling over rocky terrain and one large lake, and then had ultimately hidden herself in another, larger city. Blade found her half a day later, and Lissa quickly learned that she was free to move as often as she wanted or needed to, although that usually did not happen. Somehow, Blade always knew when they had found a safe place to ground themselves, and she never went hunting if she felt otherwise. Lissa had actually begun to feel safer when Blade wasn't around, and she'd been fighting against the sensation. She couldn't afford to let her guard down when she was on her own, but more than anything, she didn't want to break her bond with the arkin.

Now, though, as she watched Blade glare at Ashburn's arkin, she wondered if Blade would have been better off without her. Arkins were not rare, but Lissa travelled so much that Blade had never had the chance to learn what was hostility, and what was playfulness. Ashburn's arkin had approached her with the latter, but Blade had only ever been exposed to the former.

Lissa brushed her fingers between Blade's shoulders. She felt the tension beneath the smooth, black fur. She tried to soothe the arkin, but could not blame her for her mistrust.

Blade's only other encounter with an arkin had been a battle, and it was a miracle that she had come out with injuries that had healed quickly and cleanly. That dark brown beast had been a full head taller than Ashburn's arkin, probably half again as heavy. Blade was smaller and lighter than Ashburn's gray. She had grown since the first encounter with the brown, but that arkin would still dwarf her if they ever met again. Jet had been the brown arkin's name, Lissa remembered. Partner to the Seventh Sun's main tracker, an Awakened man who satiated his relentless hunger by chasing bounties under the hunting name Phantom.

If Blade survived Jet, though, this gray should be no problem if a fight comes up.

That, of course, would depend on where Lissa's opening presented itself, and how well Ashburn held up his end of the bargain.

Lissa thought back to her original assessment of the commander and scratched the *probably* from *probably intelligent*. He had managed to make her an offer that she couldn't refuse, after all.

Ashburn knew that she was Neo-Andromedan, but he had offered her safety nonetheless. He had set up the illusion of cooperation, and the Star Feds couldn't touch her. Lissa knew that they really did need her if they were going to come out of this alive, but she could survive without them. Ashburn must know that, but so long as they both kept up the performance, the soldiers could not act, not even if they all finally realized what she was.

They needed her. They needed the bargain. All she needed was a chance to slip away and find the shuttle bay. She knew that Ashburn would keep a close eye on her, a very close eye.

But he would have to blink eventually.

CHAPTER 10: ENEMIES

Back in the control room, Lance placed Myrikanj the Yukarian on the counterhack line and pulled Captain Stone, Montag, and the Shadow into a tight group around him. Looking at the Shadow's face, Lance remembered that when he had enlisted in the Star Federation, the Andromedan War had been far from his mind. The last real battle had raged just over forty years earlier, and once the true Andromedans had been chased out of the galaxy, the Neo-Andromedans had crumpled under a purge. Independents had taken it upon themselves to sniff out the surviving Nandro strongholds and break their power, and the Nandros had slipped off the Star Federation radar. When Lance had first put on the gray uniform, the Neo-Andromedans had seemed more like a myth than history.

It was the eyes that had grounded the Nandros in reality. Hard, cold, metallic eyes. Human bodies, human faces, inhuman eyes.

The Star Federation made a point of drilling the appearance of Neo-Andromedans into all its soldiers, but as the Andromedan War faded into the past, so did the heavy stress over the Nandro threat. Lance's enlistment class had received very brief Neo-Andromedan training sessions, and then had been prepared for more important matters. They had pushed the Nandros to the back of their minds readily enough, although Lance knew that he wasn't the only officer who had developed the dull habit of checking the eyes of every humanoid he arrested.

But now that the Shadow—Lissa, she'd said, if Lance was willing to believe her—was staring at him with her bright, clear, silver eyes, other bits from the information drills came back to him.

"The people who hacked your ship are part of a Neo-Andromedan organization called the Seventh Sun," the Shadow said.

The Neo-Andromedan was ripped from the genetic structure of humans without human consent.

"Contrary to what Myrikanj says, I can't tell you all that much about them. I have had run-ins with them in the past, but no major dealings."

The Neo-Andromedan was built to be faster, stronger, and more intelligent than their human base.

"What I can tell you is that they are incredibly dangerous. They'll do just about anything to reach their goals, and they hate the Star Federation more than anything."

The true Andromedans disrupted the universe when they engineered the Neo-Andromedan.

"But I don't know what they're after now. This… this might be a demonstration of sorts, a way to show the galaxy how strong they are. Or maybe it's a way to test themselves. Or maybe they just want to scare you."

The Star Federation was founded to restore order to the galaxy. It is the sworn duty of all Star Federation soldiers to eliminate galactic threats and dangers, to stand against all enemies and protect the galaxy.

"One thing I can say for certain is they didn't bring us to Ametria just to crash and ground us. If this ship is their target, then they have something much worse than a grounding planned."

The Neo-Andromedan is a danger the galaxy cannot afford.

"I'll do what I can, but Myrikanj will be more use to you right up until they try to come aboard. At that point, I'll only be able to help you if I have a weapon."

Stand and Protect.

"Are we clear?"

"Absolutely not," Lance said. "No weapons." He looked at Montag. "That goes for you and your crew, too."

Montag offered no resistance, but the Shadow faced him squarely. "Ashburn, shooting you would not further my survival in any way."

"No," Captain Stone cut in. "But helping us would."

The Shadow gave him a hard, slow look. "I thought I had already agreed to do that."

"Then tell us about the Seventh Sun."

"They're Neo-Andromedan extremists. What more do you need to know?"

"What are they planning?"

"*I don't know.*" She snapped another hard look on Stone, and her black arkin underscored the glare with a soft growl. "I'd happily tell you if I did, but my best guess is that they're going to try to come aboard. I don't—"

"How?"

"—know how." The hunter sighed disgustedly, then stalked over to the counterhack team, followed closely by her arkin. She raised her hands to her hips. Her right hand tried to close on the empty space over her weapon holster, but recovered quickly and dropped to her side again. The black arkin touched its nose to the Shadow's lowered hand, and the hunter rubbed the back of the arkin's head. The frustration ebbed out of the Shadow's stance as she watched the counterhackers, and she shifted her weight and folded her arms in concentration.

Montag said quietly, "I don't know who the Seventh Sun is, or what they've done, but if she's running from them, I'll follow her."

Stone grunted. "Right up until she runs into their open arms. Then you'll wish you ran the other way."

"She's scared of them," Montag said.

"Doesn't mean she won't run to them. Even if it is by

mistake."

Montag frowned and looked at the Shadow. "I get the sense that she knows how to avoid these people."

Stone grunted again. "She's done a hell of a job of that today."

"That…" Montag shifted, grimaced. "That wasn't her fault. They bribed us. Me. To deliver her."

Lance and Stone looked at him sharply.

"What do they want with her?" Stone kept his voice low.

"They didn't say."

"Focus on the trackers," Lance heard the Shadow tell the counterhackers. "Try to find out where they're hiding. They can't be far."

Stone started to say something else, but Lance cut him off with a sharp gesture just as a lieutenant said, "The trackers have been holding steady. The hacker never went after them."

"What do you mean," the Shadow said, "that they skipped the trackers? That's the first thing they would've gone for."

In three quick steps, Lance was at the hunter's side. She did not flinch at his sudden appearance, but she did lean away a little.

"Focus on the trackers," Lance barked. "Get them back up."

The counterhack crew jumped to work at Lance's order, but Myrikanj threw a quick look over her shoulder at the Shadow. There was no warmth there.

The counterhackers fought for the trackers for a few tense minutes, then suddenly broke through and recovered the system. The team exchanged bewildered looks, but dove back into the computer and tried to press their advantage. They were blocked everywhere else.

Lance turned to the Shadow, looking for confirmation "They let us in. They want us to see."

Metallic eyes met his, but they were somehow softer now. Sympathy? Sorrow? Fear? Lance couldn't tell.

"Yes," she said.

Lance moved away, back to the main controls, and

checked the updated tracker display. He did not register what he was seeing for a long time, and he was only dimly aware that Stone had moved to his side. "Damn," the captain whispered, and Lance nodded in agreement.

The trackers now showed signals of a massive starship stationed on the other side of Ametria. It was only a blip on the tracking display, but from the data readings, it looked like it rivaled the size of the Star Federation ship.

"At least we know where they are now," Stone muttered.

"That's not what you should be worried about," the Shadow said.

Both officers jumped slightly. Neither had heard her come up beside them.

She pointed at the tracking display, very near the Star Federation ship's location. "That's what you need to worry about."

Almost on top of the Star Federation ship were a large number of small blips surrounding a much larger one.

"Fighters," Stone said. "Escorting a gunship."

"Bring the visual display up," Lance said to the counterhackers.

The team bent over the controls, then brought up a display based on the recovered tracking system. Blood-and-shade-covered Ametria blocked the massive enemy starship, but the fleet heading right for the *Argonaught IV* was in full view. There were several small crafts—twenty-five or thirty, Lance estimated—flying in a protective, deadly cloud around a larger ship. The odd, triangular design of the smaller ships was entirely alien to Lance, but Stone had been right about them. They were unmistakably fighters. But the center ship...

"What the hell is that?" Lance whipped his gaze to Stone. "Have you ever seen anything like that?"

The captain shook his head, never taking his eyes off the display.

The center ship was squat and bulky, moving awkwardly even through empty space. Its hull gleamed deep red in the light of Ametria's sun, but there were chinks and heavy seams in the surface, a weird sight next to the small, smooth fighters.

"Is that armor?" Stone said.

"It looks like it," Lance said. "But why?"

"Driller," the Shadow said. Almost everyone in the control room turned and looked at her. "Armored driller." She turned to the counterhack team. "Watch the shields."

They stared back at her blankly.

"Shields!" she snarled.

The team jumped, whipped back to the controls. Almost immediately, three of them took on panicked looks and began to work more frantically. They struggled on, but after a few minutes, Myrikanj said, "Shields are down."

The Shadow sighed heavily. "I'm going to need a pistol now, Ashburn."

Lance looked back at the display of the advancing enemy fleet just in time to see the ships slip off the bottom of the screen. The fleet was under their hull now.

Lance checked the systems display, then turned to Captain Stone. "Get to the fighter bay. Be ready with the fleet in ten minutes. Systems say the bay force field is still up, but if it's down when you get there, contact me. Otherwise, command of the fighters is yours, but do whatever you can to take out that driller."

Stone saluted and ran for the control room door, calling for two junior officers to follow him. Moments later, a ship-wide transmission cracked over the personal communicators as Stone summoned the pilots to the fighter bay.

Lance moved back to the counterhackers. They had already focused on the fighter bay, and there wasn't much else Lance could do to direct them. He waited as Stone's summon for the fighter pilots played out again, then sent his own transmission, warning all soldiers of the forthcoming hull breach. Then he thought of Montag and he turned to secure cooperation from the renegade and his crew.

That was when he saw Orion standing at the control room door, pawing at the controls and loosing short, frustrated grunts.

Montag was gone. So were the Shadow and her arkin. Lance's hand went to his weapon holster. His pistol was still there. Myrikanj was present too, but she seemed to sense that something was wrong and glanced around the control room. She noticed the absence of Montag and the Shadow, became saturated with anger and panic, and made to rise.

"No," Lance snapped at her. "You stay."

CHAPTER 11: RUNNERS

"We shouldn't have left Myrikanj."

"No," the hunter said. "Probably not. But the counterhack team would have noticed if she suddenly got up and walked away. She'll be safe. Ashburn will protect her." She considered the control panel of the shuttle. "I could use her now, though. I'm sure I can fly this, but first I have to figure out how to turn it on."

"You got the airlock open easily enough."

"It's an emergency shuttle. It has to be easy to get into. This part, though…" She flipped a switch, then hit a button. "It looks like the Star Feds have designed their shuttles to be different from every other shuttle in existence." Another switch, another button. "I don't know if that makes them very smart or very, very stupid."

Montag watched her work. He was very aware of the arkin Blade watching him, a four-legged amber-eyed shadow. The creature unnerved him, but the hunter seemed capable of holding the arkin in check and there hadn't been any incidents. Not other than a brief run-in with a soldier shortly after they had left the control room, at least.

The soldier barely had time to register what he was looking at before Blade had slashed at the hand that held the soldier's weapon, opening a wound up and down his arm, but it had looked shallow to Montag. Or maybe he had simply chosen to see a shallow wound in order to lighten his own conscience. Montag hadn't dwelled on the issue, and the hunter had relieved the soldier of his weapon. They had left the soldier bound and gagged in one of the side rooms and then ran through eerily empty halls until they found the shuttles: a neat row of small, cramped crafts that lined the outer hull of the *Argonaught IV* and connected back to the interior by a short hallway. The hunter had hacked the entrance door easily enough, and then the airlock of the first shuttle with even less effort. No one seemed to notice the breach, if the system even had security at all.

"We're lucky," Montag said.

"You keep throwing that word around." The hunter hit more switches. "You're not going to live much longer if you keep relying on luck."

"Luck got us out of the control room and through the halls," Montag replied. His gaze flicked to the arkin, met the level amber stare, and flicked away again.

"That wasn't luck," the hunter said. "That was the Seventh Sun. We got out of the control room because the Sun decided to toy with the Star Feds. There were no soldiers in the halls because half of them are climbing into fighters, and the other half are swarming on the lower decks, preparing for the breach."

The alarm had sounded as Montag and the hunter had wound their way to the shuttle bay. Montag was certain that he and the hunter had triggered the siren, and that the shrill noise had been warning the soldiers to track them down and kill on sight. The siren turned out to be a signal for outer hull damage.

Montag could still hear the low whine even onboard the closed shuttle, but it was distant now, muted. Montag could almost pretend that they had already left, that the *Argonaught IV* and the Seventh Sun's driller were fading behind them. Almost. His imprisoned crew pulled him back. He would have to find them soon, but he kept watching the hunter, watching what she did to power up the shuttle. He would need to know how to do this later.

The hunter worked for another solid minute, then suddenly stopped and cocked her head. Montag frowned, listened, and realized that the alarm had become shriller.

"They're through the hull," the hunter said as she bent over the controls again. Her movements became quicker, frantic. She turned her head once when she reached for a far button, and Montag saw the hard set of her jaw. Then she flicked another switch, the shuttle came alive, and she sighed in obvious relief. She slumped back in her seat for a moment, then immediately straightened. "Let's get out of here."

Blade broke the stare she'd fixed on Montag, and let out a soft whine.

Montag shifted. "Are you... taking me with you?"

The hunter paused. She twisted in her seat and fixed him with a metallic stare. "You want to come?"

"I need to get my crew."

"I can't wait for you."

"No," Montag said. "I don't expect you to."

The hunter nodded and turned back to the controls. "You're not going to like this, but if you're really set on getting them, head straight for the prison hold. Leave Myrikanj. She's valuable, she'll be safe. Get who you can from the prison and then get out."

Montag stiffened. "I won't leave anyone from my crew. Not when I can save them."

"Noble, but wrong. You need to accept that some of them will be arrested." The hunter toggled a control, and the shuttle's outer airlock hissed open. The breach alarm whined louder. "And some of them will die. Move quickly and you can probably get everyone out of the prison cells. Leave your first officer behind if he's not there, and forget Myrikanj. If you hear enerpulses at any time, run. Forget your crew. And don't look back."

"I will not leave anyone."

"You will die if you don't."

"*They* will die if I do."

"Montag," the Shadow swung around to face him, "you *cannot* save all of them. Let them go."

She didn't understand. She couldn't.

Montag's crew had been with him for years. There had been plenty of fights, arguments, threats. But there had also been closeness. They were loyal, trusted, family. When had this bounty hunter, this Nandro ever known anything like that?

"When you're a smuggler," Montag said, "you sometimes have to decide if your life is worth your cargo." The hunter turned away, but Montag continued on. "Some people will kill you if you don't deliver. The Star Feds will as good as kill you if you do, but they have to catch you first. I've never had it before where you end up dead no matter what you do. The Seventh Sun is like that, right?"

No answer.

"I usually take things up with the crew first," Montag continued. "See what they think before I take a job. We did that when you came to us asking for passage off Earth, but it was my decision to deal with the Sun. We needed... I needed the money after the last job went bad. I had to pay for the cargo I had flushed. So I took the deal and didn't tell the crew until we had left Earth. They weren't happy with me, but they knew the money situation, and no one started to panic until we picked up on transmissions from the Earth Monitors and found out you'd killed a Star Fed.

"We figured you for an Alpha then, and that's when nerves started breaking. I was worried about a mutiny until you started talking about Nandros and the Seventh Sun. Turns out they were more afraid of that than they ever were of you.

"They came together again after that. They expected to fight. They expected *you* to fight. I don't blame you for running. You're not tied to anyone. But with you leaving, I'm the only thing standing between them and whatever's coming. I did that to them, and if my life is the price, then fine, but I'm not going to pay up until I've gotten them out. They've risked everything for me, and I owe them that much."

The breach alarm tore the silence apart.

Then the hunter dropped her head, said softly, "You're wrong." She pressed a fist against her forehead and frowned at her bunched fingers. "There should be weapons in one of the wall compartments. Take two or three." She pinned him with a hard stare. "Keep one in your hand at all times. And move fast."

Montag hesitated. What did she mean? That he was wrong to risk his life for his crew? Or did she—

"Go," she snapped, and Montag went.

He found the weapons easily enough. Five enerpulse pistols. They were loaded with white energy capsules. White hot, killing shot.

Good.

Montag placed one of the pistols in his weapon holster, shoved another through his belt, then took two more, one in each hand. One pistol remained. He glanced at the hunter, but she was focused on the shuttle controls with her back to him. Montag considered the final pistol again, thinking that one weapon could be the difference between life and death for his crew, and the hunter still wasn't watching him. He was reaching for the last pistol when he noticed Blade.

The arkin was on her feet, glaring at him. She flashed sharp, ivory teeth and took a step forward.

Montag withdrew his hand. He moved to the inner airlock door, and glanced back at the hunter. He needed her to open the airlock for him, but she still hadn't turned around. "Goodbye," he offered awkwardly.

"You shouldn't have taken me aboard."

Montag looked at the hunter—Lissa, he remembered—for a long time, but she did not meet his eye. "No," he said at last, "you weren't the mistake."

Lissa half-turned to him, but stopped, her gaze snagged someplace between the now and the somewhere else. "Move fast," she repeated.

"Good luck," Montag said.

She looked at him fully then. Her face was all lean angles

and rounded points, her eyes clear and bright, too unnerving to be beautiful. She shook her head, sadly almost. "Good luck." Then she faced away and opened the airlock.

The breach alarm screamed around Montag as he left the shuttle. He winced as the sound tore at his ears, but he shook off the pain and moved away from the shuttle. The airlock doors sealed and the shuttle detached from the main ship. Montag watched through the transparent airlock of the *Argonaught's* hull as the shuttle reoriented itself, hung still for a moment, then leaped away towards the distant stars. Montage waited, but no Seventh Sun fighter went streaking after her, and if there really was a starship hiding behind Ametria, it did not move. Then the shuttle was gone, and Montag left the bay.

Lissa had made a good bet on the shuttles. The Seventh Sun had been too busy with the main ship to infiltrate the shuttles' independent computers, and that would be Montag's chance for freedom. But first he had to find his crew.

He made several wrong choices before he was fairly certain he was heading for the prison block. He found one small squad of Star Feds, but they had their backs to him and he was able to slip away. The breach alarm screamed and screamed as he ran through the curving halls, covering his heavy strides, but smothering everything else as well. He tried to listen for other footsteps or enerpulse shots, but nothing could overpower the siren. His heart was pounding more from anxiety than exertion when the alarm suddenly cut off, and Montag skidded to a halt.

The silence pressed into him. It felt thick and heavy, and Montag wanted to slice it with a scream. He forced himself to stay quiet, to accept the silence, and listen.

He heard nothing. Nothing except his own breathing.

Montag crept forward. Still nothing except his own sounds, but he knew better than to let his guard down. He strained his ears and his nerves, and was rewarded with the faint sound of footfalls.

Montag moved to the inner wall. He braced himself, adjusted his grip on the enerpulse pistols, pointed the weapons down the hall, and found himself wondering if Lissa would hesitate or shoot on sight if she were in his position. Probably the latter. Montag waited with his fingers resting on the triggers.

The footsteps grew louder. A figure appeared at the end of the hall. Alone.

"Stop!" Montag called.

The figure froze. A voice drifted thinly back. "Captain Montag?"

Carter.

Montag had never been happier to see his first officer's wide-set eyes and flattened nose, a reminder of the day Montag had taken over as captain of the *Resolution*. He had to break Carter's nose to get there. Then he made the man his fist officer, and Carter had been fiercely loyal ever since.

Montag clapped Carter on his thick shoulder as they met, and Montag's relief at finding the man alive swept through him in giddy waves. He fell back into reality as he remembered that Carter was supposed to have a Star Federation escort everywhere he went, but there were no Star Feds in sight.

"One of my escorts got called to the fighter bay," Carter explained. "I knocked out the other." He grinned and took a slow swipe at the air with a heavy fist, but Montag didn't see the smile in his eyes. Instead, he saw the limpness of Carter's right arm and the scorch mark near his shoulder, cinder-black on cloth-black. Carter's smile fell. "Not as bad as it looks." He started to shrug, but winced instead. "But bad for a clip. The Star Fed got one off before I took him out."

"At least it's not your shooting arm," Montag said as he handed Carter one of the pistols.

The smile was genuine this time. "What's the color?"

"White hot."

Carter laughed gleefully, then glanced expectantly behind Montag. "Speaking of killing, where's what's-her-name," Carter asked, "the bounty hunter? Shadow?"

"Gone."

"What? Why?"

"You saw her on *Resolution*," Montag said. "She was

scared."

"We're all scared, but I'm not afraid to fight," Carter growled. "Fuck the Nandros. I'll take them down by myself if I have to." He threw a heavy frown at the floor. "She was plenty dangerous as it was, but most things get even deadlier when they're scared. We could have used her. She could have taken down ninety-nine Nandros and scared the last one shitless in a heartbeat." He gave a rough laugh. "Sending the Shadow after them would've really fucked with them. Imagine their faces, finding out one of the deadliest bounty hunters in the universe is a human."

Montag said nothing.

Carter took no notice of the silence. "Where's Myrikanj?"

"Still in the control room. I figured we'd get the rest of the crew first, then pick her up."

Carter nodded. "Then what?"

"Then we go for the shuttles and get the hell out of here."

"Good plan." Carter started down the hall, back the way Montag had come. "The crew is in the upper prison hold. This way."

Montag followed, but said, "Are you sure? I just came that way."

"This damned ship makes no sense," Carter said. "There's a weird branch in the halls near the stern, I think. It's pretty far from here." He glanced around the gray hallway. "I think." He stopped, frowned, started forward again. "No, this is right. I got turned around once but I figured out how to get back on track. The Star Fed I knocked out makes a pretty good landmark."

"Where were you going?"

"I was trying to find the control room. I thought I'd grab you and Myrikanj while all the Star Feds were running around with their heads on fire. That bitch of an alarm really set them off." Carter breathed in deeply. "You've got to love the sweet smell of silence."

Montag smiled, but it jumped nervously across his face. "They got through the hull, you know."

"Yeah, I figured that when the bitch got louder, but the Star Feds must have plugged the hole if it's off, right?"

"Right." Montag glanced behind them. The hall stretched gray and empty until the curve of the ship swallowed it. "But where the hell are they?"

Carter paused, and Montag watched as he turned the question over in his mind. His first officer didn't like what he found underneath.

"There seemed to be a pretty big demand for fighter pilots," Carter offered. "The dogfights are probably still going on."

That was a possibility, but the empty halls demanded more. Montag did not have another answer. Neither did Carter. They walked in silence until they found the prison hold.

Montag took one look at the formidable doors and immediately wished he had made better friends with the Star Feds. No one was getting into the prison hold without total authorization. "I don't suppose," he said to Carter, "you have a hack tool?"

"No," Carter said, "but someone did."

He was right, Montag saw. Someone had left a small, thin machine linked to the controls. He moved to activate the hacker, but the machine displayed symbols that he had never seen before. He exchanged a bewildered look with Carter, then both men snapped their gazes forward as the doors to the prison hold hissed open. Three men and a woman emerged.

The first thing Montag noticed was that they all wore black collars around their throats, studded with seven stars each. Then Montag noticed their eyes, and remembered that he had found Lissa's eyes unnerving. They had been cold and metallic, hard to read. The stares of these people made her gaze seem like it had been full of life and open warmth.

The woman was short, lithe, and sinewy. There was a fluidity to her limbs that made Montag think of water, but when she moved there was a rolling quality that changed the image to mercury. Shining, beaded, deadly mercury. Her hair was lighter than Lissa's, her skin paler and her face rounder, but her eyes were the same silvery gray. No, not quite the same. This woman's eyes were flecked with chilling blue.

Two of the men were of a similar height to Montag. They were both thin, but not skinny. Lean. Like animals built for speed. Predatory animals that ripped through distance. They were as sinewy as the woman, but they lacked her liquid quicksilver movements. Instead, their bodies cut through space, slicing the air.

One of them was sandy-haired with a narrow face and a narrower gaze. His face and his body were all hard angles and plains, with a sharpness in his limbs that reminded Montag of knives. And his eyes, deep gunmetal gray with a bizarre red slash near the pupils. Blood on the blade.

The man level in height with the blood-eyed man was more squared in jaw and shoulder, but that just turned him into a broader knife, something made for chopping rather than carving. His skin was much darker than the others', and his eyes were the color of burnished copper.

The last man was taller than all the others, broader and slightly thicker, but there was a hunger to him that disturbed Montag more than any of the intense stares fixed on him and Carter. The last man stood motionless, no shifting weight or even visible rise of his chest as he breathed. He gripped an enerpulse pistol in one hand, but even that hung completely motionless at his side. In spite of the immobility, he looked ready to lash out and strike at the smallest invitation. Montag found himself trying to remain perfectly still.

The last man had very dark hair, a hard-set jaw, a faint smile on his slightly parted lips, and a pale scar running from the corner of his eye down the side of his face. It was by some miracle he hadn't been blinded by that injury, and both eyes were bright, pale gold. Brighter, paler, and harder than the others'. They gleamed hungrily as they fixed on Montag, and in spite of all his effort, Montag shifted uneasily.

"Nandros," he heard Carter breathe. Montag could have strangled him.

The quicksilver Nandro rolled her eyes over Carter, then

said, "*Naro arryn terako.*"

The sandy-haired Nandro with the bloodstained eyes shook his head and responded in the same language.

"What?" Carter demanded. He took a step forward before Montag could stop him, but in spite of his firmness, Montag saw that Carter's hand was shaking. "What did you say?"

The copper-eyed Nandro ignored Carter and smiled at Montag before speaking in the Galactic Unified Voice. "Captain Montag of the starship *Resolution*, correct?" No trace of an accent.

Montag swallowed his fear. "Yes."

"Where is our cargo, Captain? We had an agreement."

"That fell apart when you commandeered my ship." Montag was surprised at the steadiness of his own voice.

The woman rolled a laugh off her tongue. "Our apologies, Captain, but you were just so slow. We couldn't wait for you."

"No," Montag said after a pause. "I didn't expect you to."

"All the same," copper-eyes cut in, "where is our cargo?"

From the look in their eyes, Montag saw that they already knew the truth, that they were toying with him, but Carter jumped in before he could respond.

"Gone."

"Gone?" Copper-eyes feigned disappointment. "How tragic."

"Yes," sandy-haired blood-eyes said. His hand cut the air as he gestured to the others. "We were looking forward to the reunion." He stabbed a finger at the last man. "Him especially."

The last man said nothing, did nothing. Not even a blink. But something far behind him, deep in the prison hold, suddenly moved, and Montag's gaze snagged as the something advanced towards them.

The woman looked at her companions. Each syllable dripped off her tongue with exaggerated care. "It's just so hard to find good smugglers these days. No sense of self-preservation."

"Mm." Copper-eyes nodded in agreement. "His crew

seemed to have stronger survival instincts."

Montag tore his eyes from the advancing something and stared in horror at the Nandros. "What did you do?"

"Nothing," blood-eyes said. "Just had a look at them."

Montag glanced behind the last man and wasn't sure he believed that.

"That's all you'll ever do to them," Carter growled.

The Nandros were amused.

Blood-eyes took a step forward. "Or what?"

Carter stood his ground. "You'll never find out where the Shadow is headed." As the Nandros laughed, Montag shot a glare at Carter. His first officer frowned back. "She left! We owe her nothing."

The laughter broke off.

"Her?" Copper-eyes stared intently at Carter, who blinked and finally took a step back. That was all the confirmation they needed.

Three of the Nandros shot alien words back and forth faster than enerpulse shots. Their tone sounded shocked, confused, and Montag heard Lissa's name more than once. He watched the Nandros as their discussion drifted into argument, and was very aware of the last man watching him. Montag dared not move.

The argument suddenly broke as copper-eyes pulled out a communicator. He sent an urgent transmission, and received a slow reply after a short pause. Lissa's name came up again. So did the planets Yuna and Phan.

They knew.

Copper-eyes spoke a few more words into the communicator, then pocketed the machine and turned to Carter. "We thank you for the information. Your contribution is..." He searched for the word. "Enlightening." He looked at Montag thoughtfully. "She went for a shuttle, didn't she?"

Montag said nothing.

Copper-eyes sighed. "Well, we know where to find her." He glanced at the last man. "Your call on the final two."

Montag barely registered the last sentence. His eyes had

gone back to the thing behind the Nandros as it emerged from the prison hold.

It was an arkin. A huge, dark brown, electric-blue-eyed arkin, one that would have dwarfed Lissa's had the two stood next to each other. The dark brown arkin's wings were massive, too large to fold comfortably against its body. They wobbled as the beast moved slowly forward under heavy muscle, jaws hanging open as it panted, and Montag's terrified awe changed to full-blown horror as he looked at the arkin's open mouth.

Its jaws were stained with fresh blood.

"Fighter is mine," the last man said. "Jet, the runner."

Montag had already committed to the lunge. He'd told Lissa that if his life was the price, he would gladly pay it. He would still pay up, knew he would have to, but not before he took something back for his crew. They were beyond help, but not revenge.

The last man moved.

The pistol shot took Montag full in the face.

Carter ran.

CHAPTER 12: ECHOES

There was the smell of blood and burning flesh and the pounding of hearts and the thick cloying stench of fear.

There were screams of pain and sometimes one of the cries would be for mercy but none was left.

There was a cold trace of a shadow and once he found it the scar on his face pulsed and burned and he wanted to follow the path but the others told him to let it go, so he focused on the warmer trails that ended in beating hearts.

There were a lot of those, and he followed them all.

There was laughter in his ears that belonged to the others. He knew it came from the others because he had stopped laughing a long time ago. Once he had been delirious with pleasure but the satisfaction had faded after the first few tastes and now there was just the hunger and he could not kill the feeling no matter how many lives he fed it.

There were growls and roars from the beast that ran beside him, but no companionship.

There was fresh blood when the beast ran ahead and chased down the runners. He took the fighters, hoping to finally satiate the gnawing emptiness inside but he was always faster and stronger and the world was sticky with time. He felt trapped outside and tried to break in but something always pulled him back before the barrier could shatter so he followed the warmer trails, hoping that the next one would be the one that would lead him back in.

There were a few moments of dull pain when something hot hit his leg but one of the others stuck a needle in him and the numbness returned.

There was a burning glare over his vision that washed out everything that did not have a heartbeat.

There were voices beating in his skull that embraced the glare and whispered, *Welcome to the Light.*

Once, there had been a voice that had screamed, *No, no! Let it go, LET IT GO!* but it had drowned itself in its own echoes a long time ago.

CHAPTER 13: DOGFIGHT

Jason pulled back from the fight. His hellhound prowled around the edge of the skirmish, and he watched as the soldiers chased after and fled from the Nandros' fighters.

They couldn't touch the driller. Fifty-four Star Federation fighters to the enemy thirty, and no one had gotten anywhere near the thing. Plenty had died trying and now the numbers had leveled out. Jason and a few others had managed to take down a couple of the Nandros, but every time Jason whipped the hellhound around, a Nandro had ripped apart two Star Federation fighters. Bits of the destroyed fighters floated around the battlefield, shattered bones of the split-wing fighters and two of the few hellhounds that had entered the battle.

The hellhounds had surprised the Nandros. Their raw power was enough to throw the enemy off, but the level of skill that the hellhounds demanded from their pilots had given the Star Federation fleet a considerable advantage at the start of the fight. One well-handled hellhound was worth five split-wings. But the Nandros had recovered quickly and, to Jason's spiking horror, they had made a point of targeting the hellhounds first.

Jason had spent the first stage of the battle evading three

Nandro ships. He was pretty sure it had been the same three fighters that kept chasing and diving after him, although they had turned him around so many times that he'd given up keeping track.

Once they had chased the hellhounds back a bit, the Nandros had switched tactics and gone after the split-wings in order to level the field a bit more. Free to go on the attack, Jason had managed to take down two of the Nandros' fighters on his own. Three more had fallen to other Star Federation pilots. That wasn't nearly enough.

Jason circled the cloud of dogfights, trying to pick the lead fighter out of the Nandro fleet. It was an impossible task. The Nandros dipped and swarmed around the Star Federation fighters, not quite moving with a hive-mind mentality but never forming up around a leader.

Jason gave up. He could not throw a fleet into chaos when it already seemed to thrive on chaos. His own fleet couldn't hold the Nandros forever, and he sent his hellhound tearing back into the fray.

Three Nandros immediately locked on to him. Two dove straight at him, and he dropped to avoid their headlong rush. The third followed him, and the hellhound howled a warning as the Nandros locked on to his tail. Jason swung the hellhound in a sharp curve, then pulled up and drove the fighter towards the *Argonaught IV*.

The flat, ugly driller hung like a leech from the belly of the starship. For the first time, Jason had a clear shot at the thing, and his hellhound barked.

The fighter bucked wildly as the forward pulse cannon fired. He didn't try to fight the motion, and instead pushed the fighter further along its momentum before pulling the hellhound into another arc. He rolled the ship over, and swung it back towards the driller. He had just enough time to see what his shot had done before another warning howled and he had to bank and swerve to safety.

Nothing.

There was a scorch mark where the shot had hit, but it was

just a faint ring on the driller's armor. No damage beyond that.

Jason snapped a frustrated curse over the communicator, then ordered the other fighters to concentrate on the Nandro fleet and forget the driller. His soldiers sounded off acknowledgement of the order, and the pattern of the battle changed.

The dogfights raged on. Jason managed to clip two more Nandro fighters, but the pilots both brought their ships under control and eagerly tore back into the battle. He was going after the second clipped fighter when his hellhound howled again. Jason didn't have time to respond, and the shot slammed into his tail.

The hellhound shrieked and bucked, throwing Jason violently against the sides of the cockpit. He fought for control, but the hellhound resisted and he had to flip the fighter twice before he'd shaken off the surprise. He held his breath as he waited for the next shot to burst through the hull and tear the hellhound apart, but it never came. The voice of one of the split-wing pilots filled the void.

"You're clear, Captain Stone, I chased him off. You all right in there?"

The hellhound screamed and screamed. "I am, but I've got to bring this hound in and trade her out." He swung the hellhound around in a gentle arc and angled back towards the fighter bay. "Don't let up on the Nandros." He hesitated for a moment. "Harls, you still alive?"

"And kicking," Lieutenant Harls barked back.

"You have command while I'm gone."

Harls acknowledged the leadership change and Jason steered the hellhound back to the fighter bay as fast as he dared go. Harls ordered two soldiers to keep an eye on him, and they chased off the Nandros as Jason's hellhound limped back to the starship. The interior of Jason's pilot gloves were slick with sweat as he pushed the hellhound through the small force field that separated the bay from space, but the fighter made it through without any trouble. Jason docked near a row of split-wings, powered down the hellhound, hopped out of the cockpit, and was greeted by an eerie silence.

Damn it, Ashburn, he thought as he whipped out his communicator. "Commander," he barked, "where is the fighter bay crew? I need them *here*, in the fighter bay."

There was a pause, then, *"Get down."*

Jason dove for cover behind one of the split-wings. Ashburn's soft but snarled order had been more than enough to put Jason on the alert, and his training pushed his questions out of mind. He crouched behind the fighter, drew his enerpulse pistol, peered under the belly of the split-wing, and waited.

Two Neo-Andromedans appeared six heartbeats later. At least, Jason assumed they were Nandros. They did not wear gray Star Federation uniforms, and Jason doubted they were from the renegade crew that had come aboard with the Shadow.

They were on opposite ends of the room, and Jason could only see the full figure of the far one. The fighter screened the closer one from the waist up, but both Nandros moved slowly, cautiously, and paused at the beginning of the row of split-wings. Jason saw the far one throw a signal across the room, then they both started forward again. Still slowly, still cautiously. The Nandro closer to Jason paused and peered around each fighter before stepping forward. The far one was not nearly as thorough as she moved down the other side of the bay, and she kept glancing in Jason's direction. Not quite at him, but she never looked more than one or two fighters away from where he hid.

Jason took a firmer grip on his pistol. He'd have to shoot the far Nandro first. She would see him long before her partner did, and there was a fighter separating Jason from the closer Nandro. He could take out both of them in two quick shots if he moved right. If they moved right.

Jason's chance never came. The Nandros' communicators burst to life, and a short transmission in an alien language tore the silence apart. The far Nandro threw another signal across the room, then turned and ran. Her partner took off after her.

Fifteen heartbeats later, Jason shifted and edged around the fighter. The Nandros were gone, but he could not shake off the possibility of a trap. Or the possibility of everything going to hell. If the Nandros were running, maybe he should be, too.

He forced himself to go slow. He kept his weapon at the ready, and checked behind every fighter he passed. He looked back often and watched for movement, but never saw a flicker other than his own shadow. His nose helped him make one discovery that put his heart in his throat, but nothing had moved then, either. Unable to do anything for them, Jason left the crew of the fighter bay as they were, walked out of range of the smell of the corpses, and pushed the image of their twisted limbs, scorched black by enerpulses, out of his mind.

Jason did not find the Nandros. They had vanished.

He paused at the doors that opened to the interior of the ship, listening, but he heard nothing. He hadn't expected to. The doors formed a complete seal between the fighter bay and the ship. Still, he hadn't been able to resist the urge to stop for a moment. He couldn't pretend to be unafraid. Out of excuses to prolong the inevitable, Jason moved to the controls and opened the doors.

He scanned the hall as fast as he could, whipping his enerpulse pistol back and forth, but there was nothing. He moved slowly into the hall.

The doors to the fighter bay slid shut behind him.

Six steps and twenty heartbeats.

Total blackness.

Jason froze as the *Argonaught IV* died. Lights, ventilation, everything gone. He held his breath, waiting, dreading. His feet drifted up off the ground as the artificial gravity faded, but then he suddenly dropped back to the floor. A soft rush of air drifted through the hallway, and the lights came on again. Dim red light supplied by the reserve emergency power cells.

Jason looked slowly up and down the hall, never thinking he would miss the color gray so much. His eyes settled on the doors of the fighter bay, and he felt his stomach drop. The force field was gone, Jason knew, and with it, the ability of the fighter pilots to come in through the bay. They were stranded outside.

Jason's communicator came alive.

"Captain Stone?" Ashburn's voice was soft, but urgent. "Are you all right?"

Jason's hand shook as he lifted the communicator. "Yes," he said. His voice stuck in his throat, but he forced himself to speak. "The fighter fleet..." He couldn't get any more out.

"Communication is down again," Ashburn said. "Outside of the personals, we can't contact anyone. Who did you leave in command of the fighters?"

"Harls."

"We'll contact him on his personal, and he can warn the fleet. They're beyond our help after that." He paused for a moment. "I don't know where the Nandros are, but if they cut the power, they must be withdrawing."

"I'll head for the breach location, cut them off."

"No." Ashburn's voice had lost its softness. "Let them go. No more deaths today."

"And the fighter pilots?" Jason demanded, suddenly angry. "Do their deaths count?"

"Anderson is on her way."

Jason swallowed his anger, and a cold knot settled in its place. He and Ashburn left the big *if* of Erica Anderson's status unsaid. There was no renegade crew to warn her of a hacking attack. "And everyone else?" he forced out.

Ashburn's voice was quiet again. "Outside of the fighter fleet, there are twelve soldiers who are confirmed alive. We haven't found everyone yet."

"How many?" Jason said. "How many of them did this to us?"

Ashburn hesitated. "Not counting their fighters," he finally said, "ten."

CHAPTER 14: ZEROS

Ten.

Ten Neo-Andromedans to nearly nine times as many Star Federation soldiers, and the Nandros had torn through the ship.

Lance hadn't been there when the driller had fully breached the hull. He found out later that they'd cut into the carrier bay, but he was still tracking Montag and the Shadow at that point. He had taken Orion and gone after the escaped hunter, but they had not been quick enough. Orion had found the trail almost immediately, and the arkin had led Lance to a captive soldier, a missing shuttle, and finally Montag's body outside of the upper prison hold. Montag's crew lay slaughtered inside, most killed by enerpulse shots, but claws or fangs had torn into a few. Lance had wondered briefly if the Shadow had done this before doubling back to the shuttles, but the kills were too fresh. He would have met her somewhere between the hold and the bay, and the trail would not have led to the shuttles first.

Montag had been right, Lance realized. The Shadow had been scared, and she'd run the first chance she got.

Looking at Montag's body and the slaughtered renegade crew, Lance had wished that they'd run, too.

Lance had received a transmission from the lieutenant in the control room just as Orion picked up another trail. As the arkin's angry growls had rumbled through the hall, the lieutenant had said that the Seventh Sun had brought up visuals from the ship's security system, and the control room now had clear image feeds of what was going on throughout the *Argonaught IV*. The lieutenant had also warned Lance of the four Neo-Andromedans that were not far from his position, and of the massive arkin moving with them. Orion had been eager to follow the new trail, but Lance called him off. He knew that he would never stand a chance against four Nandros. Not alone.

Back in the control room, Lance had stood with the others and watched the Seventh Sun's operatives rip through the remaining soldiers onboard the starship. Lance counted ten Neo-Andromedans all together, plus the arkin. He had sent private transmissions to as many groups as he could, trying to direct them remotely, but those that stood and fought were killed soon after meeting the Nandros. One of the first soldiers that Lance watched die was the lieutenant who had been so eager to take on the Shadow. He fell to the group of four.

One of the Nandros in that unit was especially ruthless, and he had cut down more soldiers than any of the others. The massive arkin had stayed closer to him than the others, but Lance saw that there was no real bond between them. He wondered if he could somehow use that against them, but the lack of closeness had not stopped either of them from taking some degree of pleasure from the killing. Whenever the tall, dark-haired Nandro with the scar on his face had made a kill, he would hesitate for half a heartbeat, and relief would touch his face for the briefest of moments. Then the look would be replaced by wild hunger, and the scarred man would tear after another life. Lance had found himself watching the behavior patterns of the scarred Neo-Andromedan and the massive arkin with growing recognition paired with horror, and it was all he could do not to rush back out into the halls and try to take them down. But he had reminded himself that if the

Shadow had outmaneuvered him with almost no effort, then the Phantom would surely kill him.

Lance had torn up his emotions and pushed the scraps away, fragments to be dealt with later. Then he had shifted tactics and tried directing the soldiers to safety, but the Seventh Sun had picked up on what he was doing and blinded the control room to the locations of the Nandros onboard the ship. The locations of the soldiers, however, remained open, and Lance and the others had to watch ambush after ambush, death after death. The crew of the fighter bay had just fallen to a pair of Neo-Andromedans when Captain Stone's transmission came through.

"*Get down*," he had told Stone, and been grateful that the far end of the fighter bay was a blind spot in the security system.

Then the Nandros had received their transmission, fled the fighter bay, and disappeared completely as the power died.

Ten.

Ten Neo-Andromedans to kill over eighty soldiers, cripple a large starship, strand a fighter fleet, and shake one of the deadliest bounty hunters in the galaxy.

Four to slaughter unarmed captives.

Anger and despair followed Lance as he and the other soldiers broke out of the control room and scoured the halls for survivors after the reserve power had kicked in. Lance and the soldiers picked up Captain Stone and a few small groups of survivors, but they mostly found the dead. Finally, there was nothing left for them to do except file through the red halls, board the emergency shuttles, break away from the *Argonaught IV*, and drift through space with what remained of the fighter fleet, waiting for Captain Anderson. No one dared speak of the possibility that her ship had been attacked as well, but one look at the soldiers onboard his shuttle and Lance knew that very few were entertaining hope.

Myrikanj the renegade put a special strain on them all. To pass the time, she put herself in a trance, but a few angry whispers broke through her meditation chants and reminded the soldiers that the Shadow was responsible for everything.

She was right, in a way. Even if the Shadow hadn't been an operative, hadn't been part of the Seventh Sun's plans, she had killed them all by running. If she had stayed and worked with them, they could've had a better chance against the Seventh Sun's forces. Maybe more soldiers could have survived.

Then again, having seen how the Neo-Andromedans had moved through the ship and gunned down trained soldiers with minimal exertion, Lance couldn't help but wonder if the Shadow would have made a difference after all. She was only one Neo-Andromedan. Deadly and powerful, but still only one.

And of course, the Seventh Sun had a player to match her. Lance would need to run the data comparisons just for formality's sake, but he was certain that he had seen the faces of two Alpha Class bounty hunters within a few hours. Of course, with the *Argonaught IV* browned out and heading for Ametria, there was no chance that they would be able to recover the data. The recordings from the ship's security would be lost, but Lance held the faces of the Phantom and the Shadow in his mind. He would never forget them.

Then there was Myrikanj. He would need to question her, find out where the Shadow had been headed after Earth, what her behavior had been like before she had come aboard the Star Federation ship, but he let the questions sit for the time being.

Instead, he focused on keeping the ragtag fleet of fighters and emergency shuttles alive. They moved away from Ametria at a slow, cautious speed, but Anderson was still beyond communication range. Lieutenant Harls had been warned of the *Argonaught IV's* brownout and the inability of the fighters to return to the ship, and Harls told Lance that the driller had detached itself from the *Argonaught IV* and fled the battle along with the Nandro fighters shortly after Jason Stone had left the battle. Lance kept up a dialogue with Harls in his fighter and Stone on another shuttle as the mismatched fleet tried to stay alive, but there wasn't much for any of them to do.

So they waited.

Lance eventually roused the soldiers on his shuttle and they divided up the food and water from the emergency supplies. He advised Stone and the other shuttle leaders to do the same, and guilt pricked at him. Harls and the other fighter pilots had to listen to that transmission and be reminded that they had no food or water. Those stranded in the fighters could survive, but Lance knew that mental breaks would come, and they would prove deadly. Space was a difficult place to be stranded, even with intense training. No good would come of dwelling on that cold fact before time had run out, and Lance turned his mind away.

Ten, he thought instead.

Ten Nandros to kill nearly eighty soldiers, and as good as kill the survivors. Then they had withdrawn, leaving nothing for the Star Federation to go on. Not where they came from, what they were planning outside of this, nothing.

Nothing except the face of the Shadow, and where she was headed. They had slaughtered Montag's crew to hide the information, but they had missed Myrikanj.

The Yukarian wouldn't want to talk just yet. Her trance had mellowed, the whispers had faded, and she was calmly mourning her dead crewmates, but Lance knew that a cold anger would set in, and she would readily tell him everything she knew about the Shadow when the time was right.

One.

One Neo-Andromedan to track and take down. One solid target. Then, from there, the Seventh Sun. Yes, that could be done.

Just under an hour later, Lance's communicator came alive. Captain Anderson had arrived.

CHAPTER 15: NIGHTMARES

There hadn't been time to see Aven.

There hadn't been time for anything, except finding a ship that could take her and Blade to Yuna as quickly as possible. Lissa had found a tiny starship manned by two sullen, silent crewmembers and one hard-blooded Hyrunian captain.

Lissa didn't particularly like the captain, but she did like the hostile sternness of her. This was someone who would grudgingly take a passenger aboard since money was money and her ship was headed to Yuna as it was, but she would never be bribed to change course. Too inconvenient, and not worth her time.

The Hyrunian warned Lissa that the ship would leave whether or not Lissa was aboard, never mind the down payment. Lissa arrived at the port an hour early, and almost missed the ship; the Hyrunian had just fired the engines when Lissa and Blade came running.

Lissa did not challenge the captain for that. She knew the Hyrunian would take the silence as a sign of weakness, but a verbal battle was beyond hope. The Hyrunians were a proud, arrogant race, and a large number of them had never seen any reason to taint their tongues with Galunvo. This Hyrunian was no exception. Lissa and the captain shared one language, and neither of them spoke it particularly well. Their few conversations were broken and stilted. Outside of chartering the ship and confirming Yuna as the destination, few other words passed between them. With that barrier, all that remained was a physical challenge, but Lissa was not too proud to admit that fighting a Hyrunian would not end well for her.

Covered in hard, greenish-yellow scales with long, powerful legs, Hyrunians were built for fighting. Their stubby arms looked a bit ridiculous and were completely out of proportion with the rest of their anatomy, but a protruding jaw lined with sharp teeth and a thick, strong tail that supported their weight when they reared back to kick provided more than enough compensation. Their toes were studded with hard nails, but if the Hyrunians lacked the necessary space to rear back and kick, they could always drop their heads and ram their opponents with the thick horns curling out from their scalps.

Hand-to-hand combat was not Lissa's strongest skillset, but even if it had been, physical combat was completely out of the question, and Lissa gladly took silent scorn over affection.

The Hyrunian's crew seemed to feel the same way. There was no bond between captain and crewmen. No self-sacrifices this time.

Lissa felt an uneasy twinge as her thoughts turned to Montag. Love and loyalty had compelled him to look out for his crew, but Lissa knew that all his efforts had been for naught. She wondered if anyone had escaped the Seventh Sun's attack at Ametria, be they renegade or Star Fed.

The Star Federation had managed to keep the sabotaged *Argonaught* a secret from the galactic media, a truly admirable feat, but information would eventually leak out. Lissa could only hope that the pinhole opened soon. She was blind on Star Fed activity without it. She was more concerned about Myrikanj than the soldiers, but a few days spent planet hopping after the bounty pickup would undercut the Yukarian's information, provided Myrikanj and a few Star Feds had survived. On the off chance that they had, the bounty would bring in more than enough to cover the travel expenses and fund Aven's treatment for a while longer. But first she had to get the money, and the pickup was always the most dangerous part of the hunt. The bounty hunting game was messy all the way through, but the rewards were well worth the risks if a hunter knew what to watch for.

Sometimes, things went smoothly. Contractors paid promptly and in full, arrogant rivals did not try to steal credit for the kill, no ambushes, nothing. Successful pickups ranged anywhere from a few minutes to a few hours, depending on where and how the contractor wanted to meet.

This time, the contractor had set up the meeting out in the deserts of Yuna, away from prying eyes and crowded streets. This time, the pickup would not go smoothly.

Perched at the far edge of the Andromeda Reach, Yuna was too remote and too hostile a planet to attract fraudulent hunters, even when the contractor wanted to make the payment within the city. Staging the pickup in the desert would ensure that only the victorious hunter would arrive to claim the bounty, and just in case, the reward would be present in full. Then, of course, would come the ambush.

If the hunter was killed, the contractor regained their money.

If the hunter survived, the fight would give the contractor just enough time to slip away, and the hunter kept the bounty.

Aven had taught her to expect these things, but Lissa didn't begrudge the contractors like he always had. It was all just part of the hunting game, an extra step to make sure she'd earned the money and hadn't just been lucky. Bounty hunters were widely feared, but rarely respected.

Aven had needed to learn that the hard way, and he never had fully grasped the lesson. He had always managed to scrape through his ambushes, but his fight over flight mentality meant that he usually returned with injuries. Towards the end of his hunting career, there had been a particularly bad ambush, and although Aven had escaped, he had lost the bounty money. He had tried to get it back, had even tracked down the contractor, but the ensuing fight had not gone well and pressure from pursuers had driven him to charter the first starship he could find. He had paid double what he should have, but the ship captain had smelled Aven's desperation. The captain took the money, and then he took Aven to Banth.

Lissa shook her head violently, scattering the memories. She wouldn't let herself think about that now. She needed a clear head, especially now that they were on the final approach to Yuna. So Lissa blocked the memories and stood quietly in the tiny control room with Blade at her side, watching the captain and two crewmen prepare the ship for the touchdown.

"Land close," the Hyrunian captain barked. Slitted yellow eyes flicked between Lissa and Blade. "Money now."

"Land one," Lissa said. "Money two."

The Hyrunian growled, but did not push further. She piloted the starship in silence, but brought up the visual display with minimal hostility when Lissa asked for it.

Yuna swelled across the image as the ship drew closer. They were arriving a few hours after sunset, and the lights from the lone city flickered in a dingy yellow circle around the small, dark stain of the planet's one and only water body, a toxic oasis that underwent rigorous purification treatments in order to barely sustain the stubborn ring of life. Beyond the huddled lights of the city, blackness stretched out hungrily, swallowing the details of Yuna's surface and still craving more. A thin crescent of light around the edge of the planet showed the rich golden sand of the deserts, a tempting change from the insatiable night, but the air blistered and the sands burned under Yuna's white sun. Better to be eaten by the single, giant shadow that was the night.

The touchdown went smoothly. They were cleared to land almost immediately and an open dock was waiting for them at the ground port. The ship landed and settled between its two larger and bulkier neighbors, Lissa paid the captain what she owed her, and then she left with Blade. The captain had fed them as per the charter, and although Blade had been less than pleased with the food, Lissa and the arkin had eaten and rested. They were strong and alert as they moved into the warm, dry night. They would need to find another ship for the return to Phan, but there would be time and money enough for that later.

Lissa glanced across the port at Yuna's lone city. Squat, lumpy buildings made from rock and heat-compressed sand filled her vision, light filtering through the dirty yellow sandglass of hovering street lanterns and the very rare windows. The city was set up in a near-perfect ring around the large oasis, with the better-kept buildings closer to the water's edge. Streets ran in circles around the city and steadily widened as they approached the outskirts. Alleyways carved through the rings in rigid lines, running all the way from the oasis to the worn and sand-beaten buildings on the outskirts. The whole city was constantly under repair from moderate but persistent sandstorms, although the buildings around the oasis were in considerably better condition. The Yuni natives, however, all were like the city outskirts: rugged and weathered and stubborn enough to survive the harsh desert.

She would find lodging in the city if she needed it, Lissa knew. No one other than the Yuni themselves stayed on the planet longer than necessary, and there was never a shortage of space for travelers within the city. No one was ever warmly welcomed, but if the money was there, so was the shelter.

Lissa frowned suddenly, then moved until her back was shielded by the Hyrunian's tiny starship. She squatted next to Blade and whispered, "Keep watch." Then she withdrew her remaining funds and counted what was left while Blade stood guard.

Without the bounty, Lissa had enough for a room and meals for two nights, three if she found a particularly rundown place and haggled the price down. There wasn't enough to charter a ship.

The realization pushed her into nervousness. A dozen ifs surged through her mind, but she pulled herself away from the flood. She had to focus on the pickup, and then she could deal with whatever she needed to when the time came.

Lissa turned her back on the Yuni city. She and Blade

walked across the ground port, weaving between starships and a few crews. They reached the edge of the hard, smooth landing area and stepped out into the desert.

The sand shifted under each step, sucking at Lissa's feet. Blade made a distressed noise a few steps behind her, but she hadn't injured herself and was shaking the sand off of her paws. Blade began to unfurl her wings, but Lissa stopped her.

"They'll see you," she told the arkin, pointing up at a sky thick with stars. Blade's black silhouette would be too easy to pick out against that backdrop. The dark ground hid the arkin, and Lissa needed surprise as an ally.

Blade looked up at the night sky, her eyes glowing dimly in the sparse light. She looked back at Lissa, sighed softly, and tucked in her wings. She silently shadowed Lissa as they moved further and further into the desert. They stopped after they had crested several dunes, and the lights of the Yuni city were nothing more than a faint smudge on the horizon.

The contractor had broadcasted the final pickup coordinates during the run from Phan to Yuna. Lissa recalled the location as she pulled out her navigator, a small black sphere that displayed holograms of planets and star systems. She told Blade to wait, then moved into the valley of two dunes. She kneeled down and hollowed out a ditch in the sand, entered the pickup destination into the navigator, and dropped the ball into the small pit.

The navigator came alive, halting its fall and hovering the breadth of two fingers above the bottom of the ditch. The inky surface flashed streaks of blue as it brought up the information, and a blue hologram of Yuna enveloped the surface of the navigator. The display showed Lissa that they were heading in the right direction, and would arrive at the pickup after about an hour of walking.

Lissa returned the navigator to its place on her belt. She took out her vacuum storage cube, activated the thing, peeled off her traveler's clothes, folded them, and swapped them for her hunting outfit. She changed into the black clothing as the cube collapsed in on itself and shrunk down to a tenth of its expanded size. Lissa replaced the cube on her belt as she slipped the hunting mask over her head. She tucked in her hair, making sure that not a single strand was loose. Not for the first time, she considered cutting it all off, but the dark color helped to soften her eyes and make them seem more human.

A different kind of luck, she thought.

She checked her equipment, making sure nothing was out of place and that the holster of her enerpulse pistol was fully secured. Then she rejoined Blade and set off again. They stopped occasionally to check the navigator and search for signs of hostiles, but they reached the coordinates without trouble.

The smooth journey made Lissa uneasy. If there was going to be an ambush, it was going to be a quick, well-coordinated attack. She wondered if a sniper waited on the crest of one of the dunes, but they wouldn't have anything close to a clear shot unless they were in the immediate area, and she could pick them out if that were the case. No sniper, then. Possibly a group attack, a headlong rush, but that she could get away from if she moved fast enough. She was familiar with both scenarios, but this peaceful silence was strange to her. Everything felt off, and tension pulled at the back of Lissa's mind.

That tension had become an almost tangible strain by the time Lissa and Blade climbed the final dune. They crouched lower and lower as they neared the top, and finally they were both crawling up the slope. They paused just before their heads broke the crest. Lissa withdrew a pair of lenses from a pouch on her belt. She tugged her mask up, placed the lenses in her eyes, blinked a few times, and tried to keep her senses intact as the world suddenly swung into infrared. Lissa settled herself, then peered over the top of the dune.

Two people waited in the deep valley. Males, she guessed, and human from the look of them. The taller one was considerably stiller than the other, although both looked fairly calm and alert. The shorter man shifted his weight and occasionally glanced around at the other dunes, but neither of them spoke.

Lissa scanned the other dunes, but no one was around, as far as she could see. Far from reassured, she moved back down the dune and took Blade in a wide, slow circle around the meeting point. They found no one else, and returned to their position near the crest of a dune.

Lissa didn't like the set up. She had expected to meet with only one person, and if they were planning an ambush, it was very well done. She'd have to watch both people as well as the surrounding dunes. Briefly, she considered keeping Blade at her side, but if there was an ambush lurking somewhere in the desert, the arkin would serve better on patrol, although they both would have to be very careful.

Lissa pulled the lenses from her eyes. They were useful for picking out hidden enemies, but they confused her vision and left her dizzy if worn too long. She rested on the dune, waiting for her eyes to readjust to the Yuni night. Starlight would reflect off of weapons, and she could listen for signs of trouble beyond that.

When her eyesight had settled, Lissa sent Blade out to scour the dunes. "Stay on the ground," she whispered to the arkin. "Stay hidden, stay safe. Listen for me."

Blade pressed her forehead against Lissa's for a moment. Then she turned and slipped away.

Lissa watched her go, but she lost sight of the arkin within a few seconds. Blade's black fur melted into the night, and she was gone. Lissa felt an uncomfortable collision of comfort and vulnerability without Blade at her side, but she trusted that the arkin would stay close. Lissa flipped on to her stomach and studied the men at the base of the dune again.

They were dressed in dark clothes, but faint starlight edged their bare faces and glinted off the firearms they held in their hands. The men were alert, but not tense. They were expecting a hunter, and were wary, but were safe to approach directly.

Lissa stood and moved to the top of the dune. The sand shifted threateningly, but she stood balanced, and waited. The taller man glanced in her direction, paused, then nudged his partner. They shifted their stances and their grips on their weapons, starlight winking off the motions, but they did not point the weapons directly at her. Lissa returned the goodwill as she slowly stepped down the dune.

The men said nothing as she descended. They stood very still as she neared the base of the dune, but the shorter one lowered his weapon as she moved towards them. The tall man keep his weapon trained on a point just over her shoulder. Lissa shifted her aim to just next to the shorter man. He would be the more dangerous of the two.

"We received confirmation of the kill soon after you took out the target," the shorter man said. "The execution was flawless, and all signs pointed towards the Shadow."

Lissa said nothing, just kept walking forward, minding her footing in the shifting sands, but she felt a creeping sensation at the sound of the man's voice. It was familiar. Maybe from a prior contract, but that was unlikely...

"Your reputation as a killer truly precedes you." There was a dim spot of brightness in the dark. A smile. "Well done, Lissa."

She froze.

A wild heartbeat passed.

Then she stepped back and realigned her weapon. The sand rolled under her feet, and sucked at her boots. In the moment it took her to regain her balance, the tall man had moved.

He came on fast, too fast, and Lissa did not have time to fully adjust her aim. She fired anyway, but the tall man slammed into her and the enerpulse scraped past his shoulder to scald the side of a dune.

Lissa and the tall man grappled together, both lost their weapons, and then her leg was swept out from under her as the tall man bore her down into the sand. He ripped the mask from her head, pushed it into a ball, and stuffed it between her teeth, killing the scream just as it leaped off her tongue. Then he grabbed her wrists and roughly pulled her up, twisting her arms behind her back. He turned her to face the short man, and held her in a bone-crushing grip as she struggled. When she kicked back at him, he tugged her arms and pain burned from her wrists to her shoulders. She buckled under the sting, and the man pushed her further down until her face was pointed at the sand. A hurt and angry cry snagged on the gag, sounding more like a whimper when it managed to escape.

"Not too hard," the shorter man said. "Don't break her before we can work on her." He drew something out of his pocket, toyed with it, then held it out in front of him. It came alive in a burst of white, and Lissa had to turn her head away as the light seared her vision. "Welcome to the Light," the man said.

Dazed, Lissa cracked open her eyes and squinted up at the shorter man. He had moved closer to her, his face thrown into shadow by the blinding object that hovered just behind him and pulsed white.

A homing beacon, Lissa realized.

The beacon rose higher into the air, and the dark shadows melted away. She focused on the shorter man as he slipped into focus, and her knees went weak with fear.

She knew this man. Once, she had considered him a friend, but that had been a long, long time ago. Now she was just afraid of him.

Rosonno's posture was strong, firm, and limitedly patient. He was someone who could wait half a lifetime for something, but not an instant longer than was necessary. His hair was smooth and dark, his brow thick and his jaw square, a close match to her memory of him. He was older now, his face softened a little by the years, but his eyes had grown harder. They were still the same gray-blue striped with gold, but there was a flintiness to his gaze, a caged wildness that made Lissa edge back into the man that held her, never mind the dull pain that pulsed through her shoulders as she shifted. One wrong move, and Lissa would unlock whatever Rosonno had become. She didn't want to find out what that was.

"We were expecting Aven," Rosonno told her, "but you surprised us." He considered Lissa for a long, silent moment.

"When did you make the shift? Six months ago? A year?" He leaned closer, stared Lissa dead in the eye. "Five years?"

Lissa stared back at him, glad for the man that held her. He kept her from moving and giving anything away.

Rosonno already knew, though. He was looking for confirmation, but he knew.

"Where is Aven?" Rosonno asked. His voice was soft, warm, and edged with malice. Something strained behind his eyes, pushing against the bars of the cage of control. "Dead?"

Lissa's gaze involuntarily dropped to the collar Rosonno wore around his throat. Seven stars stared back at her. She pulled her gaze back to Rosonno's face and saw the thing behind his eyes settle again.

"Not dead, then." His eyes narrowed as he considered her again. "Yet." He straightened up and looked down at her without any kindness. "You'll tell us where we can find him, Lissa. After we've worked on you a bit." His smile was as white and even as the row of stars on his collar. "We've brought the survival rate up to sixty-eight percent. You're lucky."

Lissa's terror boiled into anger. She wanted to scream, to rush forward and tear at Rosonno with all her strength and rage and the weight of the dead that she carried. She struggled against the man that held her, fought against him and through the pain until the man suddenly released her. He grabbed her by the shoulder, spun her around, and drove his weight into her, knocking her flat on her back. He pinned her down, closed one hand around her throat, and clenched the other into a fist.

"No!" Rosonno's snarl cut the air. "We *cannot* waste time healing her."

The fist lowered, but the Phantom's pale golden eyes stabbed into Lissa's. The same cold hunger Lissa had glimpsed three years ago still twisted inside of him. She was only mildly surprised to see him, she realized. Rosonno had stolen all her capacity for astonishment.

Rosonno stepped near Lissa's head and dropped to a knee. "We brought him here just for you," he said, smiling again.

"We let him finish up with the Star Feds, of course, then we put him on a fresh ship and pulled him over here. No wasting time with a stop off at Phan."

Lissa made another noise, and this time, it really was a whimper. The Seventh Sun had always known where to find her, and she finally realized just how helpless she was before them. All that time spent running, and the Sun had always been a full step ahead of her.

"This could be your future," Rosonno continued, gesturing to the Phantom. "A stronger, faster, brighter future." Then he finally saw the look that the hunter had fixed on her. "Five years…" He glanced at Lissa with a newfound admiration that made her skin crawl. "It must have been you that marked him."

The knife wound had left a thin scar running down the Phantom's gaunt, pale cheek. The fight had been brief, and Lissa truly had been lucky that time, but the Phantom's stare said that the grudge had not been forgiven.

"He'll want to repay you for that, but we can keep you safe until your Awakening. There is not much we'll be able to do after that, but Awake or dead, you won't need us then."

The Phantom's grip tightened around her throat, either too subtly for Rosonno to notice or too lightly for him to care. Her breath stayed steady, but there was a desperate edge to the rhythm.

Rosonno stood and moved towards the homing beacon, face turned up to the light almost in reverence. The Phantom waited for him to step away, then pressed a little further into Lissa's throat, but he lifted his weight off of her body as he made to stand. She moved.

The Phantom tried to counter her, but the soft sand weakened his footing and Lissa wriggled back and broke his stance with a solid kick to the chest. She pushed the advantage and knocked the Phantom further off balance with another kick to his chin, then pushed out from under him and surged away. She saw the enerpulse pistols lying in the sand and dove for them. Her hand closed on one, and then she was scrabbling up a dune.

A hand closed on her foot, but she flipped over and swung her free leg around. Her foot slammed into the side of a head, and Lissa was surprised to see Rosonno reel away. He didn't usually handle fieldwork. She looked for the Phantom and saw him straightening below her, the other pistol in his hand.

Lissa grabbed a handful of sand and hurled it at the Phantom as he turned his eyes up to her. She didn't wait to see if she'd hit him, but turned and tore up the dune. She heard a grunt of rage behind her, and Rosonno's yell, but then she was at the crest of the dune. She leaped over the ridge just as the enerpulse shot slammed into her shoulder.

The shot bit and burned into her skin, and pain seared up and down her arm and through the top of her chest. She started to scream, choked on the mask, but was glad to have the thing when she hit the ground. The impact jarred her jaw and she bit into the fabric instead of her tongue as she rolled down the dune. Her vision went black as she came to rest, her shoulder throbbing. She gave her head a few precious seconds to clear, then pulled the mask out of her mouth. She reached behind her, gasping, and felt the enerpulse wound.

The clothing had burned away and her skin was hot and tender, definitely scalded, but not anywhere near as bad as she had feared. The shot must have been low-intensity, meant to cripple, not kill. Which meant that the pistol Lissa had grabbed was the one she had brought with her to Yuna, was white hot, but killing shots weren't much use if she could not find the pistol again.

Lissa scraped the dark sand with her uninjured arm. She glanced up the dune as she searched for the fallen pistol, waiting for the Phantom's silhouette to appear. She heard Rosonno loosing angry snarls at the hunter, and there was a stilted but dangerous reply, but she couldn't make out the words. Rosonno's homing beacon pulsed gently behind the dune. She'd thought the beacon had been brighter, but light sometimes could be deceiving. Lissa focused on the dark ground again, and her hand closed on the pistol just as the

Phantom appeared at the top of the dune.

The enerpulse streaked towards his head, but the hunter dropped below the sand crest and the shot winked away into the night. Lissa waited, but he did not resurface. She took a deep breath, then forced herself up and started to run. Her shoulder slowed her down, but she managed to put a few dunes between herself and the two men before the sound of wing beats pulled her attention to the sky.

She saw the dark shape against the stars, saw the arkin swoop down and land a few steps away. Then she saw the flash of electric blue, and she fired the pistol again. She was still dazed from the wound and the fall, and she misjudged the arkin's stance. The shot sailed wide, and Jet charged.

The arkin rammed her, blowing her off her feet. She landed on the side of a dune and the slope carried her down. Sand ground into her shoulder, and Lissa convulsed in agony. There was a deceptively soft *whump* as Jet's paw smashed into the sand just above her head, and a fine spray of grit hit her face. Lissa flinched as Jet's hot breath touched her skin, but he yowled and lunged away from her, twisting around to snap his jaws at something else.

Blade's eyes flashed amber as she danced away from Jet's bite. The arkins blurred in and out of sight, dark bodies rearing and jumping and surging in the night. Lissa heard their hisses and snarls, but they moved too quickly for her to track Jet and take a clean shot. Even without the injury, she doubted that she'd be able to hit the right arkin. All she could see were their eyes as they flashed back and forth across the darkness.

Blade moved faster, darting around Jet and sometimes disappearing behind him, but her small size gave her the advantage as she wove between him and the dunes. Jet lumbered after her, and Lissa heard the heavy slap of his paws in the sand as he lashed out at Blade. There was an occasional yelp when he made contact. Then there was a horrible howl, but it was Jet who threw his head back and screamed at the sky. Blade's head was near his side. Lissa heard something tear, wet and meaty, then Blade turned her eyes to Lissa. The arkin came at her, and Lissa scrambled on to Blade's back as the arkin raced past. Blade surged up a dune, jumped, spread her wings, and flew off into the night. Jet's howls chased after them and a single orange enerpulse shot streaked past Blade's tail, but the darkness opened its arms and they were gone.

They stayed airborne for most of the night. Blade started off at top speed, and Lissa was tempted to let her go, but she forced herself to bring the arkin down to a steady pace. They had no water, and Blade wouldn't survive the night, let alone the day, if she kept up the wild flight.

Lissa tried not to think about her near capture. She focused on the sand below them as Blade flew on instead. She felt herself slipping out of consciousness and tried as best she could to pull herself back, but there was one moment of pure terror when she suddenly jerked awake and found herself slipping sideways off the arkin's back. She pulled herself back up, leaned a little further over the arkin's back, and pressed her cheek against Blade's neck. The arkin whined and dipped a little closer to the ground.

Near dawn, they found a rock formation with a small network of caves inside. Most of the lower-level caves had been blocked off by migrating sand dunes, but Blade found a small, deep tunnel that opened into a large, empty cavern. The air was dry but cool inside. Blade yawned, curled up on the stony floor, and fell asleep almost immediately. Lissa stood in the dark, listening to the arkin's deep breathing.

Stupid, she told herself. *Blind. Weak. Stupid.*

She had thought that the Sun had made its move on the Star Fed ship. She had thought that was the first and final strike, that their only lead when they failed to catch her would have been her charter to Phan. They had turned Montag against her and he had almost delivered her to them. Almost. That should have been it.

She had never suspected that the Seventh Sun might have reached as far back as the bounty contract itself. They must have been monitoring the Shadow, probably through the very Star Federation officer they had set up for assassination.

Rosonno had more than hinted that the Sun had taken note of the behavioral shift when the Shadow changed hands, why shouldn't they have figured out that she'd be desperate enough to take out a Star Fed this time around?

Montag, then, had been a decoy of sorts. If he had delivered her as promised, then the Sun would have had her sooner. The bounty pickup on Yuna was the failsafe.

Underestimation had saved her this time, Lissa suspected. Rosonno had once described her as soft, fragile, and too weak for an Awakening. Aven had always been the better candidate, but Rosonno must have changed his mind once he had learned that she had taken over as the Shadow. He would revise his opinion entirely if he ever found out about the virus that now burned through Aven. Then she would be the prime target.

The Phantom was another problem entirely. Lissa had known what he was the instant she had seen him three years earlier. She couldn't believe that she had met him twice and survived both times, although she knew that she was counting a premature victory. She still had to survive Yuna's daylight, and get off the planet before the Sun found her again. That would be difficult enough without the Phantom hunting her.

How far, she wondered. *How far do I have to run before I'm free of them?*

Light touches everything, Rosonno's voice cut across the years. *Nothing is faster, nothing is concealed from it.*

Lissa felt the darkness press against her. She wanted to stay in it forever, but knew the safety could not last. She could not run and hide forever, could not keep Aven hidden forever. Someday, the Seventh Sun would find him. Or her, but of course, they'd already done that.

She tried not to think about that. Instead, she focused inward, trying to calm herself. She found fear. Then anger sparked, flared into rage, spread in a hot wave over her body.

Welcome to the—

"NO!"

She did not realize that she had screamed, but she must have, for Blade came awake and jumped to her feet.

Lissa's ragged breathing filled the cave, rasping against the stone walls as she fought the wave. She couldn't lose control, not now. Not ever. Not after what she'd seen the Sun do, had seen the Phantom do, had seen Aven do.

Lissa dropped to her knees as the wave surged over her. She gasped as she fought it back, but it was too much, threatening to overpower and overshadow her. She heard Blade whine, and she answered with a pained cry of her own, holding on to the arkin's presence and her own life as her only tethers to control, and then the wave was gone, receding into nothingness. Exhaustion and despair slipped into the void it left behind, and Lissa collapsed on the ground as her vision blurred with tears.

She eventually became aware of Blade lying beside her, one wing stretched protectively over her. The arkin had fallen asleep again, but Lissa listened to her soft breath and felt her heart rate slow. Lissa curled up beside the arkin, tried to sleep, and twisted under nightmares.

She dreamed of a thousand nameless faces staring at her, with eyes that were once deep and shining but had faded to pale metals. The eyes did not blink, the emotions had all drained, the faces did not move. Not until they opened their mouths in unison and screamed, "Welcome to the Light!" Then the faces cracked, most shattered, and the rest bled through the fissures.

Lissa gasped and rolled on the hard ground, and the dream changed. The Phantom stared at her with glittering pale eyes, but behind his gaze were her dead. They twisted and shifted behind the hunter's golden stare, smoke-like wraiths that coiled around each other as they fought to tell her something. Most were the faces of targets, a blend of faces that she had never known. She could ignore them, but the familiar faces were the ones that pushed the hardest. The Phantom opened his mouth twice as two of her dead surged to the front, once for a boy and once for a fuzzy image of a woman, but only croaking sounds came out. Then one broke through the smoke, solidified, and said, "You're lucky." The Phantom's mouth moved, but it was Montag who spoke.

Lissa shifted again, and so did the dream. She was in darkness now. She was running. Blade was next to her, keeping pace with her, but there was a desperation to the arkin that Lissa had never seen before. There was a strengthening light behind them, and their shadows stretched far ahead as they ran on. Lissa did not know what they were running towards, but she did know that if they looked back, they would be blinded. "How far?" Lissa panted at Blade, but the arkin did not answer. They ran and ran after their shadows, trying and failing to catch up with them, until the ground shattered under their feet. Blade spread her wings and flew away, but Lissa fell, hard and fast and towards her death. She squeezed her eyes shut, wondering why she bothered when there was nothing to see as she fell into the dark, but death never came and she realized she had stopped falling. She opened her eyes, and found Aven looking back at her. Aven, when he had been young and healthy and looked so much like Lissa that he had once called her his reflection.

"It wasn't your fault," he whispered.

"I never thought it was," she whispered back.

"No," Aven said sadly, "not until I made you believe it was."

They looked at each other for a long time.

"You have to let go."

"I can't."

"Liar, *Arrilissa*, liar."

"You're all I have."

"And now you don't have yourself."

Lissa said nothing.

"Let me go. *Harakaa ni çyasna, Arrilissa*," Aven said. "You have the strength, Little Light."

Then he was gone.

Lissa's sleep was gray after that. Gray and dreamless. She woke to Blade nudging her. Her shoulder throbbed with dull pain, and Lissa cleaned and dressed the wound as best she could with her meager medical supplies. She searched her belt, found and swallowed an emergency nutrient tablet, and forced Blade to do the same. When Lissa checked outside, dusk had fallen. The heat from the day still shimmered on the air, but a light breeze carrying the promise of night sighed across the sands. Lissa and Blade left after darkness had fully fallen, and flew back to Yuna's lone city under a sky howling with stars.

Lissa knew that she wasn't ready to let go just yet. First she had to warn Aven's doctor. First she had to see her brother again. First she had to say goodbye.

And then?

CHAPTER 16: FLIGHT

The oasis at the center of the Yuni city beckoned to Lissa and Blade with all the seductive power of cool, deep water in the middle of sun-scarred wastelands, its scent hanging on the night breezes like unfinished promises. Thirst scraped at Lissa's throat, but she forced herself to hold her raging lust for water in check. There was danger at the oasis, and not just in the unfiltered toxins of Yuna's water.

The Seventh Sun hung over the city like a poisonous cloud. They glided through the streets dressed in dark clothes with hoods that concealed their faces and strips of cloth wrapped around their noses and mouths, not an uncommon sight on sand-blasted Yuna, but Lissa picked them out at a glance. Their postures were stiffer, their steps sharper, their glances harder. There weren't a lot of them, but they were combing the city, searching. Yuna's locals and visitors alike paid no attention to them at first, but the Sun was aggressively hostile and it didn't take long before the city began to eye them with distaste.

The areas closest to the oasis were thoroughly searched, but the main starship ground port was of special interest to the Sun. They chased off incoming ships and forced their way on to the grounded crafts. They left most of the crews alone when

121

they failed to find anything, but a few of the more physically assertive captains were left broken and bleeding on the ground, their crews too stunned to retaliate.

Lissa watched the ship raids from the flat roof of one of the sandstone buildings. Blade crouched next to her, watching the sky for the Phantom and everything else. Lissa and the arkin were relatively safe up there. They were just two more dark shapes among the hundreds of creatures that leaped across the rooftops at night, chattering and hissing and yowling at each other and at the crowds in the streets down below. Once in a while, something would saunter up to Lissa and Blade, but the arkin chased it off and there wasn't any trouble. There was one incident when a wild arkin dropped out of the sky right next to them, but it was small and sand-colored and just looked at them curiously before slipping away again.

Ignoring the creatures as best she could, Lissa watched the Seventh Sun move over the port. They had managed to completely ground the docked starships. Lissa could hear the captains yelling in protest, but they had learned from the mistakes of the others and kept their distance from the Sun's operatives.

The control could not last. The Seventh Sun was deadly, but Yuna was another breed of danger. If the visitors didn't lash back, then the Yuni natives would. There was no affection between the Yunis and the travelers and traders that came in to port, but there existed an unspoken peace treaty that the Seventh Sun was threatening.

Lissa could almost feel the tension crackling through the dry night air as the crews of the grounded starships began to form bigger and bigger packs. They began to press the undrawn borders, seething around the edges of the port and slowly boiling inwards.

The Sun ignored them, focusing completely on the ships. They missed the critical moment when a large group of Yunis blew out of the city and descended on the ground port like a sandstorm, but Lissa saw it clearly. She watched the Yunis join the crews, saw the brief hesitation as unspoken agreements filled the air, and then the Yunis and the visiting crews moved in.

The Seventh Sun agents in the port held their ground fairly well, but it wasn't long before enerpulse shots began to light up the night. Reinforcements must have been called, for several of the Sun's city combers suddenly turned and raced towards the port.

That was the opening, and Lissa took it.

She clung to Blade's back as the arkin leaped from roof to roof. They crouched low whenever they saw one of the Sun's people down in the streets, but Seventh Sun was focused on the ground port riot, and the arkin slipped by unseen. Lissa looked for the Phantom and Jet, but the Sun must have sent them elsewhere. Maybe they were searching the desert, trying to follow Blade's trail over the hot sands. Then Lissa remembered the tearing sound she'd heard during Blade's fight with Jet, and she wondered if the Phantom's arkin was even able to fly.

Lissa and Blade found what they were looking for along the southern shore of the oasis. They weren't far from the ground port, but a private dock set just at the water's edge hosted four small starships arranged in a neat line. Several hovering sandglass lanterns illuminated the area and winked off the surface of the oasis, but the private port was totally deserted. Lissa and Blade checked the closest buildings, but all they found were a few Yunis running down a nearby street. They carried enerpulse rifles, but like everyone else, they were heading for the major ground port. No signs of the Seventh Sun anywhere.

Lissa and Blade crept into the light of the private port's sandglass lanterns. They gave off a softer, yellower light than the harsh beacon that Rosonno had thrown up in the desert, and the lanterns made fat shadows around the bases of the starships. Lissa hesitated for half a heartbeat, listening to the distant noises of the ground port riot and breathing in the taunting smell of the toxic oasis, then dove into the little pools of darkness, Blade at her heels.

Blade stood watch while Lissa hacked the airlock of her chosen starship. She had picked the smallest one, but it was in great condition and she was familiar with the model. Gaining access to the starship took more time than the Star Fed shuttle had demanded, but the lock finally hissed open and Lissa climbed inside.

She checked the stores and found plenty of food and water. She cracked open a container of warm, clean water and split the amount with Blade. The arkin lapped the water slowly, relishing each drop, her eyes narrowed to two slits of pleasure. Lissa took a swig of the water and held it on her tongue. The water was blood-warm, but it softened her mouth and calmed the scratching in her throat. She took another slow sip while she worked on the ship's silent alarms.

When they had finished the container, Lissa offered part of a food ration to Blade, but the arkin turned her nose up at the sterile provision, flew off before Lissa could stop her, and returned with a small animal dead between her jaws before Lissa had time to finish fuming. Not for the first time, Lissa cursed the arkin's stubborn independence, but she did it silently. They quickly ate as Lissa finished working through the security systems and scrambled the ship's signature. When they were finished, Lissa gave Blade more water and then sipped from a small container as she worked at the ship's controls. Powering up the ship was considerably easier than breaking in. Lissa fired the engines, double-checked the systems, and brought the ship off the ground. She steered the starship out over the water, then angled up at the stars. She found and activated the ship's cloak, but she didn't put much faith in the system and kept a close eye on the trackers. Three starships took off shortly after she did. Lissa felt panic creep in, but the ships veered on to their own courses and left her alone.

The Seventh Sun must have lost control of the ground port. She knew they wouldn't take that well, and she hoped that those who remained on Yuna's surface were smart enough to keep their heads down. That was unlikely. Even if the renegades and Yunis fully understood the danger of the

Seventh Sun, they still might try to fight, but Lissa turned her mind away from the thought and focused on piloting the ship. Only when she had run through the systems again, set a course for Phan, and fed herself another half ration of food did she let herself think about what she was running towards.

She knew going back to Phan was dangerous, but she also knew that the Seventh Sun had no idea where Aven was. To them, Phan was just a steppingstone. They might have stationed a few agents there, just in case, but it was a big planet and she would be able to avoid them. And the faster she got there, the better her chances of catching the Sun by surprise. They had, after all, planned to capture her on Yuna.

The Seventh Sun's greatest weapon was their ability to outthink and outplan their opponents and their prey. They accounted for every detail, and although their slipups were rare, they learned quickly and never made the same mistake twice. But toss in a little chaos, a little unpredictability, and they could be outmaneuvered.

All Lissa needed to do was be unpredictable. But first she had to figure out what that meant before the Seventh Sun did.

And then?

CHAPTER 17: CONTACT

Phan, Myrikanj had said.

So they'd gone to Phan, but there was no sign of the Shadow.

The higher-ups had wanted him to return to the Star Federation station after the first failed search. Lance had argued with them, and won, but he knew he was pushing his luck. His superiors usually welcomed his independency and willingness to strike out on his own, but that was before he had made contact with the Neo-Andromedans and lost nearly one hundred soldiers to a small group of them.

But this was something more than just a resurgence of Neo-Andromedans. An organization like the Seventh Sun wouldn't have exposed itself for something as simple as that. A demonstration, the Shadow had called it, or a test. Something to show their superiority over the Star Federation, over the galactic alliance that had been built to end the Andromedan War and purge the Neo-Andromedan threat.

The Seventh Sun had met that goal; their agents had been far superior to Star Federation soldiers. Now Lance had to figure out their true motive. He knew the Shadow was the key.

Captain Stone did not share his opinion. Neither did Anderson. "She was a trigger for the trap," they said, although

Anderson argued the point more forcefully than Stone.

When Lance pressed the male officer's hesitation and brought up what Montag had told them, Stone said that he wasn't entirely sure what to believe, but he sided with Anderson in the end. Theirs was the more solid argument, but Lance knew that something was about to shatter. He just hoped that he could figure out the Seventh Sun's objectives before that something became his authority.

The captains were still under his command and did as he ordered, but Lance could feel his control slipping. One more misstep and the higher-ups would yank him back and give whatever was left of the mission to someone else. They warned him that they were on the verge of doing exactly that as things stood, but what they did instead was almost as bad, if not worse.

Concern over a return of the Neo-Andromedans outweighed caution, and the Star Federation sent most of Lance's captains and their command units to Phan to assist with the search. The planet was crawling with soldiers. They were undercover, but a bounty hunter like the Shadow would know how to pick them out, especially when there was such a large number of them. Their presence was beyond Lance's control, but he bit down on his frustration and made use of them as best he could.

The planet had three main ports. He gave two of them to Captains Stone and Anderson. First and foremost, Stone and Anderson were the most capable captains he had, and he could trust them with the large ports. But he also wanted to send them away and be free of their accusing stares. They would also focus better if he kept them apart. They thought that they were being subtle—and to their credit, they were for the most part—but Lance had noticed the change in their behavior a while ago and he couldn't afford to have them distracting each other at this stage.

Lance took the last and largest port for himself, but needed one of his officers to assist him as the port was connected to a major city. Captain Backélo surprised him by volunteering, but he accepted the Rhyutan's offer and sent the rest of his captains out to various smaller ports and cities across the planet. He spread them as best he could, even setting up several squads tasked with flying over and scanning the forests, but the Star Federation presence was still thick and heavy, too strong to go unnoticed. There wasn't much he could do about that, except focus on his own area and hope for the best.

They spent five Phani days looking. They checked ships and records, had patrolling Star Federation ships flag down and search potential transports, scoured the cities and wracked the ports, but the Shadow had slipped away once again.

Captain Backélo's determination to find the Shadow only seemed to increase as the trail went colder and colder, but Lance found his enthusiasm naïve and irritating. By the fourth day, Lance could not turn around without Backélo being there, ready with another question about the city or a new proposition for a search area. Normally, Lance would have welcomed that, but Backélo was one of those soldiers who was better off operating under orders than crafting his own agenda, and Lance was running out of ways to keep him busy. He was almost glad that he would lose control over the search soon.

Lance knew that he would have to admit defeat within a day at most and report back to the station. He also knew that he couldn't blame the failure on the increased number of Star Federation soldiers. The initial search had been conducted the way he wanted—small-scale and focused—but they hadn't been able to stop all of their target ships from leaving the planet. One took off nearly an hour before it was scheduled to, and Lance hadn't been able to alert a Star Federation patrol in time. He knew that the Shadow had slipped away sometime during the primary search, but he'd performed the more thorough secondary search as per his superiors' request.

Nothing.

Unsurprisingly.

Lance held on to a thin bit of hope that the hunter would return to Phan. The planet was a prime steppingstone, and the

Shadow would need to stop somewhere if she was heading out of the Andromeda Reach. Backélo agreed with the idea and threw himself into the task of narrowing down the locations where the hunter would arrive, but Lance knew that they wouldn't be allowed to remain on-planet long enough meet her if she did make the return. Or at least, Lance wouldn't be able to stay as the commanding officer.

Memorial services for those who had died at the hands of the Seventh Sun could not be put off much longer, and after that, Lance would have to work with Intelligence to piece together all the information he had on the Seventh Sun. There wasn't much, but he would be kept busy for a long while, and all for naught.

He had no idea what the Seventh Sun would do next. None of them did. The Shadow might, but she was gone.

On the sixth day of the secondary search, Lance gave command of his search area to Captain Backélo. He knew the order to return would come through that day, and he wanted to take a walk and clear his head as best he could before he returned to the station in shame. Backélo tried to give some flimsy excuse to accompany him, but Lance shot the Rhyutan a look hot with anger and Backélo backed down.

Lance dressed in traveler's clothes that day. He wanted to blend with the crowds and forget for a moment that he was a Star Federation soldier, but he'd never had much success with that the few other times he had tried. The weight of his rank pressed down on him, and a voice whispered at the back of his mind, *You wanted this. You came back for this.*

He could have stayed far away, could have lived a very different life, but he had proved unfit for the only life outside the Star Federation that had been open to him. Time spent with Red Jack had drilled that lesson into him.

"Hold this," Red Jack had said when he had walked up to Lance and handed over a small pack of hallucinogenic spices. Red Jack had been a ruthless leader of a minor gang on one of Earth's outpost planets, just barely out of his teenage years but with blood on his fingertips already. And Lance, a fresh-faced runaway Star Federation brat, had been without money, without friends, and without any idea of what he was doing. So he'd held the spices while local authorities caught and searched Red Jack and his gang. After that, Lance had been allowed to tag along, but more as a pet than anything else. An unwanted pet that needed to earn its keep.

"Shoot this," Red Jack had said next. That had been after Red Jack had gathered several more followers, and his gang had gained a bit of power as well as some new enemies. The night Red Jack had handed Lance an enerpulse pistol and told him to stand watch while the gang ran a raid on a rival's territory, Lance had shot the pistol three times. He knew that he had hit someone each time, but the darkness had washed out all identities and he felt eerily detached from the action. It was not the first time he had fired an enerpulse weapon, but it was the first time he had fired one with the intention to kill.

"Kill this," Red Jack had finally said. His gang had grown considerably by then, in numbers and in power, and Lance had been eager to officially join and feel like he belonged somewhere. Red Jack had smirked and handed him a small, fuzzy gray animal. "You want to join? Kill this."

Instead, Lance had named the last this "Orion" and gone back to the life he had been bred for. When Lance had reached the rank of lieutenant and been granted permission to craft and carry out a minor agenda within Star Federation territories, he had gone after Red Jack. That decision had earned him his next promotion.

The elimination of Red Jack had been the only personal vendetta Lance had allowed himself to indulge in. It had taken him nearly a full sidereal year to escape Red Jack and make his way back to the Star Federation, and Lance had dipped into the gray areas on both sides of the law during that time, but he had made it back, he had completed the training, and he had gone on the hunt. He had carried the smell of scorched fur and flesh with him, and the stench had lingered in his nose as he came face-to-face with Red Jack one last time. For a brief moment, there had been panic and real fear in Red Jack's eyes, and Lance had considered sparing him. Then he had remembered.

Orion had almost died when Lance had refused to kill the arkin himself. When Lance had said no, Red Jack had simply smirked, and then he had shot Orion while the arkin sat cradled in Lance's arms.

There had been no gray areas with Red Jack.

The Shadow, however, was another story. She was an Alpha Class bounty hunter, but something just did not fit. But that did not matter anymore. Not for him.

You wanted this.

Lance finished dressing in the traveler's clothes, then took Orion out for a walk, ready to get away from the fruitless investigation for however long he could.

The arkin led Lance out of the starship and through the swarming ground port, weaving in and out of crewmen as they darted around their respective ships. The docked starships stretched in two long, mismatched rows, their hulls gleaming in a thousand different neutral hues running all the way from snowy white to a black so deep it drank the sunlight and gave off no reflection. The shapes of the ships ranged from squat and lumpy to lean, predatory angles and hard, sleek edges. Most of the ships were fully grounded, resting on lowered landing gear or suspended by docking bracers. A few hovered over their spaces, either taking off or moving in for the final touch down. Between the rows of starships was a central aisle filled with a mix of faces and bodies just as diverse as the crowds found on the Star Federation space station, if not more so. There were usually more humans in Star Federation territory as a significant percentage of the soldiers were human, but Phan was an open port and traders and travelers came from all over. One thing that the Phanite visitors had in common was that they all gave Orion a wide berth as he snaked his way across the port, and Lance followed in his wake as he moved into the connecting city.

The city was not Phan's largest, and its tallest buildings were shorter than most of the broad-leafed trees that covered the planet's surface, but the city still sprawled over a considerable distance and the streets were thick with people. Orion cut his way through the crowd, and Lance followed with his mind wandering to a thousand other places. He wondered where the Shadow was, where the Seventh Sun was, where he would be after he had dealt with procedure and the higher-ups had released him back into the field. If they released him back into the field.

He could just hear them now, lecturing him on the dangers of all Neo-Andromedans. One or two of the human superiors might ask him if he had forgotten what the Andromedans had done all those years ago, even back before Earth's First Contact. Was he willing to forget about the pre-Contact exploration team that the Andromedans had abducted and experimented on? Was he willing to forget that the Neo-Andromedans were born out of the deaths of those people? Was he willing to forget about the lies the Andromedans had fed to the galaxy as they continued experimenting on humans long after the First Contact? Was he willing to forget that the Andromedans had tried to build an army, that they had meant to conquer the galaxy, that they had wanted to replace humanity with a mutation?

No, Lance might have said to those questions, *but we chased the Andromedans out a long time ago, and left the Nandros with nowhere to go.*

But that was a response for another time, another life, when his career was not on the line.

His attention was suddenly pulled back to the present as Orion halted. The arkin's ears twitched, he sniffed the air, and then he looked up at the roof of a building a little ways ahead. Lance followed his gaze, and his heart stopped.

Perched up on the roof of one of the taller buildings, head thrust over the edge and staring down at them, was a black arkin. It tensed visibly as it realized that it had been seen, then turned and leaped off the roof, on to the next building. It took off running.

Lance threw himself on to Orion's back, shouting "Move!

Move!" at the crowd in front of them. They looked back at him blankly, but an angry roar ripped out of Orion's throat and the sea of faces boiled away. There wasn't enough room for Orion to spread his wings and take off, but the line that had opened let him run.

Orion sprinted down the street, Lance shouting warnings to those ahead of them. People jumped out of the way as Orion ran parallel to the black arkin, and he kept a close pace with its rooftop sprint. The black stayed a ways ahead of them, just barely visible as it flashed along the edges of the roofs, but Orion never let the gap widen.

Strangely, the black did not take off and fly, but as he watched it, Lance realized that it was scanning the streets as it ran. It wasn't watching Orion. It was looking for someone.

The black didn't find whomever it was searching for. But it did hesitate on the flat roof of a large hospital, frantically scan the streets around the front of the building, fidget in obvious agitation, then spread its wings and take off.

Lance leaped off Orion's back, pushed and shouted people out of the way, and managed to clear an area large enough for the arkin to spread his wings. Orion tore into the sky after the black, and the two arkins disappeared into the distance.

Lance sent a private transmission to Captain Backélo as he moved into the hospital. "She's probably here to treat some minor injury from her pickup," Lance told him. "Clear the area of civilians and lock down the building. No need to maintain cover, we've got her."

Backélo acknowledged the order, and promised to be at the hospital with reinforcements in less than ten minutes.

Lance burst into the hospital and whipped questions at the first staff members he found, asking after a dark-haired woman who might have come in for recent injuries. The staff tried to ignore Lance, and then they tried to stop him when he made to move deeper into the building, but he flashed his Star Federation identification and their behavior flipped. They gave Lance access to the rest of the hospital and directed him to the wing where he would find Dr. Kyle Chhaya. Lance raced through the halls, was held up for only a moment at a decontamination checkpoint, and then passed into the correct part of the building. He met the doctor just as he was stepping out of a patient's room. Chhaya looked at Lance for a long moment, then turned and entered a security code on the door to the patient's room before turning back to Lance. He did not smile.

Lance did not break his stride. "I'm Fleet Commander Ashburn of the Star Feder—"

"I know who you are," Chhaya said. There was nothing threatening in his voice, it was just a statement, but Lance halted all the same. "I've expected you for a long time." He considered Lance for a moment. "Not you specifically, but one of the Star Federation officers. It was only a matter of time."

Lance said nothing, but confusion and alarm rustled across his mind.

"Now that you're here," Chhaya said, "you're not getting in."

Lance looked Chhaya up and down. Weight had settled around the doctor's middle, his hair was wiry gray, wrinkles pulled at the corners of his eyes, and the lines on his forehead and at the corners of his mouth were permanent, but there was a soft healthiness to his brown skin, and he was in relatively good shape. Chhaya was an average-sized man with gentle features that shattered his firmness. Lance knew that he could have easily shouldered his way around him, but he would only do that if absolutely necessary. He also needed to give Backélo a bit more time.

"Dr. Chhaya," Lance said softly but firmly, "there is a very dangerous assassin under your care."

"I can assure you, Commander Ashburn, that that is definitely not true."

"The woman you're treating, probably with minor injuries."

"I am currently treating two females, neither of which have minor injuries." Chhaya folded his arms and turned his head until he was looking at Lance sidelong. "None of my patients have minor injuries, Commander. They all have long-term illnesses."

Someone was lying to protect her, Lance knew. Either Chhaya or the person who had directed Lance to him. The Shadow might not even be in this wing. Better to check, though, than risk her slipping by again.

Lance pushed past the doctor, ignoring Chhaya's protests, and looked through the thick pane of glass set in the door. He peered through the decontamination chamber. The view of the patient's room was slightly warped by the second glass pane, but not enough to distort the faces of the man and woman inside. They both caught Lance's movement, and snapped their heads towards him simultaneously.

"… not have you harassing my patient," Chhaya was saying, but Lance barely heard him.

For a long time, Lance just looked at the man, at someone who had once been strong but now lay thin and weak on the hospital bed, all the strength melted off his bones. His dark hair had a dull sheen to it, and there was the slick gleam of fever sweat on his forehead. His lips were thin and parted as he breathed heavily through his mouth. His cheeks were gaunt and drawn, his skin bleached by sickness, but his eyes were bright and fierce as they looked back at Lance. They were sunken and there were dark smears under them, but that only intensified the metallic gaze.

Lance met his stare, and saw just how similar the man and the woman were. Same black hair, silver eyes, straight noses, angular faces, firm jaws. Same startled, angry, predatory gaze.

So, his mind finally offered, *shadows have brothers.*

CHAPTER 18: ASLEEP

"I don't know," Aven panted, "which I prefer. The Star Feds, or the Sun."

Lissa shot an angry glance down at him, but he was fixated on Ashburn and did not notice.

The commander had broken his crazed stare and was saying something to Aven's doctor, who was shaking his head and mouthing "no" over and over again.

"Chhaya will keep him out," Aven said. He swung his head towards Lissa. The fire in his eyes faded, and he looked up at her tiredly. Each breath rattled in his chest, and he had grown so frail that Lissa was worried that his ribs would shatter if he inhaled too deeply. The many machines in Aven's room filtered the air and kept the room smelling flat and sterile, but the faint stench of decay edged one of Aven's exhales. "Now that he's here," Aven continued, "nothing we can do."

She knew that Aven was right, no matter how much she did not want to admit it. The Star Feds had finally caught up with them, and they were stuck. Even if she hadn't been there, Lissa still would have been caught. She had come to say goodbye, to let go, but one look at Aven and she couldn't bring herself to do it. He had wasted away and had given up, but he was still her brother and she still owed him a chance at life, even if he didn't want to take it. If the Star Feds had captured him, she would not have been able to let him go.

Take care of him.

Aven seemed to know what she was thinking. He smirked at her. "What are they going to do? Move me?" His smile fell as a violent coughing fit came on, and he dropped back when it had passed, exhausted. "Let them try." He closed his eyes and was silent for so long that Lissa thought he had drifted out of consciousness. "Might be nice," he said suddenly, startling her. "Having Star Fed security. Keep the Sun off me."

Lissa hesitated. She'd started telling Aven about the Seventh Sun's ambush at Ametria and then again on Yuna, but Ashburn's sudden appearance had interrupted her. She'd gotten as far as her charter with Montag after the assassination of the Star Federation officer, and Aven probably figured that the Star Feds had trailed her to Phan as the result. He seemed content with the idea, and really was drifting off to sleep this time, ready to let her deal with Ashburn and whoever he had with him on her own.

He really had given up.

"Aven," she said softly, "Rosonno found me."

Aven's eyes fluttered open. He stared up at the ceiling for a stunned moment, then looked at her and tried to sit up. Several machines beeped in protest, and out of reflex, Lissa put a hand on his shoulder and gently pushed him back down. It took almost no effort.

"Where?" Aven rasped. "When?"

Lissa folded her arms and paced back and forth beside the bed as she quickly relayed Montag's betrayal and her brief capture by the Star Federation. "Humans." Aven spat the word as thought it were a vicious curse. "Can't trust any of them." Lissa glanced at him, then continued on. She told him about her escape, Rosonno's ambush and the Phantom, about the riot on Yuna and the ship she'd stolen. She finished with the return to Phan, and admitted that she currently had no idea where Blade was. She looked at Ashburn again, and wondered if his arkin had gone after her. At the moment, the gray didn't seem to be with him.

Aven had closed his eyes again, but he was frowning hard and Lissa knew he wasn't sleeping. She left him to his thoughts and kept an eye on Ashburn as he argued with Chhaya.

The doctor stood firm against the Star Fed. Ashburn made angry gestures at her and Aven, but Chhaya just shook his head and talked him down. Finally, Ashburn folded his arms and stood staring at her silently through the locked door. She looked back at him. They both knew she would have to come out eventually.

"The Star Fed contract," Aven said suddenly, "must have been planted. Rosonno put it out."

"I figured that," Lissa said, not turning away from Ashburn. "I'm fairly sure the target was an informant, too. He was probably feeding the Seventh Sun information on the Shadow's movements from Star Fed data, and once the Sun had enough to go on, they put a high enough bounty on his head to make the risk worth it."

"So you took the bait, and offed their contact, and destroyed the Star Fed's best lead, all in one quick shot." Aven sighed with resigned admiration. "Smart. On their part."

Lissa's eyes narrowed in disgust, but she said nothing. For all his fear and hatred of the Seventh Sun, Aven held a healthy amount of respect for them, but in the worst way. Before his sickness, there had just been fear and hatred, but now that the Banthan virus was gnawing away at his life, regret was seeping into the holes that the disease left behind.

"The Phantom," he said, "is another problem."

"We knew that he was collared," Lissa said. She reached up and touched the shoulder that had been struck by the enerpulse shot. Chhaya had healed the wound completely before letting her in to see Aven, but the spot still itched a little with the memory of the pain. "And we knew that he'd been Awakened."

She heard a soft rustle and knew Aven had glanced at her sharply. "We did?"

No, she remembered, *we didn't.* "I did. I saw it the night I fought him, three years ago. He got to the target before I did and I…" She swallowed hard. "I shouldn't have moved in, but I needed that bounty." She felt Aven's eyes on her back. *I didn't do it for you,* she wanted to say, but she bit down on the words and the memory.

"You should have told me," Aven said.

"You wouldn't have stayed in the hospital if I had, let alone on Phan."

"What wonders my stay has done for me."

She looked at him then, saw the hardness of his eyes and his grip on the thin blanket covering him. Once, she would have tried to sooth him, but now she just waited for him to wear himself out. Another coughing fit came on, and the rage seeped out of him as he dropped his head back and lay flat.

"It's done now," he said weakly. He stared up at the ceiling again. "What's he like? The Phantom?"

Lissa heard the curiosity edged with regret and a little bit of envy in his voice. She felt as though she'd been slapped across the face. She turned back to meet Ashburn's gaze again. He was taking in everything, all the trouble between her and Aven, storing the tension away for later use.

"Strong," Lissa said. "Fast." The Phantom's golden eyes flashed across her vision for a moment. "Hungry."

"And he's hunting you now?"

"I suppose."

"He'll find you."

"Maybe."

"He finds everyone."

"He didn't find me for nearly three years."

"Maybe he wasn't hunting *you.*"

Lissa said nothing.

Aven broke the silence after a few moments. "It's good you have a ship now." His words were almost as heavy as his breathing. "Haven't had our own since… since…"

"Since you got sick and I had to sell it." Lissa had funded Aven's first few treatments with the money from the sale, a decision she would come to regret once she realized that she had limited herself to dead-or-alive bounties and straight assassinations, but then again, jumping from charter to charter made her difficult to track. In the end, she'd been glad to be rid of the starship *Lightwave*, especially since it constantly reminded her of the trip to Mezora. She'd gone for repairs and restocking back when Aven was still the hunter, and she had not returned to Earth in time to retrieve him after the pickup that went sour. He'd already gone to Banth.

"You can go places now," Aven said after a long pause. "Anywhere. Like I used to."

Lissa glanced at him, saw that the sweat on his brow had thickened. A monitor confirmed that his temperature had risen a little and she knew he was slipping away into fever dreams. "I don't think that's going to be possible," she murmured as she faced the door again.

Both Ashburn and Dr. Chhaya were watching her now. Ashburn had resigned himself to Chhaya's authority over his patient, but he would wait for her as long as he needed to.

Lissa wondered how he would react if she were to tell him everything she knew about the Seventh Sun. She could spark a panic in the Star Feds, throw them back into war. They just might be strong enough to stand against the Sun, but only if the Phantom was the only Awakened Neo-Andromedan.

She shifted uneasily, remembering Rosonno's words. The survival rate was up to sixty-eight percent.

He could have been lying, but she didn't think he was trying to scare her. Not intentionally. Not with a bluff. He knew that she'd rather sleep forever.

The Seventh Sun must have successfully Awakened others by now. The Sun might be hiding them, or training them, or maybe the Awakened had secretly been unleashed on the galaxy like the Phantom when his hunger had threatened to tear him apart. Awakened Neo-Andromedans could only avoid starvation for so long. They needed to kill.

Sixty-eight percent.

The Star Federation would crumble under that survival rate. But it was the aftermath that worried her.

Be unpredictable, she thought. She looked at Ashburn for a long time. *Well, they might not predict that.*

Lissa took one last look at Aven. His eyelids fluttered lightly, and his breathing was still heavy and ragged, but he had finally fallen asleep. He had been right about one thing: the Star Federation wouldn't be able to touch him now that the Banthan virus had claimed him completely. That would keep the Seventh Sun at bay, too. For the first time in his life, Lissa realized, Aven was safe.

Time to let go.

CHAPTER 19: DECEPTION

Lance drew his pistol as the Shadow approached the door. She raised her hands in response, showing him empty palms, then reached for the controls for the decontamination chamber. She stepped inside, waited for the automated chamber to sweep her clean, then glanced at Chhaya. The doctor sighed softly and shook his head with resignation and sorrow. The Shadow offered him a simple stare in return. Then she opened the second door and slowly stepped into the hall. "His fever rose, Dr. Chhaya," she said.

Before stepping inside, Chhaya threw a hard look at Lance, who nodded once. As long as he had the Shadow, Lance would happily leave the brother alone. Chhaya knew, of course, that the Star Federation would keep an eye on his patient, but Lance had promised to keep the soldiers at bay and let the treatment continue uninterrupted. Chhaya had accepted the promise, but reluctantly. He very clearly did not trust Star Federation promises.

Lance left the doctor to his patient and focused on the Shadow. She was dressed in traveler's clothes again: layers of light but durable clothing that concealed her frame. Lance made her stand with her palms pressed to her head and quickly but thoroughly checked for weapons. She wore the thick leather belt with the pouches slung all along its surface, but Lance did not find anything lethal, and her pistol holster was empty. He was not all that surprised. Carrying weapons into a hospital was not easy without a Star Federation badge.

He bound the Shadow's hands behind her back with a set of lasercuffs, then sent her down the hall, back towards the hospital's main entrance. She did not struggle, and walked slowly ahead of him. The few members of the medical staff that were not too busy to throw them a passing glance merely looked at them curiously, then dropped their attention back to whatever they were doing.

Lance regarded them suspiciously. "How many of them know who you are?" he asked the Shadow in a low voice.

"Just Dr. Chhaya," she replied softly. "But plenty of them have had stranger things happen to their own patients than a visitor getting arrested." They walked in silence for a few steps, then the hunter glanced over her shoulder. Her eyes were hard and metallic. "Dr. Chhaya has done nothing wrong. You know that, right?"

Lance met her gaze calmly. "Who pays for your brother's treatment?"

"Aven," she said. "My brother's name is Aven. I pay for his treatment."

"What happens now that the funds have been cutoff?"

"Chhaya continues until the reserve funds are gone." The Shadow faced forward. "Then the treatment stops."

Lance heard sadness in her voice, but also acceptance. "That's unfortunate," he said.

"No," she said, "it's not."

Lance glanced at her in sharp surprise but said nothing.

"The Banthan virus is a vicious thing," the Shadow finally offered. "Aven's been fighting it for years. He… he might have won out, but he's given up. This is…" she dropped her head and watched the floor as she walked. "Better."

Better than what? Lance wanted to ask. The Star Federation would drill her later, though, and he'd find out then. For now, "Why is Aven sick? Why aren't you?" He saw her shoulders tense slightly. Guilt. Interesting.

The Shadow raised her head and watched the ceiling this time. She took a deep breath and let it out in a strained huff. "Because I had the money for the vaccination. He didn't."

Younger brother, Lance decided. *Probably sent to wait somewhere while his sister hunted. But why Banth?*

"He was running," the Shadow said before he could ask. "Running, running, we were always running." She slowed her pace, and ignored the barrel of the enerpulse pistol that Lance pushed against her back. "I'm so tired of running."

"Lucky you," Lance said, giving her a light shove forward. "You won't be running anymore."

"No," she agreed. They stepped around a corner into an empty hall, and she came to a sudden halt. "Now I make a stand."

Lance took three quick steps away from her, out of range of a kick. He took a firm stance and pointed his pistol at her heart.

"Not against you," the Shadow said. She half-turned towards him and blinked tiredly at him. "*With* you."

"Of course," Lance said. "Just like last time."

The Shadow considered him for a moment, never once dropping her eyes to the pistol. Then she shrugged. "You actually should be thanking me for that."

Lance's eyes narrowed, and he tightened his grip on his pistol.

The Shadow smiled, but it did not touch her eyes. "Who do you think the Seventh Sun went running after when they left the *Argonaught VII* or whatever number it was?"

Lance's anger flared. "Almost a hundred soldiers are dead because of them. Because of *you.*"

"But you're alive," the Shadow said softly. "And…" she studied his face for a moment. "So are some your soldiers. Did you ever stop and wonder why?"

He had not, truthfully. He and the other officers had just assumed that the Seventh Sun had planned to cut the power and crash the ship, and had left the soldiers for dead when they pulled out. Could their retreat really have been because of her? Had they run after her so fast that they forgot about the possibility of survivors? He found that hard to believe, but he could not drop the idea all at once. "You're that valuable to them?" he asked.

Another hollow smile. "I'm that valuable to you. Why not to them?" She turned away and started down the hall again, pausing at a decontamination checkpoint. "But all Neo-Andromedans are valuable to the Seventh Sun," she threw over her shoulder.

Lance went after her, enerpulse pistol still at the ready as they passed through the checkpoint. A red alarm went off at Lance's pistol, but he scanned his badge and they passed through. "Nandros valuing other Nandros," he said as they emerged. "Shocking."

The Shadow's smile was bitter this time, and so were her eyes. "Not for the reason you think."

"Why, then?"

The hunter frowned at the floor and said nothing for a long time. They had almost reached the main lobby, and doctors and patients with minor troubles were walking up and down the halls within easy earshot when she finally stopped and turned to him again.

"Soon, the Seventh Sun is going to have the strength they need." She spoke in a whisper, so softly that Lance had to lean close and strain to hear her. He pressed the barrel of his pistol into her belly, not taking any chances, and she kept very still. "They will come forward. When they do, the Star Federation will fall."

"And you're going to help us prevent that," Lance whispered back, "by turning on your own people, and handing them over to the Star Federation."

"I'm trying," the Shadow said, strained, "to save them. As many as I can."

"From what?"

The hunter opened her mouth, paused, and swallowed the words. She looked away from him, frowning.

145

Lance gave her a few moments, but when she did not offer anything else, he drew out his personal communicator and sent a private transmission to Captain Backélo, saying that he was bringing the Shadow out. The Rhyutan would be waiting outside with reinforcements, ready to escort them back to the ground port, and the sooner Lance put the Shadow in the ship's prison hold and set off for the Star Federation station, the safer he would feel.

Lance did not believe all this talk of joining with the Star Federation in order to bring down the Seventh Sun. More likely the Shadow was stalling, trying to make time for herself or someone else. Maybe Anderson and Stone had it right, maybe she really was working with the Seventh Sun and was just very skilled in deception as well as assassination.

But the fear had been real, he remembered.

The Shadow was afraid of the Seventh Sun. She'd never work with them willingly, but had they somehow gotten to her? Maybe through the brother? Whatever the case, Lance would not wait long enough for them to strike. He took a firm grip on the Shadow's upper arm and pushed her forward, trying to steer her across the lobby and out the door, but she refused to move.

"Ashburn," she hissed. "This could throw the galaxy back into war. Neither side can afford that. Too many people will die, innocent or not."

Lance pushed again, and this time the Shadow took a step forward.

"You can't lead the Star Federation back into war," she said, still softly but desperately.

Lance forced another step, then another. "Even if I wanted to," he told her in between struggles, "I could not promise that."

The Shadow planted her feet, coming up short and driving her shoulder into his chest. It wasn't a hard hit, but Lance felt the power behind it and knew that she had softened the blow. She gave him one last look over her shoulder, a hard, gleaming, metallic silver stare that cut into him. "Then the Star

Federation will fall," she said.

She whipped her head forward and marched out of the hospital, nearly jerking free of Lance's grip, but he held firm and went after her.

As they stepped outside, shock jolted in Lance's gut. The street was still crowded with civilians. Backélo should have cleared the area, should have been standing at the ready with at least twenty soldiers to escort him and the Shadow back to the ground port.

"I know you're one of the better officers," the Shadow murmured, "but I expected the Star Feds to send more than just you." She threw a quick glance at him. "And you did too, apparently."

Ten minutes, the Rhyutan had said. Lance had been inside the hospital much longer than that. He tightened his grip on the Shadow, then glanced quickly up and down the street. Not a single soldier in sight.

Lance took out his personal communicator again. He contacted Backélo, but the Rhyutan did not accept the transmission. Lance tried again, but there was still no answer. He was about to send a transmission to Captain Anderson when the Shadow suddenly breathed, "There!" and dove into the crowd. She slipped right out of his grasp, and wove through the swarm of multicolored bodies.

Lance went after her, but he quickly fell behind. It was all he could do to keep track of her dark hair as he caught glimpses of it over shoulders and in between faces. He sent a quick transmission to Anderson, but the message was muddled by his shouts of "Move!" and he could only hope that she'd understand him. He tried to send one to Stone as well, but someone bumped into him and he lost the communicator. He did not try to retrieve it, did not look back to see where it had fallen, but kept after the Shadow.

She led him in a serpentine path across the street but always heading for a narrow alleyway between two buildings. Slanted, hazy light from the Phanite sun threw the alley into shadow, and Lance did not immediately pick out the very tall figure standing against the wall, so tall that he would've stood head and shoulders above most of the Phanite crowd. His dark clothes and hair had hidden him at first, but his pale face finally emerged from the gloom and Lance got a good look at the Rhyutan.

As he drew closer, Lance saw that Backélo was speaking into a communicator, one hand darting excitedly through the air as he spoke. He looked up suddenly, throwing a gleeful stare across the street at the hospital, and broke off mid-sentence as he saw that Lance and the Shadow were gone. Backélo glanced quickly at the crowd, locked eyes with Lance, turned, and ran down the alley.

Lance redoubled his efforts to get through the crowd, but the Shadow reached the edge long before he did. She shouldered her way through the last few knots of people, burst into the alley, and tore after Backélo.

With the lay of the Phanite city, there was a neat grid of narrow alleyways between each block of closely packed buildings. Most of the buildings were connected by overhead walkways, and very few people traveled through the alleys. Lance met two mangy animals and one exhausted-looking human as he picked his way through the gloomy maze, searching for the Shadow and Backélo. By the time he found them, the Rhyutan was sprawled unconscious on the ground.

The Shadow crouched over him. She turned her head and looked at Lance as he drew near. Her hands were still bound together by the lasercuffs, but they were in front of her now, and she held Backélo's communicator to her ear, listening. Her expression was dark, but her eyes shone bright, clear, and angry. She watched Lance advance, but only let him take three steps towards her before she dropped the communicator and ripped Backélo's enerpulse pistol out of its holster.

Lance had his pistol up and at the ready, but before he could put any pressure on the trigger, the Shadow had fired. The shot collided with his pistol in a burst of pale blue, and the weapon went spinning out of Lance's hand in a charred mess of metal. He gasped in pain and clutched at his fingers, but there was no damage beyond a shock of pain from the passing heat.

The Shadow stayed where she was, hovering over the unconscious Rhyutan. A muffled transmission recording played over Backélo's communicator, but she ignored it and kept her eyes and the barrel of the pistol on Lance. "Move," she hissed, "and I will kill you."

CHAPTER 20: REASONS

For a brief moment, it seemed as though Blade had shaken off Ashburn's gray. She burst out of a silvery blue cloud alone and came barreling towards the ground port. She caught sight of the Yuni ship and angled towards it.

Lissa watched her from the inner airlock, but kept her enerpulse pistol fixed on Ashburn. She wasn't too worried about him. He'd been exhausted by dragging the unconscious Rhyutan through the narrow alleys, but she kept the weapon pointed at him all the same.

They had been waiting for the better part of an hour, and Lissa was beginning to worry that she would have to leave Blade behind. The Star Feds would come looking for Ashburn soon, and Lissa had to get them off-planet before then. She'd taken the tracers off of Ashburn and the Rhyutan and left them in an alley well away from Aven's hospital, but soon the Star Feds would close the ports. She was just beginning to accept that she'd have to leave Blade behind when the arkin tore through the cloud.

Lissa immediately saw that Blade was fatigued. Her wing beats were erratic, and even when she glided she could not hold herself steady. Ashburn's gray followed her out of the haze a few heartbeats later, and as Lissa squinted up at him, she saw that he looked just as tried as Blade.

Lissa moved back into the ship as the arkins came on. "Keep your gray under control," she told Ashburn as she took up a position across the hall from him.

He looked at her, then at the enerpulse pistol, then back out of the open airlock at the approaching arkins. Ashburn would cooperate, she knew, but one wrong move and he'd break free and Lissa would have half the Star Federation bearing down on her.

Neither arkin touched down gracefully, and both were panting heavily as they scrambled into the ship. Blade managed to take a few unsteady steps towards Lissa before Ashburn's gray blundered through the airlock, but the arkin barely glanced up as he stood shaking in the hallway. Both arkins had scratches, but they were superficial wounds and the bleeding had stopped a while ago.

Ashburn moved to the gray, saying softly, "Easy, Orion." He talked the gray down to the floor, and the arkin yawned and closed his yellow eyes. Blade took her cue from him and slowly sank down as well. She was already panting less deeply than Orion, but Lissa saw the heaviness in her eyes and let the arkin rest.

"Come on," Lissa said as she closed the airlock. "Time to go."

Ashburn glanced at her, realized she was speaking to him. "I'm staying here."

"You're coming."

Ashburn rested his hand on Orion's head.

"He'll be all right," Lissa said, pointing to Blade. The black's eyes had slipped fully closed, and she lay sprawled on the floor. "No trouble there."

The Star Fed still would not move.

"Fine," she said, turning. "I'll talk to the Rhyutan myself."

That brought him to his feet. For all his resistance and unease, Ashburn dreaded another betrayal within the Star Federation most of all. The last one had led to almost a hundred dead soldiers and a lost starship. Now that he had the chance to counterbalance a new attack before disaster spun out, he would cooperate, but Lissa knew he'd be watching for an opening, too.

In the small control room, Backélo the Rhyutan was still unconscious. He remained firmly in that state as Lissa powered up the ship. The departure went smoothly, aside from a brief moment of tension when Ashburn tried to take the enerpulse pistol. Lissa moved quicker, and he slowly sank back into his seat as the barrel of the pistol pressed into his chest.

"You're alive," Lissa told him, "because you're not with the Sun. But don't stretch your luck."

They cleared the hazy Phanite atmosphere, and slipped away from the planet. Lissa engaged the cloak and scrambled the signal, set the ship to coast at quarter-speed, then sat with her attention divided between the trackers and the two Star Feds.

As Phan winked off the edge of the ship's starmap, Ashburn began to question her about the Seventh Sun. She noticed that he avoided personal questions, perhaps because he knew that she would not answer them. He stuck to broad inquiries, trying to get a better grip on the Sun as a whole, and Lissa fed him as much information as she dared. Too much, and the fragile calm would shatter. Lissa was faster, but if he got in close Ashburn could overpower her. She had learned a few defensive combat techniques a long time ago, but years spent successfully sniping had rusted her abilities. Of course, Ashburn did not need to know that.

Lissa told him about the Seventh Sun's ultimate goal of establishing Neo-Andromedans as the most powerful race in the galaxy. As a Star Fed, Ashburn accepted that without hesitation. He knew enough about the Andromedan War and the role Neo-Andromedans were meant to play.

The Seventh Sun had been founded a few years after the end of the Andromedan War and the final stage of the Star Federation's failed purge. The organization was fueled by a desire to prove that Neo-Andromedans were strong even without the help of the original Andromedans, and deserved a place as the leaders of the galaxy. They needed the Star Federation out of the way for that, but if the Sun succeeded in bringing down the Star Feds, they would quickly take over more territory and decimate those who stood against them. They had the technology and the mindset to start and follow through with another war, but they lacked the numbers. They were close now, very close, but their current strength was not enough to defeat the Star Federation in open war.

"Ten of them took down a hundred soldiers," Ashburn said quietly. "How many do they need to bring down the entire Star Federation?"

"I don't know," Lissa answered truthfully. "But more than they have."

What Ashburn did not know was that at least one of the Seventh Sun's operatives on the *Argonaught IV* had been Awake. The commander had told her about the Phantom being onboard the ambushed ship, but she did not tell Ashburn about the hunter's status. The threat of a Neo-Andromedan army slowly building up somewhere on the outskirts of the galaxy was enough to convince him that the Star Federation needed to be on the alert. If the Star Federation ever found out about the Awakenings and what that would mean for warfare, then the Star Feds would scour the edges of the galaxy and destroy the Sun's base on sight.

If taking out the Sun was as simple as that, Lissa would gladly send the Star Feds off with her best wishes. But Rosonno and the other heads were too smart and too cautious to keep to the base all at once. They would be scattered, and if the base fell, they'd find out and disappear almost immediately. It wasn't the locations of the heads that concerned her, though. If the survival rate really was at sixty-eight percent, there were bound to be other Neo-Andromedans on the Seventh Sun's base, candidates for Awakenings that the Seventh Sun had found. People who would be killed alongside the Sun. Uncollared people who were still asleep.

Aven had been right, Lissa realized. The Phantom had not spent the last three years hunting the Shadow. With his help, the Sun might actually have the number of Neo-Andromedans needed to attack the Star Feds, but not enough that had been Awakened.

Lissa had no grand illusions of saving them all. She could not storm the base, take out the Seventh Sun, and free the Awakening candidates. Not alone. With the full force of the Star Federation behind her, she might have a chance at the first two, but the Star Feds were just as likely to kill the candidates as they were the members of the Sun. Teaming up with a Star Fed or two and hunting down Rosonno, however, would slow their plans, and then maybe a few very precise, very quick shots could crumble the Seventh Sun from within.

Maybe.

"So," Ashburn said once Lissa had told him as much as she dared about the Sun, "now what? Where do you expect to find them?"

"That depends on your friend," Lissa said, glancing at the unconscious Rhyutan.

While they waited for Backélo to rouse himself, Lissa considered Ashburn. He hadn't been pulled into the Seventh Sun, that much she knew. They would never place a collar around a human neck, but they might have tried to dupe him into working for them. They had done as much with Captain Coleman, why not with Fleet Commander Ashburn? But the commander had meant to deliver her to the Star Federation, nothing more, and Backélo's betrayal had caught him completely by surprise. Ashburn was curious and concerned enough about the Seventh Sun to cooperate with her for the time being, but he'd be more comfortable with the Star Federation behind him. There was no calling for reinforcements this time, and he'd have to get used to working alone.

The arkins eventually wandered into the control room. They still looked tired, but they were more alert now and were eying each other suspiciously. There was no open hostility, though, and they left each other alone for the most part. Lissa let Ashburn search for a medical kit and treat Orion's wounds once he found the supplies. When he was done, he wordlessly handed the kit to Lissa and watched as she took care of Blade.

As she cleaned Blade's cuts, Lissa's mind replayed the transmission that Backélo had sent back on Phan.

Target confirmed, sir, the Rhyutan had said, his voice heavy with excitement. *Will escort back to designated vessel. Starship is medium in size, easy to overtake but difficult to overpower. Departure likely to occur within the hour. Current location is—wait. Where...?*

The transmission ended there.

She had not been able to trace the contact back to a location, but the Seventh Sun was at the other end of the frequency, that much she was sure of. They knew that she had been on Phan, but she might be able to sneak away this time. The Sun hadn't recognized the stolen ship from Yuna, hadn't set their sights on it, but she kept a nervous watch on the tracking system all the same.

Backélo swam back into consciousness just as Lissa finished treating the last of Blade's scratches. He peered groggily around the room, not quite seeing Lissa, Ashburn, and the two arkins. He tried to bring his hands up to his head, but found them bound behind his back with the lasercuffs Ashburn had used on Lissa. The discovery seemed to ground him in reality, and he bolted up into a sitting position and focused a wild stare on Ashburn. "You!" he breathed. His eyes darted to Lissa, paused, then settled more fully on her. "And... you?"

"Us," Lissa said. "We're all a little confused, and a little upset. Some more than others." Out of the corner of her eye, Lissa saw Blade's lip curl back in a silent snarl. Backélo cringed, and Lissa had to fight back a smile of relief. This would be easier than she had hoped, but she would have to start with the basics. "Back on Phan, who did you contact?"

"The Star Federation," Backélo said at once. "Admiral Moore himself."

That was not what Lissa had expected to hear, and judging by Ashburn's sudden rigidity and dark expression, the response had caught him by surprise as well.

The Rhyutan relayed the rest of his story readily enough. He claimed to have been contacted by the admiral just after the *Argonaught IV* had been ambushed at Ametria. Backélo had been told that Neo-Andromedans were involved, but for some reason, Commander Ashburn was remaining oddly silent about that fact. Ashburn had dodged the questions of his superior officers, and after seeing how easily the organization known as the Seventh Sun had overpowered the *Argonaught IV*, the admirals suspected foul play. Backélo had been told to keep a close eye on Ashburn and report all developments in the Shadow investigation back to Admiral Moore. Moore and the other admirals were concerned that Ashburn had gone rogue and begun working with the Neo-Andromedans. There was no other explanation for his behavior, or the Seventh Sun's ability to infiltrate such a secure and powerful starship. In order to confirm this, however, the admiral had asked Backélo to keep a close but quiet eye on Ashburn and avoid tipping him off at all costs. Backélo finished his story by spitting at Ashburn, "Nandro-loving traitor."

Lissa's spine tightened at the Rhyutan's closing words, but she bit down on her rage and turned to Ashburn. "Your thoughts on this?"

Ashburn shook his head darkly. He looked ready to strangle the Rhyutan, and his fists were clenched so hard that his knuckles had turned bone-white.

Lissa eyed him warily. His pride as a Star Federation officer was much stronger than she had initially thought. She would need to watch out for that.

Backélo's allegiance was another problem entirely. There was no way Ashburn had gone rogue, but the Rhyutan was so dedicated to the Star Federation that he had blindly stumbled into the Seventh Sun's hands. Lissa doubted that any of the Star Federation admirals had ever contacted Backélo. The Sun must have paraded under Star Fed colors, impersonating an admiral that most soldiers had probably never spoken to in their entire careers, and the Rhyutan was so eager to serve that he had relayed information back to them without any hesitation.

Lissa wondered if Backélo was the only soldier that the Seventh Sun had contacted. Anyone who had been aboard the *Argonaught IV* would never believe that Ashburn had gone rogue, but if the Sun had convinced one captain, then they could have snared others.

Panic touched Lissa on the back of her neck once again. *Did they know I would try to convince Ashburn to work with me?*

But no, that had been spontaneous, and Ashburn had found her purely by coincidence. The Seventh Sun must had been monitoring Ashburn as a precaution, just in case he had stumbled across Lissa again and managed to arrest her, but they had gone a step further and turned the commander into a traitor. He was a failsafe against more unpredictable elements, much like Montag had been. Time to find out what the Sun had planned beyond that.

Lissa stepped to where the Rhyutan sat and dropped to a knee in front of him. "I am the Shadow," she told Backélo, "and I am Neo-Andromedan, but I am not your enemy." She glanced over her shoulder at Ashburn. "Neither is he."

Backélo snorted.

Lissa ignored that. "Why do you think Ashburn did not move against the Neo-Andromedans?"

The Rhyutan's slitted blue pupils flared and contracted. He fixed Ashburn with a hard stare before spitting, "Because he is a traitor. He is working from the inside to bring down the Star Federation and let Nandro scum like you back into the galaxy."

"Actually," Lissa said softly, "the Nandro scum like me never left." She held Backélo's gaze for a long moment. "So if Ashburn was working against the Star Federation," she ignored the disgusted sigh behind her, "and he had taken me aboard his ship, what would have happened?"

"I would have alerted Admiral Moore on a private frequency," Backélo hissed begrudgingly. "Then the rogue ship would have been overtaken and subdued by a larger starship."

"From the Star Federation?"

"Of course."

More likely from the Seventh Sun, masquerading under Star Fed colors.

"Then what?" Lissa asked.

"Transfer of the Shadow to the larger starship, then transfer to a prison planet."

Star Fed prison planets are on the far side of the Viaz.

Lissa frowned at the Rhyutan. "With a relay point?"

There was a flicker of confusion in the Rhyutan's dark eyes. "Yes," he said.

"Where?"

Backélo set his jaw and said nothing.

"Ametria?" Lissa guessed.

Backélo's surprise was confirmation enough.

The death planet again.

They wouldn't have moved the base, Lissa told herself. *Not to Ametria, let alone into the galaxy.* She frowned, wondering. *There's something there. There has to be. They wouldn't bring me there twice if there weren't.*

Unless the Seventh Sun really was just trying to kill her, but an enerpulse shot on Yuna would have sufficed for that. And did they really have enough candidates to justify wanting her dead without attempting an Awakening?

Sixty-eight percent.

There was a rustle as Ashburn leaned forward in his seat. "I called for reinforcements when I made the arrest." His voice was soft, but edged with steel. "Why the hell would I have done that if I was going rogue?"

The Rhyutan shifted, brought himself up to kneeling. He jabbed his chin in Lissa's direction when he said, "You were going to loose that Nandro on the ship, have her kill the soldiers, but you needed to keep up appearances. I would not let you have those soldiers." He grinned suddenly. "And without the soldiers there, you had to make your move sooner. You showed yourself for what you are." Backélo edged forward. "A traitor, working for Nandros."

Ashburn was on his feet now. He started forward, a look on his face that Lissa had seen many times before, but behind other eyes. This time, Lissa stopped Ashburn with a hand on his shoulder rather than a pistol aimed at his vital organs.

"If there's one thing I know for certain about you, Ashburn, it's where you've thrown your loyalty."

Ashburn's eyes were flinty green as they slid towards Lissa.

"He really believes that you were going rogue," she continued. "Ask yourself why."

She could feel the tension under her hand as Ashburn stared at her, but he said, "The Seventh Sun?"

She nodded.

"So in less than five days, they re-infiltrated the Star Federation, impersonated one of the admirals well enough to convince a captain that I've gone rogue, and set up another trap at Ametria." He screwed up his face as though thinking hard. "Right. That's believable." Sarcasm dripped off every syllable.

Lissa dropped her hand. "You still don't fully understand what we're up against."

Ashburn raised his eyebrows. "We?"

Lissa smiled hollowly. "Star Fed commander or rogue partner to a bounty hunter, you're in this now."

Ashburn's gaze did not soften, but this time, his eyes really were narrowed in thought. He folded his arms and tapped out a decision against his upper arm with a finger, then pushed past Lissa and stood over Backélo. "You didn't come up with the no soldier trick," he said, glaring down at the Rhyutan. "I know you. You're not that smart."

There was a stunned moment of silence, then Backélo's mouth worked furiously as he spat out profanity in the Rhyutan language.

"All right, enough." Ashburn turned back to Lissa. "If the Seventh Sun really is trying to turn the Star Federation against me, why put that idea in his head? It sounds like they already had the ship overtake planned."

Lissa folded her arms across her chest in consideration, but made sure to keep the enerpulse pistol free and clear. "If you'd gotten me on the target ship, then yes, they would have overtaken it."

"And if you'd gotten away?"

Then the swarm of Star Feds searching around the hospital would have told them where to look for Aven.

Lissa said nothing.

"Oh," Ashburn said, pulling her gaze back to him. The commander stood with his mouth partly open, frowning. "Oh, they don't know where…"

Lissa felt a hot wave rush over her. Her body tensed, and she felt the anger burning at the back of her mind. *Steady,* she told herself. *It's all right if he knows, he already saw. Keep control.*

Ashburn's eyes flicked over her as she reacted to the sudden strain. He studied her for a moment, then closed his mouth and nodded once, almost imperceptibly.

The Rhyutan's head whipped back and forth between them. "Know where… What?"

"Nothing," Ashburn said, folding his arms. *For now,* his eyes said to Lissa.

Backélo frowned up at Ashburn, opened his mouth to say something else, but Lissa recovered her voice and cut in quickly.

"Where is the intercept point?"

Backélo's attention snapped to her. "What?"

"The intercept point where the first Star Fed ship was supposed to overtake the rogue target. Where is it?"

The Rhyutan hesitated, considering her. One of the arkins shifted in the middle of the silence, and Backélo quickly gave her the coordinates.

"That's far," Lissa said to Ashburn. "Just far enough to give us the time we need."

"For what?" Ashburn's gaze hardened again as realization hit him. "You can't be serious. No, we are *not* going to—stop!"

Lissa entered the destination and pushed the ship up to high speed.

CHAPTER 21: DOUBT

Dr. Chhaya had been very cooperative, and Jason let him go after a few questions. Commander Ashburn had been at the hospital, the doctor had said, and he had arrested a woman that Chhaya had treated for a shoulder injury. "Enerpulse wound," Chhaya had said. "But not a serious injury, just a surface burn." Ashburn had shown up just as Chhaya had finished treating the shoulder, and then the commander had escorted the woman out of the building and that was the last the doctor had seen of either of them.

"Thank you," Jason said. "I won't keep you from your patients any longer."

Chhaya nodded. "Goodbye, Captain Stone."

Jason watched Chhaya as he receded down the hall. He knew that there was something the doctor had not told him.

Chhaya had looked like he was expecting someone from the Star Federation. He had eyed Jason's uniform without any of the uneasy respect that flickered behind the gazes of most people pulled aside for questioning, but when Jason started asking about Commander Ashburn, there had been a moment of hesitation. Chhaya had looked as though he'd been prepared to answer different questions. Jason knew he had caught the doctor off guard, but Chhaya adjusted quickly. Rather than give anything away, he did not volunteer information and only answered Jason's questions as tersely as possible. He was polite, and he seemed to be telling the truth, but something had been left unsaid.

Jason let Chhaya get halfway down the hall before he contacted Erica. He relayed to her what the doctor had told him.

"I've got another dead end here," Erica said. "We found his tracer, but no sign of Ashburn."

Jason grunted. "The Shadow must have taken him."

"Well," Erica hesitated, "we also found Backélo's tracer."

"Then the Shadow must have taken them both."

"Right."

Jason heard the jagged edge in her voice. He glanced around the hallway, saw that he was well out of earshot of the few doctors in sight. "Good to speak free?"

"Yes."

"You don't really think Ashburn's gone rogue, do you?"

"No," Erica said at once. "Well, I didn't at first. I thought the order from Moore was just a precautionary thing since Ashburn has been acting strange ever since the Nandro ambush. There was something a little off about it all but…"

Jason saw Chhaya step into a room at the end of the hall and took note of the door. "But?"

"But now that Backélo's missing, I'm not really sure what to think," she admitted.

Jason couldn't fight off the smile. That had to be a first for her, but he couldn't pretend to know what was going on any better than she did.

When the admiral's transmission had come through, coded to only reach the captains that were headed to Phan with Ashburn, Jason's thoughts had turned to the commander's decision to let the Shadow roam free when the *Argonaught IV* had been ambushed at Ametria. He also thought about the Shadow's apparent fear of the Seventh Sun. The hunter had seemed to welcome Star Federation support, and she had been willing enough to help, but the instant Ashburn had resisted her methods, she had fled.

Ashburn, on the other hand, had been just as flustered by the Nandro attack as Jason, but the commander also had been determined to save as many soldiers as he could. Jason had survived thanks to the commander's warning, and he could not believe that Ashburn had willingly sacrificed all those soldiers. He also wasn't ready to think that Ashburn had turned rogue in the few days since the incident, but Backélo's disappearance was a problem. There was no clear-cut explanation for it, unless Ashburn really had betrayed the Star Federation. Or was dead somewhere, burned away by enerpulses, but they should have found the body by now.

"I watched Ashburn climb the ranks," Jason told Erica. "He couldn't take orders for shit and he had his own agenda even when he was a lieutenant, but he was a Star Fed kid through and through." He saw Chhaya emerge from the far room and disappear around the corner. Jason started down the hall. "Rogue isn't in his blood."

"I hope you're right," Erica said. "We can't afford a traitor now." She cut the transmission.

Jason reached the room at the end of the hall just as Chhaya came back around the corner. He was frowning down at a datapad and did not notice Jason until he had reached for the door controls. Then there was a burst of nervous surprise before he fixed Jason with a hard stare.

"Was there something else you needed, Captain Stone?"

Jason looked over the doctor's shoulder, into the patient's room. She was a middle-aged Phanite, short and possibly stocky once but very thin now. The characteristic purple-red hair of the native Phanite population had fallen out of her scalp in large chunks, her skin was covered in dark blotches, and she lay with her head resting heavily on her pillow, her breath heavy with sedated sleep.

"Yes," Jason said. "Directions."

Chhaya smiled, but there was something more than just friendly humor behind it.

CHAPTER 22: CONTROL

Ametria's cracked, hell-red surface was just as terrifying to look upon the second time, maybe even more so because they had returned willingly.

Well, Lissa thought, *two of us did.*

Ashburn had not had much choice in the matter, although he had argued for contacting the Star Federation and calling for reinforcements. Lissa destroyed the suggestion for a number of reasons, but the one she gave Ashburn was that a fleet of Star Fed ships would be impossible to hide. The small Yuni craft could cloak itself and scramble its signal, but anything larger would give off too much energy and show up on a Seventh Sun tracker immediately. Ashburn had accepted the reasoning with his eyes on the enerpulse pistol in her hand.

Watch him, she reminded herself.

Backélo, on the other hand, did not exert himself to hide his glee. He was expecting a Star Federation ship to be waiting for them, ready to overtake and overpower the smaller starship, and then the good captain could send an Alpha Class bounty hunter and a rogue commander to the prison planets.

Lissa would have welcomed the Star Federation with open arms, but she knew that they would not be waiting at Ametria. She did not know what she expected to find, but she knew it would not be as easy as the Star Feds.

She had been right about one thing, however: the small Yuni starship was able to sneak by the trackers. Lissa skirted the ship around the night side of the planet, and as they came into the daylight, they found something between bloody Ametria and one of the planet's smaller moons.

The Seventh Sun was bold enough after all.

The base was small, dwarfed by the Ametrian moon, but larger than the Yuni starship by far. The structure was simple, nothing more than a slowly rotating disk around a long central spike, and the whole base gleamed red under the light of Ametria's sun. From a distance, it looked like nothing more than a child's toy, but there was nothing innocent about it in Lissa's eyes. Everything about it was eerily calm, as though it had every right in the world to exist this close to so much danger and not suffer for it. There was no activity around the base. It just hung in space between the massive planet and the tiny moon, turning on its axis and glowing in the light of the dying star.

"That's not right," Backélo said from the floor. His wrists were still bound by the lasercuffs and Lissa had not let him rise, but he craned his long neck and stared at the tracker's visual display in total shock. "That's not right," he repeated, the words slow and sticky.

"Why here?" Ashburn asked.

Lissa shook her head, her own voice too gummy to escape her throat.

A Seventh Sun base within the galaxy could only mean one of two things.

First possibility: it was a resting point for Sun starships. Although small, the station easily could have docked a fleet of lesser starships, and if it really was a military base, then the Seventh Sun was closer to striking against the Star Federation than Lissa had thought.

Second possibility: the base was a holding point for Awakening candidates.

Would they risk that? Lissa wondered. *Risk all of them?*

As far as she knew, Rosonno and the other heads had always Awakened candidates at the main base. Situated outside of the galaxy somewhere beyond the Andromeda Reach, the main base was ideal for the Awakenings. Far from the danger of roaming starships, the location was virtually inaccessible. Only the members of the Seventh Sun and a handful of uncollared Neo-Andromedans knew where to find it, and the other uncollared may not even be alive any more.

Sixty-eight percent.

Rosonno must have achieved that number through multiple Awakenings, very few of which would have yielded live results. Once, he had said that the Seventh Sun always learned more from failures than successes. Lissa was certain that the Sun's primary candidates would have been the uncollared Neo-Andromedans who knew where to find the main base. She did not know about the others, but she and Aven had managed to escape thus far. Of course, neither of them was a threat to the base any longer, even if the Sun did not know it. Aven lay captive to disease and Lissa's memory had been fuzzed by the years. She once had asked Aven where the base was, and he had screamed at her and gripped her arm so hard that she'd carried fingerprint bruises for days afterwards.

Could this small station really be an Awakening site? Lissa hoped that it was not. More likely, it was a relay point between the main base and the ships the Seventh Sun had sent into the galaxy, no more than that, and yet…

That's an awfully small military base.

She had to get in there, somehow, to look around and see what the Sun was up to. She was toying with the idea of bringing the Yuni starship in closer when Ashburn broke her out of her thoughts.

"How did we not find this before?" The commander had moved closer to the tracking display, staring at the Sun's base. "This must have taken years to construct. We should have picked it up on a run across the Viaz, and definitely when Captain Anderson gave us a tow a few days ago." Ashburn shook his head in horrified awe. "What else is hiding out here?"

"We should scan the area," Backélo said.

Lissa saw with alarm that he had climbed to his feet while she had been lost in thought. She realized that the Rhyutan also seemed to have forgotten all about his claim that Ashburn had gone rogue, and the two had snapped back into their ranks. Duty as Star Feds had trumped all else, and that meant trouble.

"We can find out what else is out here," Backélo continued.

"No scans," Lissa said. "We're barely slipping past them as is." She hesitated, realizing how true that statement was. Stealth drives could only do so much, and the extra power required for a long-range scan would draw attention to the Yuni ship at once. And even without a scan, there was no way they could bring the ship closer to the base. It would become too visible. "We should turn back, return to Phan."

Backélo eyed her suspiciously. "What are you hiding?"

"Us," Lissa snapped back. "I'm hiding us."

"We need to know," Ashburn said quietly. "We *have* to know what else is out here."

"Really? That's not enough for you?" Lissa gestured to the display of the base.

Ashburn faced her squarely. "What about the dreadnaught that we picked up on when we were out here? A ship that size could not have docked at that station, so where did it go?"

Lissa shrugged and said acidly, "Away," but she thought back to the display from the *Argonaught IV* all the same, back to the fleet of fighters swarming around the driller and the one massive starship behind Ametria. A display that the Seventh Sun had let them see. Even then, she'd had her doubts about the dreadnaught, but if the Seventh Sun really did have a vessel that size, they would not have risked it in a dogfight with a nearly equal-sized Star Federation ship. The fighter fleet and the armored driller could have come from the base, and if the Sun had manipulated the trackers whenever the Star Feds passed by on a run to their prison planets, the station easily could have disappeared behind a hacked data reading.

Backélo never gave her the chance to say as much. He moved far faster than Lissa thought he could, and it was all she could do to keep herself from firing the enerpulse pistol as he dove across the room and slammed his shoulder into her. She managed to keep the weapon under control, and her relief was so strong it was almost solid; the barrel of the weapon swept clean across Blade. A single shot would have mortally wounded the arkin, if not outright killed her.

White-hot, Lissa thought as she spun with the momentum Backélo had thrown into her. She let the Rhyutan slide past her, then brought her elbow up and jabbed at his face. With no way to block her, Backélo took the full force of the blow. He fell to the ground, dazed.

"Never do that again," Lissa hissed, standing over him. She turned to face Ashburn, ready to counter him next, but instead she vaulted over the Rhyutan, nearly tripped over Blade as the arkin rose with a growl, and actually tripped over Orion. She fell into Ashburn, driving him away from the controls and pulling him down to the ground through sheer force of momentum, but it was too late.

Ashburn had initiated the scan.

The Yuni starship's scanners ran across the surface of Ametria. They returned with the location of the crash site of the *Argonaught IV*, but Ametria's surface held nothing else for the initial quick scan. There was nothing between the Yuni starship and the Seventh Sun's station, nothing between the station and the moon, nothing just beyond the moon. That was all the scanners had time for before they cut out.

There was a terrible silence as Lissa, Ashburn, Backélo, and the arkins waited. Then the tracking display snapped out of sight, the ship shuddered violently, and the navigation system swung the nose of the starship directly towards the Ametrian surface.

Lissa could have killed them right then and there, Ashburn and his arkin and especially Backélo. Three quick shots—

No. I might need them.

She felt anger settle in her stomach, but it was a cold anger entirely unlike what she had felt on Yuna, and it did not spread. That did not stop her, however, from slamming her fist into Ashburn's jaw.

She caught him by surprise. He looked back at her with stunned anger, but though he tensed, he made no move to retaliate.

Orion jumped to his feet and snarled at her, but Ashburn called the gray arkin off. He stood rubbing his jaw with narrowed eyes and a look of disgusted shame and rage on his face.

Backélo rose cautiously, keeping his eyes on Blade as she growled and flashed her fangs, but as he came fully upright, he swept his gaze over the ship's controls. "What happened?"

Lissa rubbed her knuckles and shook the ache out of her hand as she glared at him. "Do you really not know?"

The Rhyutan frowned back at her, angry now. "No one could hack a ship that fast. This is a set up. You must have let them into the system somehow."

"You mean just now, when I did not touch the controls?"

"Earlier, before we left Phan, you must have rigged the ship." Backélo glowered at her, all traces of fear gone. "You *wanted* us to get caught."

The anger grew hot, melted into blind rage, and Lissa suddenly found herself in front of the Rhyutan, the barrel of her enerpulse pistol shoved up against his jaw. The world around her felt very still, very quiet, very empty, but she slowly came back into herself. She heard her own breathing and the tenser rhythm of the Rhyutan's breath, Blade's soft growls and Orion's anxious grunts. Ashburn was the only source of silence now. She found herself focusing on that as she regained control.

"If I were you," Lissa said, "I would keep as quiet as possible for the rest of my life, however long or short that may be."

Backélo swallowed, and the barrel of the pistol bobbed as

the motion traveled down his long neck.

"And you," Lissa said fiercely as she turned away from Backélo and stalked towards Ashburn. "You've seen what they can do. You've seen them overtake a fully manned Star Fed dreadnaught. *You should have known.*"

"I know there's something you're not telling me," Ashburn said softly.

"There will always be something I'm not telling you," Lissa snarled. "*Always.* But what I do tell you will be the truth."

Ashburn held her gaze for a long, silent moment. She saw him run through everything he knew about her, about her brother, about the Seventh Sun. She saw him remember the soldiers that had died under his command, and she saw him remember that she had run. She saw him struggle, and then finally accept.

"All right," he said. "Now what?"

Lissa's gaze darted to the navigation system. They were still set on a headlong rush for Ametria. The Yuni ship would crash within the hour. They'd never survive the impact.

"Now we wait until we're in the atmosphere," Lissa said quietly. "Then we hope we can get the airlock open."

"You're going to jump?" Backélo asked, his voice raw with distress.

"Something like that."

Blade grunted and rustled her wings.

Smart girl, Lissa thought.

CHAPTER 23: MAW

Waiting for the crash was mental agony, but they tried to busy themselves as best they could. They filled most of the time by searching for supplies that they might need, although Backélo's ability to help was restricted. The Shadow deactivated his bindings long enough to let him bring his hands out from behind his back. Then she reactivated the lasercuffs and his wrists snapped together again. Lance considered trying to convince the hunter to at least free the Rhyutan while they prepared for the crash, but thought better of it. At this point, he wasn't sure if even he could trust Backélo.

As they went through the ship's stores, Lance thought about Backélo's betrayal. The Shadow had been right. Captain Backélo really did believe that Lance had gone rogue. Lance had been hurt and angered by the accusation; it was a wild insult to him and his integrity as a Star Federation officer, especially if Backélo was not the only one of his captains who would have acted on such a charge. He wanted to believe that only Backélo had accepted the information the Seventh Sun had sent, for Rhyutans had always made far better soldiers than they did leaders, but Lance found that he could not fully blame the other captains if they had entertained the possibility beyond the level of a necessary precaution.

Lance was responsible for the deaths of nearly one hundred soldiers, he had not acted the way he should have when faced with a Neo-Andromedan, he had let an Alpha Class bounty hunter slip away, and he had travelled to Ametria in order to help that Nandro Alpha Class bounty hunter. Granted, he had not had much choice in the final matter, but he had not tried as hard as he should have to escape, either.

Part of him was glad that he had not. He had been right, there was more to the return of the Neo-Andromedans than the Star Federation had anticipated. War had always been expected, but not one on the scale of the Andromedan War. Although deadly, Neo-Andromedan numbers had been depleted and the Star Federation expected to overpower them through brute force. The attack involving the driller suggested otherwise, but there was another advantage that the Nandros had, something about the Seventh Sun and the Neo-Andromedan race as a whole that the Shadow was not telling him.

There will always be something, she had said. *Always.*

Lance believed that wholeheartedly.

The supply search proved fruitful. They found food and water in the starship's small galley, but agreed that loading up on food may not be the best idea. Although a virtually inhospitable planet, what did live on Ametria was violent, aggressive, and terrifying. The Shadow, Backélo, and Lance had all agreed that they did not want to risk attracting unwanted attention. They made water the priority and only took a few fully sealed packs of food. No one said it, but Lance knew that they had also reached an agreement regarding death. They were not likely to stay alive on Ametria long enough to starve.

They found breathing devices in one of the wall compartments of the starship's control room. Data scans performed by the Star Federation several years ago had informed Lance and Backélo that they would be all right in terms of atmospheric pressure and radiation protection, but breathing was another matter entirely. None of them trusted the Ametrian atmosphere with their lungs.

Fitting the arkins out with the breathing devices proved to be a challenge. The masks had not been designed for non-humanoid faces, and Lance and the Shadow spent quite a bit of time modifying them. When the time came to tailor the masks to the arkins' heads, Blade the black arkin stood sullenly while the Shadow fixed the mask over her face. She turned her head away in displeasure at one point, but the Shadow pulled her muzzle back up and finished fitting the mask. She made a few small adjustments, then pulled the mask off and released the arkin with the warning that she would not be free for long. Blade made an angry noise and fixed the Shadow with a dirty look, but there was no escalation beyond that.

Orion, on the other hand, was especially defiant. Lance had to wrestle him to the ground before he could get the breathing device anywhere near the arkin's head, and even then he could not properly fit the mask. The arkin bucked and tossed his head violently, nearly throwing Lance across the room twice. When Lance did manage to reasonably secure the mask, Orion tried to paw it off. Lance tugged hard on the arkin's ear as a reprimand, and Orion sulked for ten minutes.

After that, they returned to searching the ship. They found a few small sandglass hover lanterns that gave off a dingy yellow glow when activated, and the Shadow insisted on taking them.

"If we can't get to the crash site by sundown, we will want them."

"Those things will draw the attention of every Ametrian out there," Backélo shot back.

"We're not going to travel by them," the Shadow returned calmly but with a hard edge in her voice. "But the light may be useful somewhere."

Lance sided with the Shadow on the matter and that was the end of that.

There was not much else in the ship that would prove useful to them save for the small store of enerpulse pistols and rifles. When they broke open the locker, the Shadow forced

Lance and Backélo away and kept a careful watch over the weapons. Backélo tried to argue with her, but Lance told him to keep his mouth shut. If the Shadow wanted them dead, she would have already killed them. She was the one with the pistol, after all. The Shadow left Blade to guard the store even with Backélo's sullen agreement to leave the weapons untouched.

They spent the rest of the journey near the airlock, breaking open the independent control panel and examining the interior. Backélo suggested a trial run, but Lance and the Shadow both shot the idea down. One wrong move and they would eject themselves into space. Better to start working on one of the airlocks once they had broken the atmosphere.

After they had studied the airlock controls thoroughly, the Shadow sent Backélo back to the control room and told him to keep a close watch on the navigation system. He did not have to go far, and the Shadow was content to monitor him from the hall. With the size of the starship, she had a clear view into the control room from the central hall. She sat on the floor near the branch that led to the airlock, across from Lance and Orion.

"We can get off Ametria in a shuttle," she said after a brief silence. "I slipped by the station in one when I fled the *Argonaught*. I think they're too small to trigger the hacking signal. Not enough power to register."

Lance considered that. The shuttles were even smaller than the starship they were on, and they had slipped by the station twice before. Once when the Shadow stole one, and once when Lance had led the soldiers off of the *Argonaught IV*. And come to think of it... "Our fighter fleet was operational during the Seventh Sun's attack. Whatever they have set up, it must deal only with individual ships, not swarms."

Which means a base could be overpowered by a fighter fleet, Lance thought. *If the Star Federation finds any more of them, we'll have that advantage.*

The Shadow seemed to read his thoughts. "That might be a decoy weakness. Make you and the other Star Feds think you can get a fleet in close, just in case you ever did find a base. If you're brave enough to try it, then..." Her hand slashed the space in front of her.

"Is that something they would do?"

The Shadow nodded without hesitation. "The problem with the Sun is that by the time you've come up with a plan, they've already thought of it a week earlier. You can't outsmart them, just outmaneuver them. You have to be... unpredictable."

Lance stretched his legs out. "Is that why we came here?"

The Shadow grinned hollowly. She let the smile fade, to be replaced by deep thought. "A small group of cloaked fighters might be able to sneak up on them, but not a full fleet." She glanced around the hallway. "Our stealth was destroyed when you triggered the scan. Go over a power threshold and you become as bright as sunlight to the station." She paused. "That's my theory, at least."

Theory or experience, Lance considered her words all the same. "I suppose it would explain the range of the hacking attack when they went after the larger ships. I don't know when they infiltrated our ship, but they took over Montag's *Resolution* while we were still very far out."

"Yes," the Shadow said. She frowned darkly at the floor. "Although I think that was a more calculated move. They knew exactly where to find that ship."

A small silence played out.

"What you told me," Lance said softly, "back at the hospital. Was it true?"

"Yes."

"All of it?"

"Yes."

Then the Star Federation will fall.

"So when you said that you were trying to save as many people as you could," Lance pressed on, "what did you mean by that?"

The Shadow shut her eyes. Her frown deepened, and her grip on the enerpulse pistol tightened. When she opened her eyes again, they were harder than Lance had ever seen them, harder even than when she had pointed the pistol at his heart in the Phanite alleyway and threatened to kill him if he moved.

"Ashburn," she said, softly but fiercely, "when I tell you that the Seventh Sun is your enemy, that's what I mean. I don't mean Neo-Andromedans, I mean the Seventh Sun. Never forget that."

Lance waited, but she did not offer anything more. He wanted to ask, but instead found himself saying, "Is your name really Lissa?"

"Yes."

They sat in silence until Backélo came back to the airlock. He said that they had entered the atmosphere and were making a rapid descent towards the Ametrian surface. He also said that they looked to be heading for one of the many canyons.

Lissa deactivated Backélo's lasercuffs and gave him and Lance access to the enerpulse weapons.

"Don't try to pull what you did in the control room," she warned them.

They nodded in agreement, then took two pistols each and slung rifles across their backs. Backélo wanted more, but Lance warned him against weighing himself down. Blade was too small to carry an extra passenger, and Orion would only be able to stay airborne under so much weight.

The ship shuddered violently as it tore through the atmosphere, and it was all Lance and Lissa could do to work on the airlock controls. They succeeded in opening the outer airlock, and red light from the planet's sun spilled through the transparent inner doors, bloodstaining the ship. Backélo made an uneasy noise, and Lance paused to look out at the Ametrian landscape.

Sunstained stone stretched as far as they could see, barren of plant life. There were rock formations everywhere, dark shadows pooling in the crevices and under the outcroppings. There was a winding canyon that slowly slunk into view as the ship screamed towards the surface, a dark maw that stretched wide in anticipation.

"Masks," Lissa said, tearing Lance away from the view.

He and Lissa pulled their breathing devices on and secured the respirator packs, then turned to the arkins. Blade once again was more cooperative than Orion, but Lissa took a firm grip on Orion's head once she had outfitted Blade. She held the gray arkin still while Lance fitted the mask and secured the respirator pack around his neck. Orion snapped at her hands when she released him, a useless gesture with the mask on, but Lance thanked her. Then he and she dove back to the airlock controls.

The starship was only a few lengths above the surface when the inner airlock burst open. Angry wind flooded the hall and shoved them all off balance, but the arkins stood their ground and kept their footing. They flattened their ears along their skulls and pulled their wings in tight as Lance and Lissa climbed on to their backs. Backélo awkwardly lowered himself on to Orion, and Lance felt the arkin buckle slightly under the additional weight. There wasn't time for Lance to worry, for Lissa had already moved Blade to the airlock's edge.

They paused for a moment, a black silhouette against the Ametrian sun, a shadow framed in blood. Then Blade leapt into the air and was gone. Orion went after her, and he jumped as soon as he reached the edge.

The wind bent around the starship, throwing Orion's flight pattern into an erratic struggle for balance. Backélo's additional weight did nothing to stabilize him, and the Rhyutan was almost thrown from his back. He grabbed Lance's arm and held tight as the arkin fought the wind, and the Rhyutan settled heavily against Lance's back as the arkin leveled out, spread his wings, and glided.

A shadow passed over them as Blade flew by overhead. Lance looked up and saw that Lissa was watching the starship. He turned his head just in time to see the ship disappear over the lip of the canyon. For a while, there was just the rush of the wind around Lance's ears. Then there was a muffled crash followed closely by another, then a burst of light that faded quickly as the canyon swallowed the burning starship.

They landed shortly thereafter on top of a low rock formation, Blade touching down considerably more gracefully than the overburdened Orion. She was also breathing easier, Lance noticed, and he checked Orion's mask to make sure it was properly fitted. This time, Orion did not struggle.

While he worked on Orion's mask, Lissa pulled a small, shiny black ball from her belt, toyed with it, and then held it out in front of her. It rose up from the palm of her hand and was enveloped by a blue hologram sphere that flickered in and out of sight for a few minutes, then solidified into a display of Ametria's surface. Lissa touched the hologram, entered a set of coordinates when prompted, then looked at Lance and Backélo. "Are these right?"

Lance squinted at the coordinates. They were from the small piece of data that the brief scan had returned: the crash site of the *Argonaught IV*, or very close to it at least. "I think so," he said.

Backélo nodded in slow agreement.

Lissa confirmed the coordinates, and the navigation sphere pointed them into the Ametrian wilderness. They set off on foot, not wanting to exhaust the arkins. They slowly picked their way over the uneven terrain, the closeness of the Ametrian atmosphere pressing in on them. The air was hot and heavy as the red sun slid across the thick sky above them, and the world felt very dense in spite of the lifeless stillness. Lissa led the way, the arkins close behind her, followed by Lance and Backélo.

They walked in silence for the most part, but Backélo gripped Lance's shoulder at one point.

"Ashburn," the Rhyutan said, his voice small and distorted by the breathing mask. "I want to apologize. For doubting you."

"We can talk about this later," Lance said.

"No," Backélo said. "No, I was… wrong. About you."

"I've made mistakes."

"Yes, you have made a lot of mistakes and are unfit for command," Backélo said, and either ignored or was oblivious to the look Lance gave him. "But you are not a traitor, Ashburn."

"Captain Backélo," Lance said, "until the admirals see fit to strip me of my rank, I am still your commanding officer. You'd do well to remember that.

Backélo looked very much like he wanted to say something, but he shot a dark look ahead instead. "I don't trust the Nandro, Commander."

Lance heard the heavy distaste that Backélo put on the final word, but he let it go this time. "Neither do I, but she's keeping us alive."

"For a reason."

"Probably, but for now, she's our best chance for survival."

They had almost reached another canyon, this one much narrower than the one that had swallowed the starship, when Blade and Orion both froze. They looked at each other with their ears standing straight up, then hunched down in unison, their thick tails sweeping the ground nervously. Lissa caught Lance's eye and they exchanged a bewildered look, then jumped as a loud, low roar rumbled over them. Deep and throaty, the roar churned the air before fading away into echoes.

"A bull?" Backélo asked.

Lance shrugged and shook his head, then moved to help Lissa urge the arkins on. As he stepped up next to her, she grabbed his wrist.

"It's close," she said. "Whatever roared like that, it's very close."

"What do you want to do?"

"Fly."

"Until we're across the canyon, sure."

"And then beyond there, as far as we can. Then we touch down somewhere safe, rest the arkins, and then fly again."

Lance shifted uneasily. "Orion won't last very long under all that weight."

Lissa looked over his shoulder at Backélo, then adjusted

her grip on her pistol.

"That is not an option," Lance snapped.

"I did not say it was." She met his gaze again. "I want you to know, though, that if the sun starts to set, I'm not going to wait for you."

"Thanks for warning me this time."

She looked at him without malice, then glanced around, shuddering a little. "It's nothing against you. I just have a feeling that most of this planet wakes up when the sun goes down."

There was another deep roar, softer this time, more distant.

"There are monsters in the light, too," Lance said.

Lissa had turned her head towards the direction of the second roar, but she tensed sharply at his words. She did not meet his eye when she said, "More than you know."

They picked up the pace after that, alternating between flying, walking, and briefly resting. When Lissa showed them the navigation sphere again, the sun was low in the sky and they had stopped on top of one of the higher rock formations between two canyons.

"Not much further," she told them. "Maybe about an hour." She glanced up at the low-hanging sun, then froze. Lance saw her go rigid, and he followed her gaze.

Ametria's moons had begun to shine through. Two of the larger ones had slipped over the horizon, a blazing red and orange display, but one of the smaller moons had appeared as well. It hung soft and purple near the top of the sky, but there was a large red thing suspended in front of the moon, just close enough to Ametria for Lance make out the disk-like shape rotating around the long central axis.

Lissa stood looking at the Seventh Sun's base for a long time. Then she made an angry, cutting gesture with her hand and swung herself on to Blade's back. She steered the arkin over the edge, and the black slipped into a low, easy glide over the stony ground, but both Blade and Lissa suddenly snapped their heads to the side. Blade's wings ballooned out as she pulled up short. The arkin twisted in midair, shrieking, and Lissa clung tightly to her back as she rolled and surged in a new direction. She hit the ground, pushed off, and beat her wings furiously as she climbed back up into the sky.

A set of jaws closed over the air where Blade had been a moment before, barely missing the stiff, tufted fur at the end of her tail. The creature's head emerged in full, followed by the thick neck and shoulders, and then Lance was diving on to Orion's back. The arkin flinched as a throaty roar ripped the air apart, but Orion forced himself forward at Lance's frantic urging. Orion took off as soon as he found the edge of the rock, and Lance turned him skyward. Orion climbed, wings beating hard but evenly, and leveled out well above the Ametrian's reach. Or at least, Lance hoped they were out of its reach. He got a good look at the creature as Orion circled overhead, and he pushed the arkin a little higher, just in case.

The thing was huge. The body itself was small in proportion to the creature's height, the head roughly half the size of the torso, but the Ametrian's four legs were long and thick, built for climbing and fighting. It scrabbled up the rock after Lissa and Blade, long claws hooking into existing crevices and carving new ones with no visible effort, but Blade had a head start and she quickly slipped out of reach. Lance could see the power bunching beneath the Ametrian's leathery skin as it swiped the air where Blade had been, and its thick neck was corded with muscle as it craned its head and snapped at the empty air again.

The Ametrian was dusty red in color, with darker red and brown splotches patterning its body. Two wickedly sharp horns curved out of its long, sloping skull, and when the Ametrian turned its head to glance up at Orion, Lance had a clear view of its oversized, yellow teeth. The Ametrian's eyes were deep red as they traced Orion's movements, the pupils a thin white slit.

The Ametrian crouched low, watching, then surged and jumped. Its jaws closed dangerously close to Orion's belly, and the arkin climbed higher into the air.

Lance looked for Lissa and Blade, but found an escape instead.

There was a canyon not too far from them. They could cross the gap and lose the Ametrian if Orion did not sink under the extra—

FUCK.

They had left Backélo.

Orion gave a distressed whine as Lance turned him back. The arkin tensed noticeably as the Ametrian watched them swing around, and Lance felt his own fear threaten to shatter his resolve, but he could not leave the Rhyutan.

Backélo was where they had left him, perched on top of one of the higher rock formations. Lance picked him out by his pale skin and angled Orion directly towards him, but as they drew closer, Lance realized that he would need more time than the Ametrian was likely to give him.

Backélo had crawled to the edge of the rock. He crouched there on his hands and knees, staring transfixed at the Ametrian as it slowly lumbered towards him. The creature was still below his level, but if he did not move back from the edge, it would see him without any trouble, and for all his speed and agility, the Rhyutan would never be able to get away. Even if he managed to break his fear paralysis.

Lance swung Orion around in another loop over the Ametrian's head, trying to catch Backélo's eye without pointing the Ametrian directly to him, but the Rhyutan was too terrified to fracture his attention.

The Ametrian lunged at Orion again, and again came terrifyingly close. Lance knew he would either have to leave Backélo, or send Orion in a dive for the Rhyutan and hope for the best, but coming out alive was a little too much to hope for.

Then there was a flash of black as Blade shot across the Ametrian's line of sight. The Ametrian lost all interest in Orion and went after the black arkin. Lance paused long enough to see Lissa twist around and fire off an enerpulse pistol shot at the Ametrian's head.

Backélo seemed to come back to his senses as the Ametrian chased after the black arkin. He shakily rose to his feet, still staring after the receding Ametrian, but he caught sight of Lance and began to show signs of comprehension.

As Orion touched down, Backélo jumped on to the arkin's back, nearly driving Orion to the ground in the process. The arkin grunted under the strain, but righted himself and took off again.

Lance knew that their survival would depend entirely on how long Lissa was willing to dangle Blade in front of the Ametrian. Though he beat his wings furiously, Orion's speed was slow and he was only able to rise a little above the highest rock formations. Even then, he kept sinking, and he was forced to carve his way through the space between the jutting rocks rather than fly over them and risk scraping his paws and belly.

Orion managed to bring them through the rocks unharmed, and the formations suddenly dropped off into a low plain for the final stretch. The canyon gaped wide ahead of them. To their left, Lance saw the Ametrian dancing on its back legs as Blade darted above its head, always just out of reach, but Lance's relief was short-lived. The black arkin was tiring, and Lissa was letting her drift further and further away from the Ametrian. All too soon, the Ametrian fell back to all fours, gave a frustrated roar, and dropped its head to rake its horns across the stony ground. When it looked up, it looked straight at Orion, and Lance saw its rage flare.

"Go!" Lance screamed as the Ametrian tore after them. "Go, Orion! GO!"

Orion grunted, but did not push himself to go faster. Fear snaked its way through Lance's gut as he realized that the arkin was far too tired to outstrip the Ametrian, but he saw Orion turn his head to watch the oncoming Ametrian. Lance let himself hope that the arkin would be able to work his own way through this, and just did his best not to disrupt Orion's movements.

The Ametrian had lowered its head as it charged across the

plain, ripping across the distance at a heartstopping speed. It started to raise its head as it drew closer to Orion, but its timing was off and its jaws had only just begun to open as it reached the arkin. Orion angled in towards the head, let his body collide with the Ametrian's snout, and was pushed over the creature's skull. He avoided the teeth cleanly, but his back legs hit the base of one of the Ametrian's massive horns. Orion jolted and spun, fought for balance and won, but Backélo was thrown off his back.

Lance felt Backélo leave. He twisted around, flung his arm out, and caught hold of the captain. Orion lurched again as Backélo came up short and then dropped towards the ground, but Lance held tight and the soldier did not fall.

Lance's shoulder was on fire as Orion frantically fought for height and balance. Backélo's weight threatened to pull Lance over the arkin's side, but he would not let go.

Just a little further, he told himself. *Just across the canyon. Just a little further.*

He focused on Orion's wing beats, on the rush of the wind around him, on the arkin's panting and the hammering of his own heart and the red light against his clamped-shut eyelids as he kept telling himself to hold on.

Backélo slipped a little further down Lance's arm. Then he screamed. Then he was ripped from Lance's grip, and he was gone.

Lance was very aware of three things as Orion flew on. First, the beating of his own heart. Second, tingling relief in the fingers of his now-empty hand. And third, the gleam that had appeared on the horizon as they crossed the canyon, light bouncing off the hull of the crashed starship *Argonaught IV*.

Just a little further.

CHAPTER 24: BURST

Losing the Rhyutan had been hard on Ashburn, but when they reached the ship and saw that the impact had smashed the shuttles along with a good part of the hull, Lissa worried that the commander might snap.

When Orion touched down on the hull of the ruined starship, Ashburn slid off his back and stood looking out at the barren land, back the way they had come.

"Ashburn," Lissa started, then, "Lance…"

But he shook his head and she left him alone. It took him awhile, but he finally turned his back on the dead land. "I'm going to check the hull." He swung on to Orion and took off before she could stop him.

Let him go, she told herself. *Let him grieve, whatever he needs to do, then he can let go and we can get off this planet.*

Except the shuttles all looked to be destroyed, and even if the ship's remaining fighters were still intact, they would never make it back to Phan. If they could power up the communications system, they could signal the Sun's base, but Lissa would have preferred to stay on Ametria. Maybe they could reach the Star Feds with an encrypted message, but with the base so close, she doubted it. All the same, she took Blade along the hull, searching for an access point.

She found the wide hole where the Seventh Sun's driller had leeched on to the ship. Perched on the lip of the hole, she scanned the dark interior through her infrared eye lenses, but nothing seemed to be living down there. She took Blade into the ship and flew in a slow, wide spiral down to the bottom, but the room was clear. She removed the lenses, waited for the dizziness to fade, then activated the three sandglass lanterns she carried. Though small and dim, they cast just enough light for her to see that she was standing in the docking bay.

Montag's *Resolution* loomed in front of her, nearly shaken loose from its physical restraints in the crash. The ship's hull was battered and dented, but it was a renegade craft and it had been designed to take some damage. Lissa went over the ship as best she could, a difficult task in the faint lantern light, but the *Resolution* looked to be mostly intact. More importantly, the ship looked flyable. Lissa was about to try to gain access through the airlock when she remembered that the *Resolution* had been on the verge of blacking out when the Star Feds took the smuggler ship in.

So much for that.

When Lissa and Blade emerged from the interior, they found Ashburn and Orion waiting for them. Lissa took one look at Ashburn and her hand went to the enerpulse pistol on her hip. She did not like his smile at all.

"Any luck with the shuttles?" she asked cautiously.

Ashburn shook his head, still smiling. "They're all completely trashed, but I did find something that we can use. Two things, actually."

"What things?"

"Two of the ship's pulse cannons are still intact."

Lissa eyed him. "And what are you going to do with a cannon?"

Ashburn pointed straight up.

The Seventh Sun's base hung red in front of the purple moon.

For a long, stunned moment, Lissa had nothing to say.

Part of her agreed with Ashburn. The base needed to be

destroyed. It was the Seventh Sun's and nothing good would ever come out of it.

The rest of her thought of the candidates that might be on the base, of the unknown Neo-Andromedans who might be forced to scream *Welcome to the Light*. That was the part of her that found her voice.

"There's no way you'll have enough power to fire a cannon. I don't know what the Sun did to this starship, but even if you—"

"The Sun cut the power," Ashburn said, still smiling. "They stranded us in space, but now that we're on a planet, we can fire those cannons."

"How?"

"The Star Federation redesigned their weapons systems a while ago. They put individual power supplies in the pulse cannons so that we wouldn't drain ourselves and risk a blackout every time we needed to fire a gun. If we can access the control line, I can manually calibrate and fire the cannons."

Panic nibbled at Lissa's spine as she looked up at the base again. "Ashburn, that is not a close target."

"It's not far, either."

"But all that power… Couldn't we transfer the cells?"

"To where? The shuttles are trashed and we won't make it far in the fighters."

"What about the *Resolution*?"

Ashburn paused. "What?"

"Montag's ship. The Sun's driller hit the carrier bay, and the *Resolution* is still inside. It took a bit of a beating, but it looks flyable. If we can power it up, we can get out of here."

Ashburn frowned and rubbed the back of his neck. "We can't take the *Resolution* off-planet, anyway. Not if that base is still up."

He was right, she realized. The base had to go. But if there were candidates…

"Lissa," Ashburn said, his voice surprisingly gentle. "What are you not telling me?"

If there were candidates, she could never hope to save

them anyway.

"Look," Ashburn said, still gently but firmer now. "I have the protection of the entire galaxy on my shoulders, and you put that on me. You pulled me into this, and now that I'm in, I'm going to act. That base is a threat, and whether or not I can actually do it, I'm going to try to take it out." He looked at her closely. "But if you know some reason why I absolutely shouldn't, then you need to tell me."

Still nothing.

"Are you... protecting someone?"

Lissa looked up at the base again, at the purple moon in the slowly darkening sky. Red against lilac, lilac against indigo, and a small white blaze beyond the crescent horns where a single brave star had managed to cut through the atmosphere. It was a surprisingly beautiful sight. "No," she said softly. "I'm not protecting anyone."

It took her longer than it should have to realize that Ashburn had moved to her side and placed his hand on her shoulder. She jumped suddenly, and shied away from him.

Ashburn dropped his hand. "I know that this is a hard decision, but you said yourself that the Seventh Sun is our enemy." His eyes hardened under the weight of his dead. "And they have a lot to answer for."

Lissa glanced up at the base one last time.

Let them go.

Ashburn led her back into the interior of the ship, to doors that were programmed to remain open in case of power shortages, to storage lockers where they found the tools they needed to open the armored casings of the pulse cannons and access the control lines. Ashburn focused on the larger cannon, and said that if that one didn't bring down the base, he doubted the smaller one would be able to do it. "Besides," he added, "we'll want the power cells for the *Resolution*." He smiled at her over his shoulder, but quickly dropped it when she did not return the gesture. "As soon as I get this cannon up, be ready to move. We don't want to be in the area when it fires."

There was not much Lissa could do to help once Ashburn had gained access to the control line. She did not know much about pulse cannons other than their destructive power, and she settled on the hull to watch. Blade lied down next to her, Orion on her other side. Lissa looked at the gray in surprise, but he just blinked at her. When the time came to swap the depleted respirator packs for the reserve set, Orion offered no resistance as Lissa changed his pack out.

Ashburn worked for a long time. Lissa tried not to follow his gaze every time he looked up, but she knew he was tracking the Sun's base. It was still fixed in front of the small moon, and their orbits were slow enough that there was no risk of losing sight of either.

The Ametrian sun had nearly set by the time Ashburn had finished. Their shadows were long and thin under the light of the three new moons that had crept over the horizon; a few of the brighter, more determined stars were shining through the thick sky; and wild sounds were running across the darkening land. As the planet came alive, so did the pulse cannon.

"Move!" Ashburn shouted as the cannon swung up towards the base. He ran for Orion and jumped on the arkin's back. Lissa and Blade followed them as Ashburn pushed the gray into flight, and he led them over the edge of the hull as the pulse cannon fired with a deafening roar.

As Blade followed Orion's tail in a wild dive towards the ground, Lissa looked over her shoulder. She saw five blue-white energy pulses tear into the sky and streak towards the Sun's base. They quickly disappeared into the distance, and the pulse cannon died. An eerie silence settled over Ametria as the last rays of red sunlight faded away and the world slipped into darkness.

Ashburn brought them back up on top of the hull. They stood with their eyes turned skywards and the muscles in their necks tightening in protest, and they waited. They watched, waited, and waited—

The Seventh Sun's base exploded in a burst of silent light.

Ashburn sighed heavily, partially in awe but mostly in relief and triumph. He turned to Lissa, but she was staring up at the destroyed base and only registered him at her peripheries. The dead base filled the rest of her vision.

One pulse cannon, from one Star Federation starship, had done that.

"And you wonder why I won't tell you everything," Lissa said softly.

CHAPTER 25: FOCUS

One good thing about Ashburn going missing, Jason had to admit, was that it made time alone with Erica considerably easier to come by.

They had thoroughly searched the Phanite streets, but neither had come up with any hard evidence and they had known that they would have to let the case drop. Frustrated with the cold trail and with the time they'd spent apart, they agreed to meet on a small ship docked at the ground port, the same one Erica had taken to the city. They both needed it, and they came together with more than enough passion and energy to make up for the long dry spell. When it was over, Erica lay with her head on Jason's chest, tracing small circles on his shoulder with her finger. She only did that when she was thinking, and he retaliated by playing with a lock of her short, blonde hair.

Erica sighed after a while, and Jason knew he had lost the battle. "Do you really think that there's no chance Ashburn's gone rogue?"

Jason dropped his hand to her shoulder. "I meant it when I said that rogue isn't in his blood." Her skin was very smooth and soft under his hand.

Erica sighed again, and started tapping in the center of the rings she had traced out. A bull's-eye of concentration. "There's just something that's off. It's like... there's something missing."

"Commander Ashburn, maybe?"

Erica gave him a light tap on the cheek, then went back to tracing targets on his shoulder. "We should go back to that hospital. You said that you thought that the doctor wasn't telling you something. What was his name?"

"Kyle Chhaya."

"Right, him. We should talk to the rest of the staff, see what we can find out about Dr. Chhaya, then double back to see what he has to say once we've got a better idea of how he operates."

"Mm." Her head rose and fell as Jason took a deep breath. "We've probably let him sit long enough by now. He may think he's safe. We can catch him off-guard, maybe get more out of him this time."

"Right." Erica pushed herself up and climbed over him. Jason watched the bend and curve of her back as she dressed. "I want to find out more about his patients, if we can. We'll probably only get restricted access, but maybe if we—"

Erica's personal communicator cracked to life. She finished fastening her uniform, then picked up the small machine. She moved away from the cot, careful to keep Jason out of range, and accepted the transmission.

"Commander Keraun," she said with obvious surprise as the Hyrunian's head flickered into focus. Jason looked up sharply but Erica made a small gesture behind her back with her free hand. "How can I help you, sir?"

"I've heard Commander Ashburn and Captain Backélo have gone missing," the Hyrunian growled. "I want to know what's going on."

"I am trying to figure out exactly that as we speak, sir."

Keraun snorted. "What is your next move?"

"There's a doctor at a local hospital that witnessed Commander Ashburn arresting the Shadow," Erica said. "We talked to him but we think he's hiding something."

"Good, find out what. I want you to keep me updated, Anderson."

"Yes, sir."

"On everything, especially if it concerns this Seventh Sun group."

"Yes, sir."

"And Anderson, if you find a Nandro—" even via hologram, Jason saw the gleam in Keraun's yellow eyes, "—kill it."

"Yes, sir."

Jason rose from the cot and began to dress himself as Erica put away the communicator. "What are we going to do if Keraun comes to Phan?"

"He won't come."

"But if he does—"

"There's nothing for him to find," Erica said, combing her fingers through her hair and smoothing out the tangles Jason had created. "We've been all over this planet and we've got nothing. Keraun knows that. He'll leave us alone. Besides, the higher ups trust us to keep things under control. Even with a Nandro threat, there's no reason why they should send another fleet commander in to babysit us."

Jason's frown deepened as he realized that Erica was focused on their authority over the case and nothing more. She had always been strong and ambitious, and he loved her for that, but at that moment, he wanted to turn her away from the Star Federation. "Ric," he said softly. "I meant what—"

"You know, I really hate it when you call me that."

Jason came up short, the top half of his uniform only partly fastened near his hip. "What?"

"My name is Erica. 'Ric' is not a nickname for that." She brushed her hands over the sleeves of her uniform, pushing out the wrinkles. "It wasn't as of eight months ago, and it isn't now, just because you keep using it."

"Fine," Jason said, frowning. "But what I meant was, what are *we* going to do."

She looked at him then, almost in bewilderment, and it

took her a few heartbeats longer than Jason thought it should have to answer. "If the soldiers catch us, we're fine. They don't know how long we've been together, and they won't care so long as we're back in time to give them fresh orders." She held his gaze for a moment. Then she sighed. "If Keraun comes and he thinks something's up, then we act a little cooler and meet a little less often. He's not going to do anything if it's just sex."

"I thought we'd passed that point a while ago."

"Of course we did," Erica said, returning to straightening her uniform. "But Keraun doesn't know that."

"Ashburn figured it out."

"No he didn't. You think he did because he's got you paranoid for some reason, but he doesn't know." She wrestled with her boots. "If he did, one of us wouldn't be here right now."

When they had both finished dressing, they left the starship. They passed a few soldiers, but other than the customary salutes, Jason and Erica were not given any special attention. They emerged from the ship quickly enough, into the slowly rising Phanite dawn. Pale sunlight seeped across the hazy sky, drowning the few stubborn stars that hung low on the opposite horizon. Lights were flicking off across the ground port as the daylight grew stronger, and shapes gained color as the world came into focus. The starships brightened into a thousand different shades of gray, the soft light pooling on the hard angles of the tri- and split-wing ships and sliding across the rounded noses of the shuttles. Faces and bodies as diverse as the two rows of starships came into focus as they darted around the ships.

Jason paused for a moment, breathing in the cool dawn and feeling the morning air against his face and his hands, the only bits of skin that the Star Federation uniforms left free. Then Erica touched his arm. She pointed his gaze to a soldier stationed outside of the starship.

The soldier stood with his arms crossed and an enerpulse rifle slung across his back, speaking with a woman. They were not terribly close to where Jason and Erica were, but the ground port had not come fully awake and bits of the conversation threaded their way to Jason's ears. He stiffened sharply when he heard Ashburn's name.

As Jason and Erica emerged fully from the starship and headed for the soldier, Jason saw the woman glance at his and Erica's uniforms. Her gaze lingered on the captain insignias, and she broke off what she had been saying to the soldier and turned to meet Jason and Erica head on. She smiled uncertainly as they drew near.

She wore plain traveler's clothes, Jason saw, and was dressed warm against the cool morning. Her jacket was fastened all the way up to her throat, her hands pushed snugly into her pockets, but her cheeks and ears were flushed pink from the bite of the dawn. She looked harmless enough, but Jason made a point of scoping out the areas around her hips and waist, looking for the telltale snag of fabric on a firearm. He did not see anything.

"Captain Stone, Captain Anderson," the soldier barked as he straightened and saluted them before gesturing to the woman. "She has a report of Commander Ashburn."

"Mara Turner," the woman introduced herself, still smiling. The name rolled off her tongue and dropped like beads to the ground.

Jason saw Erica shoot the soldier a hard look before focusing on the witness. "I'm Captain Anderson of the Star Federation. What can you tell us, Ms. Turner?"

Turner looked back and forth between Jason and Erica as she spoke, brown eyes rolling from face to face. "I saw a man and a woman yesterday. The man was tall and blond. The woman was shorter than him, and had very dark hair. I thought that they were behaving strangely, but I did not do anything about it until I saw the Star Federation soldiers here at the ground port. I thought it best to report the incident, and—"

"Sure," Erica said, and Jason heard the edge of annoyance in her voice. "And where did you see them?"

Jason did not blame Erica for her shortness. They must

have had at least six dozen reports of Ashburn and the Shadow come in over the course of the night, all of them pointing to the hospital Jason had visited. One more report would just add to the noise.

Mara Turner, however, had not seen them at the hospital. She claimed to have seen them on the other side of the city, jumping across the rooftops. "They had some sort of animals with them. Big cats with wings." Turner frowned and rolled her head to one side. "I don't know what they were, but the man and the woman were riding on their backs. They flew down out of the sky and landed on a building, then went running and jumping along the roofs."

This was new. All of the reports of Ashburn and the Shadow had been distinctly lacking in sightings of the gray and black arkins.

"Were the creatures chasing each other?" Jason asked.

Turner frowned and shook her head, short brown hair swinging back and forth. "They did not go fast, and if one pulled ahead they would wait for the other."

Jason felt Erica glance at him, but he kept his eyes on Turner. "Where was this again?"

"On the far side of the city, near the political district and the embassies."

"What else can you tell us?" Erica asked.

Mara Turner's hands rolled out of her pockets and spread with the fluidity of water into a light shrug.

Not water, Jason decided. *Something else.*

"I can't tell you much, I'm afraid. I only saw them for a minute at the most." Turner frowned again, thinking hard. "They looked to be heading into the political district. I can't say for sure, but if I had to guess, that would be it."

Erica nodded thoughtfully. "Thank you, Ms. Turner." She turned to the soldier. "Have you recorded this?"

The soldier held up a small datapad. "I have her earlier report and this conversation, Captain."

Erica nodded again and released the witness. Mara Turner walked away, and just before she disappeared into the growing ground port crowd, Jason realized that the rolling fluidity of her movements had reminded him of mercury.

"Clean up the witness report and send it to Commander Keraun," Erica told the soldier.

Jason felt a twinge of anger and nervousness as the soldier hurried off, but said nothing. One report was not likely to bring Keraun running.

"What do you think?" Erica asked in a low voice once they were alone. "Any credibility to that?"

"She said she saw the arkins," Jason said. "That's a better lead than we've had so far. I can't think of what they would be doing in the political district, though."

Erica pushed her hair behind her ears. "Do we have an Earth ambassador on Phan?"

Jason thought for a moment. "We must. I have no idea who it would be, though."

Erica crossed her arms. "It may be time to seriously consider the possibility of Ashburn going rogue." Jason looked at her sharply, but Erica nodded as though he had agreed. "We should get over to the embassies. I think this is the better lead, but I want to go back to that hospital, too."

"Mm." Jason pulled a small disk out of his pocket and drew his arm back, ready to toss the disk into the air. It was one of the ten hologram disks that the Star Federation doled out to its soldiers, but he doubted he would miss the one and he could get a replacement easily enough. "Shoot for first pick?"

Ten minutes later, Erica's transport shuttle left for the political district. Jason was already well on his way back to the hospital by then. He had left the hologram disk on the ground where it had fallen, reduced to a scorched black mess by the enerpulse shot. Erica had hit it on her first try.

CHAPTER 26: PRICE

Night had fallen in full by the time Lance and Lissa had finished transferring the power cells from the second pulse cannon to the *Resolution*. They worked as fast as they could by the light of the sandglass lanterns, connecting the cells to the energy converters more by touch than by sight, but before they were done, Orion and Blade had to chase off a few of the more aggressive creatures that had decided to explore the interior of the *Argonaught IV*. The creatures stayed outside of the faint bubble of light, but Lance could make out leathery wings and gleaming teeth as they circled closer. Then the arkins bared their own fangs and drove the monsters away.

When the power transfer was complete, Lance, Lissa, and the arkins slipped inside the captive starship. The *Resolution* blazed with life from the new power cells when they activated the systems, and they pulled off their nearly depleted respirators as the ventilation came back online. Orion was especially pleased to be free of the breathing mask, and he tossed his head and took one prancing lap around the control room. Blade watched him.

The ship was just small enough to slide through the hole left by the Seventh Sun's driller. They pushed the *Resolution* out and angled up into a night sky dotted with a few scarce stars and heavy with moons. Two new moons had risen to claim their places above the horizon, fiery orange and red giants, but the small purple moon still hung near the top of the sky. It swung across its orbit almost perfectly in synch with Ametria's rotation, and the dark debris field stood out clearly against the soft color.

Lissa looked at the destroyed station on the visual display for a long time. She had not said much about the annihilation of the Sun's base. She had not said much of anything, really, other than the necessary conversations about transferring the power cells. She knew the model of the *Resolution* better than Lance did, and she had only emerged from her concentration to point him to a far line that he needed to hook up or a heavy cell that took the two of them to properly align. Her silence made Lance nervous.

For someone who so clearly hated the Seventh Sun and who was so used to ending a life from a distance, she was holding the destruction of the base awfully close to her heart.

Had he been wrong about her? Was she really one of the Seventh Sun's operatives, playing him into some trap? He doubted it.

She had been torn between approving the use of the pulse cannon and fighting him to the death before he could get near the control line, that much was obvious, but that could not have been part of a plan. If the Sun wanted Lance alive, that could not be worth the destruction of a full space station, especially not a station that they had worked so hard to keep hidden.

No, Lissa was not part of the Seventh Sun. But the decision to destroy the base had broken something, and it might drive her away from the Star Federation, possibly even to the Sun. He had to call her back.

He watched her tear herself away from the visual display and chart a course for Phan. If he was going to pull her away from whatever she had turned to, it had to be now. He'd never be able to do it once they'd returned to Phan; the Star Federation would pounce on them both the moment they entered the atmosphere.

He considered her for a long moment, and he knew that she felt his eyes. He could see it in the tenseness of her movements and the way she tried to keep her back to him. She never would have done that before the pulse cannon ripped the Seventh Sun's base apart. Now she either trusted him to not put the barrel of an enerpulse pistol against her skull, or did not care if he did. He did not think it was the former.

He let her work for a while, hoping she would speak first, but as the *Resolution* sped on and Phan drew closer, Lance knew he had to do something. He jumped into the void. "We have a problem."

She glanced over her shoulder, at the systems he was monitoring. "What is it?"

"You," he said simply.

There was a heavy silence as she finally looked at him. Something flickered behind her eyes, a brightness that unnerved him even more than her quiet had. "I risked my life for you on Ametria," she snarled. "I got you off that planet and I helped you murder I don't even know how many Neo-Andromedans and—"

"And that's the problem," Lance said softly but firmly. "Suddenly, it's murder. Suddenly, it's not right to strike at the Seventh Sun."

Lissa frowned, shut her eyes, and turned away.

Too far, he realized. *Pull back. Be gentle.* "Look, I know there's something you're still not telling me." He leaned forward in his seat, rested his elbows on his knees, and watched her as he spoke. "If that's how it has to be, then fine, but don't lose sight of why you brought me into this."

She barely moved when she said, "I haven't."

Lance sighed, very quietly, but behind the breath there was the weight of broken trust that had never been whole to begin with. "I think you lied earlier, when you said you weren't protecting someone."

Lissa shifted in agitation, but the thing behind her eyes had died and she seemed emptier now. "No, I wasn't protecting anyone." A short pause. Then, "I couldn't."

Lance thought that he was beginning to understand what she had not told him, but he could not shake the feeling that there was more. He decided to focus on what was there, for the moment. "I know that there were probably people on that station that were not part of the Seventh Sun. I've been a Star Fed long enough to know when and where to expect civilian casualties. It's never easy, dealing with that."

"Except when they're Neo-Andromedan, right?" She looked at him then, fiercely and challenging, but he did not drop his gaze.

"It's never easy," he said again. Then, after a short pause, "Is there any way we could have helped them?"

She did not immediately answer, just looked sadly at the control panel. When she spoke, her voice was so soft that he had to strain to hear it. "No."

"Even if we'd gone back for reinforcements?"

She shook her head.

"I won't pretend to know how much the Seventh Sun has taken from you, but I know that I've already lost more to them in five days than I have to anyone in my entire career. I put some of the dead to rest today, but I just made more graves for you, didn't I?"

She said nothing.

He decided to change tactics, try to nudge her back to her roots. "Your brother is the reason you got into the hunting game, isn't he? Aven, right?"

"Yes."

"Tell me about him," Lance invited.

She bristled at the words. "Why?"

Because maybe then you'll remember why you hate the Seventh Sun so much, he wanted to say. Instead, he asked, "He's your younger brother?"

"Older."

Lance felt his brow furrow in surprise, and he cocked his head a little, but he waited for her to speak again.

It took her a long time, long enough for a minor system to

malfunction. Its alarm gave three short beeps, and Lissa rose from her seat to find the maintenance panel. Her gaze snagged on him as she stood, and she frowned. "Look, Ashburn, I'm not going to give you my history." She moved out of the control room, and Lance jumped up and followed her. "You don't need it," she continued over her shoulder, "and once Aven is dead, most of it won't matter." Lance opened his mouth to protest, but she ran ahead of his stunned voice before he could get a syllable out. "I haven't forgotten why the Seventh Sun needs to be brought down." She reached the access panel in the floor, yanked it aside, and hopped down into the shallow pit. "I know who they are, what they've done, and what they're still doing. I will never forget that." She glowered at the red light highlighting the faulty power line, reached for it aggressively, and stopped herself before she did more damage. She sighed softly, then began to work more gingerly with the malfunctioning area. "It's just that, for the first time, I finally realized just how powerless I am against them."

Lance dragged his voice out of hiding as he kneeled next to the access point. "We just destroyed a space station while grounded on Ametria. I wouldn't consider that powerless."

"No, the Star Federation destroyed the base. A Star Fed cannon on a Star Fed ship operated by a Star Fed fleet commander. I didn't do anything. I wanted to, but I couldn't, and I'm afraid that that's how this is all going to end."

Lance felt a twinge at the back of his mind, but he pushed it away and kept his voice gentle when he asked, "What would happen if it were all up to you?"

"There's no point in fantasizing, Ashburn."

"What would happen?"

Lissa finished the maintenance repair. She swung herself out of the pit and slid the access panel back into place, sealing up the floor. She rested her hands on the panel for a long moment, then pushed to her knees and swung to face him. "I'd take out the heads of the Seventh Sun. Track them down, blast them out of existence."

"So more heavy strikes on their bases?"

"No," she said at once. "Small scale attacks. Infiltration and assassination."

Lance could not pretend to be surprised. It was something that the Shadow could do, and would do very well. "Would that kill the organization?"

"No, but that would cripple it, maybe beyond full recovery." She reached up and rubbed her shoulder, as though massaging an injury that was not there. "There would be... loose ends, but without the leaders, whoever was left could not move against the Star Federation. Not immediately."

"Would anyone else rise up in the leaders' places?"

"Maybe." She frowned, rubbed her left shoulder harder, a habit she seemed to have whenever she considered the future. "I don't know. It's possible, and honestly, I really don't think that killing the heads will do anything more than slow things down, but maybe time is all that's needed for things to change."

Change who? he wanted to ask. *Change what?* He knew he would not get an answer. Instead, he asked, "Could you do it? Could you take them all out?"

"I'm an Alpha Class bounty hunter, aren't I?"

"True," Lance said, but he wondered just how true. The destruction of the base had cracked the Shadow, and now something was a little broken loose inside Lissa. There was also the issue of her brother. Lance had figured him as the younger sibling, but Aven was older than Lissa. Would he have really let his little sister take up bounty hunting all those years ago? She would have been very young at the time. Too young. And there had been a predatory shade to Aven that the illness had not managed to completely wash out.

At the very least, the Shadow had two faces. That much Lance knew for certain.

"So," he said as they made their way back to the control room. "How many bases does the Seventh Sun have?"

"I don't know." She slipped back into her seat next to Blade, who pressed her nose against Lissa's leg for a brief moment before dropping her head back to the floor and shutting her eyes. Lissa reached down and scratched the arkin between the shoulders, and Blade sighed contentedly. "There's a main base, but I don't know how many of the smaller ones they've set up."

"Where's the main base?"

Lissa's hand paused. Blade cracked her eyes open and glanced up, but Lissa sat up and looked at Lance squarely. "I don't know."

"So we're flying blind." Lance felt agitation grab hopelessness and dance around his spine. The galaxy was an awfully large place to search in the dark.

She glanced away. "Not exactly. Aven..." She choked on the next word, tried again. "Aven knows where the main base is. I tried asking him about it, but he would never tell me. Even before he was dying."

Lance felt a twinge of guilt. He kept forgetting the price she was paying for all of this. He'd lost soldiers, he'd lost Captain Backélo, he'd almost lost his own life. But he was still alive, there had never been any warmth between him and Backélo, and his soldiers had risked their lives bravely to defend the galaxy, just as all Star Federation soldiers were sworn to do, and not all lost soldiers could be avenged. That was a simple truth that Lance had learned to accept a long time ago.

But she was losing her family, probably her only surviving family, and had been losing him for years. She was allying herself with the organization that had nearly annihilated the Neo-Andromedan race after the Andromedan War, and the Star Federation would work very hard to finish the job now that the Seventh Sun had become a threat. He had to remember that. If he forgot, he really would drive her away.

"I suppose that we may as well try talking to Aven since we're heading back to Phan anyway," Lissa said.

"If we showed up with a squad of Star Feds, would he be more cooperative?"

She laughed. "Ashburn, there's no way he'll tell you or any

other Star Fed." She hesitated, smiled bitterly. "No, that's not true. If you could guarantee total destruction of the Sun's main base, he might tell you."

Cold surprise tightened around Lance's chest. "He wants that?"

"Yes."

"But you don't."

"No."

Lance relaxed a little, but he was still unnerved. "Well, given that plenty of people saw us come out of that hospital, there are bound to be several soldiers in the area, looking for Backélo and me."

Lissa froze. "You're right." She leaned back and stared up at the ceiling. "And that means the Sun will be there, too."

So we led them to him after all. "Would they take your brother, in his condition?"

The way she looked at him made Lance feel like a small child. "Ashburn, Aven's not the one who just destroyed their station at Ametria with a Star Fed pulse cannon. He's not the one I'm worried about."

Lance held her sharp gaze for a long time. "I suppose we'd better see if this ship has any firepower, then." Another minor maintenance alarm sounded off. "I'll take care of this one," he offered, and started to rise.

"No," Lissa said, and stood. "You stay here and check the pulse cannons. You know weapons tech better than I do." When she reached the door to the control room, she hesitated. "The Sun probably knows we're coming. They know Phan is the logical destination, and they'll be waiting." She looked at him squarely. "Make sure your soldiers are, too."

Lance checked the weapons first, arming and readying the *Resolution* for a dogfight before broadcasting their destination to the Star Federation and whoever else was listening.

CHAPTER 27: TRUTH

The hospital staff did not seem surprised to see Jason back, nor did they seem to care about the lieutenant and four cadets that accompanied him. The staff was cooperative and pleasant enough when he asked where he could find Kyle Chhaya, but Jason ran into wall after stubborn wall of denial whenever he asked after the doctor's patients. He wasn't quite ready to use Star Federation force to break his way into the database, and he took the pleasant but firm smiles and set off to find the doctor. The off-duty surgeon that Jason's team met in the halls was more helpful, although exhaustion made him curt and he barreled off after spitting back two bits of information.

Dr. Chhaya currently had five patients in total, all with long-term illnesses.

Three of them were from the native Phanite population.

Jason wasn't quite sure what to look for in the other two patients, but he would know it when he found it. Until then, he focused on finding Chhaya again. He took his team through the halls, through the heart of the building, and into the proper wing. They reached the decontamination checkpoint, were given the customary run down on proper safety procedures when interacting with the patients, and three of the soldiers had to suffer through immunity booster shots. They found

Chhaya a few corners away from the checkpoint. The team started down the hall, but Jason halted the soldiers with a quick gesture and they stopped short.

The doctor was not alone. He stood in front of two men, his back to the small team of soldiers, and Jason felt alarm prick at his neck as he saw the inflexibility of Chhaya's posture. He remembered that the doctor had been firm but relaxed when Jason last saw him, ready to deal with trouble but easy with confidence. Now, Chhaya stood rigid, his arms stiff at his sides and his feet shoulder-width apart and staggered, as if ready to spring forwards into an attack, or backwards away from a strike. Jason eyed the two men, and could not blame the doctor for his nervousness.

The men were both fit and lean, like predatory animals built for speed. They were a bit sinewy, but there was a sharpness to their limbs. Their bodies did not occupy space so much as they cut through it, slicing the air.

One of the strangers was sandy-haired with a narrow face and a narrower gaze. His face and his body were all hard angles and plains, and although Jason was too far down the hall to see the man's eyes, he could tell that the stranger did not look at Chhaya with kindness.

The other man looked more bored than anything, from what Jason could see. His skin and his hair were darker than his companion's, and he was more square in the jaw and the shoulder, but he still had the lean, predatory look to him.

Jason did not like the look of either of the two men, but before he could signal his soldiers forward, a door opened next to Chhaya and a woman stepped out. She shouldered her way past the doctor, pulling out her communicator in a smooth, fluid movement. Jason led his soldiers forward as she spoke tersely into her communicator, and he saw shock roll across her body as the response came. Even the men looked sharply at her as the response played out, and Jason strained to hear. It was too faint for him to fully pick out the words, but he did not think that the transmission had been sent in the Galactic Unified Voice, or any language that he could have recognized.

But he did recognize the woman as he drew closer. Her eyes were different now, hard metallic silver instead of soft brown, and her jacket had been unfastened to reveal the black collar around her throat.

Jason's hand went to the enerpulse pistol on his hip as he drew closer to the group. The two men had metallic eyes as well. Jason could see the copper gaze of the darker man and the red-stained gunmetal stare of the paler one. There were collars around their throats as well, and Jason drew his pistol just as the Nandro who had called herself Mara Turner turned to say something to the men. Her gaze snagged on Jason, and anger washed over her face. Two short words dropped out of her mouth, and then she turned in one fluid motion and took off running. The two men took one look at the approaching Star Federation team, and then they cut around after the woman. Jason sent the lieutenant and the four cadets after the Nandros. He darted to Chhaya as the soldiers slipped around the corner.

The doctor did not move as Jason rushed into the space next to him, and he did not seem to feel Jason's hand on his shoulder. His eyes were shut tight and he did not open them when Jason said, "Are you all right? Dr. Chhaya, are you hurt?"

He waited, but Chhaya did not say anything. He did not even seem to be breathing. Then enerpulse fire ripped the air apart and Jason turned away. He took a quick step down the hall, but a hand closed with surprising strength on his elbow. Jason looked back at the doctor, and saw pure terror in his dark eyes.

"No," Chhaya whispered, shaking his head. "No."

Jason hesitated, but when another enerpulse shot sounded, he wrenched his arm free and took off. He raced through the halls, trying to reach the fight, but all he found were the bodies of the lieutenant and the soldiers scattered around a few corners. He slowed enough to see that they had all been taken out by a single enerpulse shot to the face, and he moved forward with caution. A few frantic staff members who had been shoved out of the way pointed him in the right direction, but he never found the Nandros. They had disappeared. Again.

Jason traced his way back to the fallen soldiers and stood in grim silence as he watched the hospital staff confirm their deaths and cover the bodies. They tentatively asked him if he wanted to leave the scene as it was for investigative purposes, but he shook his head and the staff removed the dead. As they took the last body away, he sent a transmission to Erica, telling her to get out of the political district. "That report was a fake," he told her. "Our witness was a fucking Nandro and she fed us a dead lead."

"There were Nandros at the hospital?" Erica asked sharply. "Were they Seventh Sun?"

Jason thought about the collars around their throats. Then he thought about the transmission from Keraun and the threat of that commander coming to Phan. "I don't know," he told Erica.

She made a discontented noise. "Do you know what they were after?"

"No." Jason turned and started down the hall. "But I'm going to find out."

He found Dr. Chhaya almost exactly where he had left him. The doctor looked calmer now, but it was a resigned calm and he stood with his hands clasped behind his back and gazed sadly into the room the Nandro woman had come out of. He did not glance around as Jason stepped to his side, just kept looking into the room. Jason followed his gaze and felt his heart stutter.

"I try very hard to save all of my patients," Chhaya said after a brief pause. "Sometimes, that means helping them fight more than just diseases." He looked away then, and waited for Jason to meet his eye. "His name is Aven. The Seventh Sun has been after him and his sister Lissa for years. I don't know if they'll be back for him, but if they try to move him, he will die. They know it, he knows it, and Lissa knows it, too. Aven is beyond their reach, but now that they're aware of his condition, the Seventh Sun will go after Lissa." Chhaya turned to face Jason squarely, and his gaze intensified. "'Stand and

Protect.' That's what all Star Federation soldiers are sworn to do. If you mean to serve as you promised, then you'll do everything you can to keep Lissa out of their hands."

Jason's anger flared. "She's a cold killer who abandoned us when we needed her. We asked for her help, and she left us to the Seventh Sun. As far as I'm concerned, she can rot in whatever hell they throw her into."

Chhaya tightened his mouth. "And what about as far as the rest of the galaxy is concerned?"

Jason grunted disgustedly. "The galaxy will be a lot safer with one less bounty hunter on the Alpha list."

"Not if the Seventh Sun has that hunter."

"You mean if she's not working for them already."

"No, that's not what I mean."

"What, then?" Jason glared at the doctor. "What does the Seventh Sun want with the Shadow? What makes her so special?"

"It's not just her," Chhaya said quietly. He looked into the room again. "It's also him, and every other Neo-Andromedan out there."

Jason glanced at the dying Nandro, but turned his attention back to Chhaya almost immediately. "But what do they want?" Impatience and rage were making him edgy, and he had to force each word out.

"When Lissa brought Aven to me, she warned me about his temper." Jason crossed his arms impatiently, but Chhaya ignored him and continued on. "It took her a while to tell me about the Seventh Sun, but her main concern was for her brother, and the risk of triggering a dangerous instinct during his treatment. I never hit it, but Lissa called it an Awakening." Chhaya paused, but this time, Jason found the patience to wait for him to speak again. "Awakened Neo-Andromedans are very dangerous, from what I understand. Under extreme mental or emotional distress, a killer instinct kicks in, and it threatens to destroy them if they don't kill first. Lissa said that when a Neo-Andromedan is Awake, his or her senses are heightened, and they become even stronger and faster than they are naturally."

Jason swallowed his rage. If that was true, then the Neo-Andromedans were a greater threat than anyone had ever realized. Jason was not quite ready to believe it, but the potential risk that posed was too great to be ignored. "And she knows this because...?"

"Because she's seen it before." Something hard appeared behind the doctor's eyes. "Several times, from what I understand."

"So that's what the Seventh Sun is after?"

"Candidates for the Awakenings, yes." Chhaya nodded at the dying Nandro. "Aven was a top candidate, from what I understand. Now that he's dying, Lissa will be at the top of the list, or very close to it."

Jason shifted, wondering just how much deadlier an Awakened Neo-Andromedan could truly be. He thought back to the Nandros that had ambushed the *Argonaught IV*. Ten of them had ripped through the ship, killing every soldier they found and leaving only a small handful of survivors. Had any of those Nandros been Awake? With the ship stranded on Ametria and the survivors only alive because they had not met the Nandros, that was a question that only the dead could answer. *The Shadow may know,* Jason realized, *but she could be anywhere. Ashburn too.* To the doctor, Jason said, "Why didn't you tell me any of this sooner?"

Chhaya sighed quietly, then turned to face Jason again. "Because I should not have been the one to tell you. But time is running out, and you need to be ready to make some decisions."

"About what, exactly?"

"About Aven, and Lissa, and every other Neo-Andromedan you may happen to meet. But please, if nothing else, remember that some of them would rather be asleep."

Jason looked into the room at the sick Nandro again. At Aven.

The top half of his mattress had been raised, and he was braced against the elevated part, his back pressed into the mattress and head thrown back over his pillow, staring relentlessly up at the ceiling. Jason saw exhaustion in Aven, but also muted anger. The Nandro's hands clutched at the thin blanket spread over his chest and legs, and although there was not much strength in his fingers, Jason saw intensity in his grip.

Chhaya sighed again. "I need to check on him and make sure his latest visitor hasn't caused him too much stress." He gave Jason one last searching look. "I know that you'll have some questions for him, but please remember his condition when you bring in the interrogation team." Chhaya moved into the room then, leaving Jason alone with his thoughts.

He didn't have much time to think. His communicator came alive and a lieutenant told him that they had received an emergency transmission from the starship *Resolution*. Ashburn and the Shadow were on a headlong rush for the ground port of a city on the night side of Phan, and they were under attack.

CHAPTER 28: CATCHER

Lissa knew the Sun was coming for them long before Phan came within easy reach of the ship's trackers. There was no activity around the planet that suggested that the Star Federation was moving to receive them. She wondered if the Star Feds had even received the broadcast Ashburn had sent. The Seventh Sun could have blocked the transmission if they were expecting a ship to return to Phan.

If, she thought wistfully. *No way they're not.*

By now, the entire organization must know that the Ametria base had been destroyed. They might not have been expecting the *Resolution* to escape the planet, but they would be watching and waiting at the nearest ports. The Star Feds, on the other hand, looked blissfully unaware of the approaching *Resolution*. If the Star Feds did not move soon, the *Resolution* would be an easy target for the Sun.

Three small starships came streaking towards the *Resolution* as Phan came within striking distance. A quick scan revealed that the advancing ships were not from the Star Federation, and Ashburn fired a warning shot. The hostiles did not balk. They raced towards the *Resolution*, and Lissa and Ashburn began the evasive maneuvers as the three hostiles opened fire.

Piloting the *Resolution* was difficult with just two people.

Montag's crew had consisted of over twenty members, and even that was small considering the size of the ship. With just Lissa and Ashburn, it was all they could do to bend the *Resolution* to the controls. Ashburn focused on the weapons and Lissa took the brunt of the piloting operations. Ashburn managed to keep the pursuers at bay as they raced towards Phan, but something within the ship rattled loose as Lissa pulled the *Resolution* out of the line of enemy fire. An alarm sounded off, and Ashburn had to abandon the pulse cannons and find the problem, but he came sprinting back to the control room after only a few minutes.

"The shield generators are coming loose," he panted lightly as he slipped back into his seat in front of the weapons controls. "I can't fix them."

He would need a steady hand and a steadier ship to secure those generators without damaging them, Lissa knew. At this point, he could not have either. The generators broke loose after another couple of evasive maneuvers, and the *Resolution's* defenses dropped to nothing. Enemy fire tore into the stern almost immediately. The arkins hissed and scraped their claws on the floor as the ship shuddered violently, and Lissa heard Ashburn snarl a curse but the new alarms drowned out the words.

Lissa sent the ship into a headlong rush for the Phanite surface. She pointed them at the first city she saw, hoping to land near at least a few Star Feds. The city lights pulsed with life, glittering hazily through a small gap in the cloudy midnight sky, and Lissa threw all her hope and luck to those lights.

The *Resolution's* stern bucked and rolled as the hostiles kept up the pursuit. Ashburn answered with less agile but much more powerful pulse cannons, but he had to give up the counterattack. The *Resolution* was no top-of-the-line Star Fed cruiser, and the pulse cannons were draining the power supply. Ashburn switched his attention to communications after that, and sent an emergency transmission across as many frequencies as he could.

Good, Lissa thought as she rolled the *Resolution* over again.

One of those was bound to reach the Star Feds now that the ship was this close to the planet. That was too much noise for the Sun to contain.

The *Resolution* rumbled and growled as more enerpulse shots slammed into the hull. More alarms screamed, and minor systems began to fail. Then the ship tore into the Phanite atmosphere, and the ship bumped and bucked its way through the clouds. The hostiles followed, but they stopped firing and fell back a bit as the *Resolution* screamed towards the surface.

Lissa hit the reverse thrusters. The starship slowed and stopped thrashing, but the ride was still rough. Rain lashed at the hull, audible even over the alarms. When the ship hit the treetops, one of the arkins roared, Blade from the sound of it. The ship was slammed back into the air, and Lissa knew that they were moving far too fast to touch down safely at the ground port. She activated the emergency crash settings of her seat, let the thing secure her against the forthcoming impact, told Ashburn to do the same, screamed for the arkins to get away from the walls and brace themselves, and then let the ship fall back into the forest.

The ship burned its way through the trees, smashing a long trail of broken branches and shattered trunks as the forest dragged the speed down. The *Resolution* put up a hard fight, but the trees finally took the ship and broke the wild charge with several thick, sturdy trunks. Lissa considered it no small miracle that the ship had not flipped, but as the ship came up short and fell to the ground, the pain that rattled up her spine was enough to make her forget about miracles all over again.

When she slid out of her seat's restraints, she found that she was mostly unharmed, just had some tenderness in her neck and back that flared into agony when she moved too much. Ashburn suffered the same, although he had hit his knee and would be limping to the city. Orion was all right save for a few bumps, but one of Blade's wings hung limp and bent at her side, broken. One look at the wing, and Lissa bit through her own pain and set off to find the medical supplies.

"We don't have time," Ashburn snapped at her, taking her

by the elbow. "We can heal Blade once we reach the Star Federation."

Lissa pulled out of his grasp and found a small supply of pain relievers in the control room. She wanted to look for something more, but she knew Ashburn was right. The three hostile starships had already reached the crash site and were circling overhead, searching for a clearing large enough to land in.

Lissa gave herself and Ashburn a half dose of painkillers each, and a full one to Blade. The arkin whimpered a little when they set off through the halls, but the drug had taken hold by the time they reached the airlock. Lissa was relieved at first, but then she saw the dazed glaze spreading over the arkin's eyes and concern drowned out all else.

The drop from the airlock to the forest floor was not far, but there was enough distance for Lissa to worry about Blade's wing. The arkin barely paused, however, and jumped down after Ashburn. Her wing hit the ground, hard enough for her to yelp, but she settled again and slowly turned her amber eyes skyward to watch one of the Seventh Sun's ships loop over the crash site. She swayed uneasily as her head traced the flight path.

The fallen leaves mushed under Lissa's feet as she hit the ground, soft and spongy from dampness and rot, and slick with the Phanite rain. Lissa and Ashburn tugged their hoods up, but the rain plastered their jackets against their skin and soaked the arkins.

Light from the *Resolution* spilled out of the open airlock and signaled their position to the circling starships, and Lissa saw one break its flight pattern and angle back towards them. She did not wait for it. She grabbed Blade's head and pulled the arkin through the trees, following the *Resolution's* broken trail back towards the city. Her hands kept slipping on the arkin's wet fur, and Blade ripped her head out of her grip all too easily. Ashburn helped Lissa usher the black arkin along, although Orion was a bigger help. He pressed his shoulder to Blade's uninjured side and pushed her along. When she turned to snap at him, he nipped her shoulder and turned her forward again.

As they moved away from the *Resolution*, the night pressed in. The rain fell freely as they stumbled along the *Resolution's* trail through the dark forest, but the light from the hostile starships illuminated the ground in short bursts as the Sun's ships swung overhead. The trek slowed to a crawl as the mud bogged them down, and Lissa had to lead them off of the *Resolution's* trail when the fallen trees became impossible to navigate. The ground firmed up a bit, and the overhead leaves blocked a surprising amount of rain, but the world was still soaked and dark and sucked at their feet. The Sun's prowling starships lost sight of them and disappeared from the sky quickly enough, but that made Lissa nervous. Their ships surely had scanners, but the Sun already knew where they were heading and did not need to follow them. And now Lissa had no idea where the Seventh Sun's operatives were.

Slowly, very slowly, the glow of the city appeared against the storm and the looming trees became easier to separate from each other. Lissa wanted to pick up the pace but Blade was quickly becoming too hard to manage, even for Orion. They had paused for a short break, hoping the rest would clear the arkin's head, when Lissa heard the *snak* of a misplaced footstep. She whipped her head towards the sound, and the stillness held for three tense heartbeats. Then she saw the shadow move.

"DOWN!" she screamed, and threw herself into Ashburn. She drove him to the ground as the enerpulse shot seared the empty space where his head had been a moment earlier.

They scrambled to their knees as a low growl washed through the trees. Lissa saw a flash of electric blue and heard the massive arkin blunder forward as he leaped for them. Through the sudden terror, she wondered dully how Jet had moved so stealthily before this, but then Orion was between them, roaring at Jet and stamping his paws on the ground. Jet recoiled slightly, surprised to meet a larger arkin than Blade, but he still had a considerable size advantage and he came forward again. Orion met him head on, and the arkins snarled and snapped and scratched their way through the trees. From what Lissa could tell, Jet was trying to get past the gray, but Orion was holding his own and was pushing Jet further and further away.

Lissa rolled off of Ashburn and surged to Blade, crouching over the arkin's head and trying to persuade her to lie down. Blade would be safer on the ground, would blend with the dark leaves and branches and attract no attention if she kept her eyes shut.

Out of the corner of her eye, Lissa saw Ashburn draw an enerpulse pistol and rise up in one smooth motion. He kept his head down as he moved to Lissa's side. He scanned the forest as Lissa tried to whisper Blade down to the ground, and he saw the shadow a split second before she did. He flipped his enerpulse pistol to the shadow and fired. He scored a hit, but he had straightened too much and exposed his chest. The next shot came from a new direction, and hit him in the lower ribs.

Ashburn went down.

Lissa's vision had been seared by the enerpulse shot, but she heard Ashburn's soft *umph* of pain and there was a soft thud as he hit the ground. Blade's head thrashed in her arms and the arkin moaned softly, and then a hand closed on the back of Lissa's jacket and she was yanked away from Blade.

Lissa stumbled backwards under the force of the tug. An arm wrapped around her throat, pinning her head in place, and then there was hungry panting in her ear and the cold bite of a knife blade at the corner of her eye. Someone called out "No!" as the Phantom started to take revenge for a three-year-old wound, but if the someone said anything else, the sudden drunken roar cut them off. Blade's eyes appeared near Lissa's face as she sunk her teeth into the Phantom's arm, and then the knife and the panting and the pressure were gone.

There was a deep cry of pain in Lissa's ear and Blade scratched Lissa's hip as she scrabbled at the Phantom. Lissa yelped and slipped away from the arkin's claws. She took three steps away, tripped over something, *Ashburn*, crawled off of him, checked his injury.

Lissa could not see it, but she knew the wound was bad. She smelled burned cloth and flesh, and she gingerly felt the scorched edges of the wound. There was heat under her fingertips, and the skin felt too soft and slippery, but she also felt that Ashburn was still breathing. He might pull through, she realized, if he could get medical attention quickly enough.

If.

Lissa drew her pistol as she scanned the forest, looking for more moving shadows. She saw Blade dancing with the Phantom, jaws still locked around his arm, and she saw trees and trees and trees and then a leap and dodge as Orion chased Jet even further away. And then there was a screech.

She looked back at Blade and the Phantom. The arkin had released his arm. The Phantom was supporting her weight, but he slowly let her drop. There was a wet sucking sound, and then a *whump* as Blade hit the ground. She landed on her broken wing, but did not cry out.

The Phantom dropped his arms. The knife flashed in the faint light, and something wet dripped off the blade. Not rain. Fresh blood.

Something inside of Lissa broke.

She lost track of her own body. She did not remember moving, but she must have because her blood was running wild and her breath was ragged and angry. Outside of all that, there was only the bright light of the Phantom's heartbeat and her burning desire to snuff it out. There were other heartbeats around her, but she only cared about the one, although several of the others were pressing in and she had to drive them off again because they made it hard to see. Then one heartbeat came too close and something snagged at her hip and something else collided with her head. And then there was a burst of light brighter than all the lives around her. Her vision faded and there were close soft voices and distant shouts and the cloying smells of rain and death and then the world cracked.

CHAPTER 29: BREAK

There was darkness, but Lance could not say for how long. Sometimes, hazy white would swim across his vision, and he would hear voices and fuzzy faces would almost slip into focus. When there were things to almost see, they would seem familiar, and Lance would try to reach out to them with both body and mind, but then the pain would return and the world would fade again. There was always a moment, though, between the pain and the recession of the darkness when everything felt soft and warm and Lance knew he was floating. He could never enjoy those moments because there always seemed to be questions buzzing around his ears. He never fully registered the words, but the questions sounded urgent and he wanted to answer because he knew that there was something important lodged in the back of his mind and he wanted to tell someone about it, but when he focused too hard, the pain would wash back in and he would ebb back out of consciousness.

The darkness wasn't so bad, he decided at one point. There were no questions in the dark, and he was safe and at peace and nothing could touch him. He wanted to stay there forever, just drift through the darkness with nothing else around him. He thought that it would be all right for him to just fall asleep in the dark, just sleep and sleep and never wake up.

He almost did just that.

He drifted through the dark until something hit him in the ribs. Then he just let himself drop to the ground, felt the spongy soil and wet leaves soak up the force of the fall. He shut his eyes and tried to sleep, but something was growling and something else was roaring, then someone was screaming and he had to open his eyes. Dim light filtered through the trees and glowed on the fog, and Lance saw two shapes fighting. The bigger shape was stronger, he saw, but the smaller one was faster and flickered in and out of space like a shadow thrown by candlelight. There were voices in the night and more shapes that moved in to overwhelm the quicker shadow, then the world shattered and Lance's eyes shot open.

He was breathing very hard, he realized, and his vision had been taken over by the light haze again, but everything slowly came into focus: stark walls, immobile wall cots, hovering medical equipment, and very thin blankets.

Starship infirmary, Lance guessed.

He lay on one of the extended wall cots. There was a dull pain in his chest, constant but not unbearable, and he reached up to touch the thin metal band around his head that monitored his vitals.

Still alive, he decided.

He sat up too quickly, and cried out as the pain pierced through him. Dizziness clamped down on his brain and his vision swam in circles, but he managed to stay awake.

I was shot, he remembered. *We were ambushed, and Orion fought the big arkin and Blade was already hurt and Lissa... And Lissa...*

And Lissa.

He looked, but she was not there. Lance was alone. Completely alone.

Part of him wanted to believe that Lissa and the arkins had somehow come through the ambush, that their wounds had healed quicker than his and they did not need any more medical attention. The rest of him remembered the way the ambushers had melted in and out of the darkness, and he just could not bring himself to entertain the maybes.

He moved to the edge of the cot and slowly dropped his bare feet to the ground. He felt the cold shiver up his legs, and the thin garment around his hips did little to keep him warm, but he welcomed the chill. He liked feeling something other than lonely pain.

He pressed his hand to the thick bandage wrapped around his chest, ready to test his pain threshold and see what it would take to knock himself unconscious again, and then the infirmary door hissed open and Captain Stone walked in. He carried a bundle of clothes under one arm and looked at Lance without any sign of relief to see him awake. Lance felt a little colder.

"Don't mess with that," Stone said. "You're healing, but the wound needs a little more time before you can rip the bandage off and go prancing around the galaxy again." He moved to the foot of Lance's cot and glanced at the readings on some of the medical equipment. He nodded before focusing on Lance again. "Just so you know, we found Orion and brought him aboard. He had a few tears and scratches, but nothing serious and we've treated his wounds as best we could, which is pretty good, considering he would not let anyone get close enough to give him a full examination."

Lance had to smile in spite of everything. "I can calm him down if your doctor is willing to take a closer look at him."

"No need," Stone said. "We figured out that he'll stay pretty calm if we kept him in the same room as the black arkin."

Lance did not try to hide his confusion.

"Our search team met with some resistance in the woods, and they were thrown off by the attack, although the ambushers never pressed their advantage and they disappeared after a few quick scuffles. The search party lost the trail after that, but Orion found them and led them back to you and the black arkin. I think he knew that we'd take care of you and him, but he refused to move until we'd taken the black arkin with us."

"And how is she?"

Stone dropped the bundle of clothes on the edge of the wall cot. "She was almost dead when we found her. Nearly bled out from a knife wound in the chest that had almost pierced her heart. The med team patched her up and reset her broken wing, too. They think she'll make a full recovery, but they said something about her being depressed." Stone shook his head. "We put Orion in with her, hoping he'd cheer her up, but all that did was calm your beast down."

"You know why she's upset," Lance said, turning his gaze back to the floor. "We lost Lissa." Out of the corner of his eye, he saw the captain shift his weight back and forth.

"You confirmed as much during your interrogation."

Lance did not move for a long moment. Hazy faces and furry voices drifted across his mind. Then realization dawned on him and he turned to face the captain. "You drilled me while I was under."

"Yes."

"You couldn't wait?"

"Captain Anderson was... growing impatient."

Lance tensed in anger, but pain shot up and down his side, forcing him to calm himself again. "How long was I out?"

"Four sidereal days."

Lance stamped his heel on the ground. Lissa and the Seventh Sun would be light-years away by now, their trail cold.

"We don't have the whole story," Stone said slowly. "Just bits and pieces."

"Well now that I'm awake, what else do you want to know?"

There was no point in hiding anything now, and Lance told the captain about Backélo's death on Ametria, the discovery of the Seventh Sun's base, and the destruction he and Lissa had wrought. No, that *he* had wrought. Lissa had not wanted him to, he explained, but there was no other choice.

Stone listened to the new information with rigid eyes and a

solid frown. When Lance finished the Ametria account with Lissa's reluctance to tell him something, the captain folded his arms. "I may know what she was not saying."

So Lance listened to Stone's recount of the fake report and the encounter with the Seventh Sun's operatives at the hospital, the discovery of Aven, and Dr. Chhaya's warning about the Sun and the Awakenings. By the time the captain had finished, the cold had crept all the way up Lance's spine.

"That must be what they were doing on that base," Lance breathed, "and what they're going to do to her." He thought back to Lissa's fear of the Sun, and knew that if he had been in her position, he would have been terrified, too. Even now, sitting on a starship surrounded by Star Federation soldiers with painkillers nibbling at the edge of his mind, Lance felt a little afraid. "They're building an army."

"From what I understand, it's an army that does not feel pain unless it does not kill."

Lance shut his eyes tight and tried to ignore the sudden throbbing in his head. "This is enough to reinstate absolute military rule across the galaxy and trigger another purge."

Stone sighed, very quietly. "Once, I might have said that another purge might not be such a bad thing."

"And now?"

Another sigh, heavy this time. "Now, a doctor's told me that some Nandros would rather be asleep." He began to pace across the length of Lance's cot, his footsteps surprisingly light for someone of his height and build. "The Nandros that work for the Sun should be enough to make me scream, 'That's not true,' but I keep thinking about the Nandro we met on the *Argonaught IV*." He stopped pacing. "The Shadow. Lissa, right?"

Lance nodded.

Stone was quiet for a long time. When he spoke, his voice was just as heavy as the sigh had been. "If one of the deadliest people in the galaxy is afraid of being Awake, there is no way there aren't a bunch of other Neo-Andromedans out there shitting themselves in terror. If we purge because of the

Seventh Sun and their plans, we are going to kill a lot of innocent people."

"Exactly. And more likely than not, we will drive the survivors to the Sun. Then we will have war."

Stone sighed again, and he looked as though he carried the weight of all the living and the dead throughout the galaxy on his shoulders. "I just don't know what our next move has to be."

Lance knew. "We need to talk to Aven. Small-scale interrogation, one-on-one would be best." He slowly pushed himself to his feet, waited for his head to clear, then reached for the clothes Stone had brought for him. "I should be the one to—" He stopped when he realized what Stone had given him.

Traveler's clothes. Not a Star Federation uniform. Lance was not just a patient in the infirmary. He was a prisoner.

Stone shifted again. "I'm sorry. I should have said something sooner, but…"

"Expulsion?"

"Suspension, at least until the higher ups have a better idea of what's been going on."

Lance breathed a sigh of relief. "If I can talk to them, that shouldn't take long at all." Stone's silence was enough to make him go cold all over again. "This isn't a normal suspension, is it?"

"I told you that Erica was getting impatient. We should have waited for you to regain consciousness on your own, and then asked you questions, but she…" Stone's voice caught on something, and Lance saw how hard the captain struggled to get the next words out. "Commander Keraun has asked her to report directly to him. Based on what you'd told her, and what she's relayed back to him, he's decided to take over the mission himself. He has full approval from the admirals. He's coming from half-way across the galaxy, and he's dropping the body of the bounty hunter Starcat at the main space station first, but he's coming."

"I'm sorry," Lance said. He knew what this meant for

Captains Stone and Anderson. Erica Anderson was doing her duty as a Star Federation soldier, but from Jason Stone's face, Lance knew that he had placed more value on their relationship than she had. That relationship was something that might have died on its own within a year if the two had not learned to balance their clashing goals and personalities, but with someone like Keraun around, a year could shrink to a single day.

Stone grunted and shook himself back to reality. "If Keraun finds out about the Awakenings, he will initiate the purge."

Lance frowned at the captain. "If?"

Stone shrugged. "I may not have helped Anderson with the interrogation as much as I should have."

Stunned, Lance managed to ask what it was exactly that Keraun did not know.

"You and I are the only Star Feds who know about the Awakenings, and Aven. Everything else is on record, or will be, once I fill in the gaps about how you destroyed the base and how Backélo died, but that's all."

"Does he know that there is a main base?"

"Yes."

"And possibly several other smaller bases?"

"Yes. But as far as the Nandros are concerned, that's all that he has to go on. It's not enough to initiate a purge."

Lance nodded. That wasn't much, but it was something.

Stone refolded his arms. "You said you wanted to talk to Aven?"

He shrugged. "I'm not going to have that chance now, am I?"

"But if you did?"

"Then yes, I'd talk to him about finding the Sun. But I'd also talk to him about finding Lissa."

"You'd go after her?"

Lance considered the clothes sitting on the cot again. He reached for the bundle. "Aven is your best chance of finding the Seventh Sun. Lissa is your best chance of coming out of the encounter with your lives."

"How would you find her?"

Lance laughed without humor. "I'd ask a shadow. Or half of one, at least." He saw the confusion on the captain's face, and smiled hollowly again. "Aven was the Shadow before he got sick. Lissa only took over five years ago."

Jason Stone did not even try to hide his surprise.

"Make sure Keraun does not find out about that, either."

"No, definitely not." Stone shook his head. "That makes Aven more of a threat than I thought he was, but we don't need Keraun storming a hospital. Aside from the fact that Aven would not be able to defend himself, how would that look, the Star Federation attacking a half-dead victim of the Banthan virus?"

"That's a smear the Star Federation can't afford." Lance sank back on to the cot and began to struggle with the clothes, but the pain in his chest stopped him every time he stretched his arms or bent his torso too far. "Aven might know where they've taken Lissa. Or he might at least be able to give you a lead." He tried to dress again, but again the pain pulled him back. "You'd have to be careful, though. He probably won't like a full interrogation team, and if Keraun finds him..." He gave up on the clothes, panting.

"Here," Stone said, stepping to his side. "Let me help."

"No, I can—"

"Ashburn, we don't have time for this." He picked up the shirt. "Stand up."

Lance sighed once, very quietly, then swallowed his pride. When he was finally dressed, Stone helped him struggle into his boots.

"Aven probably won't talk to anyone from the Star Federation, will he?" Stone asked as, with a team effort, they fastened the last buckle.

"No," Lance said, his voice stiff with embarrassment.

Stone ignored the shame, picked up the jacket and helped Lance haltingly fight his way into it. "What about you, then?"

"Me?"

"Yeah."

"Why?"

"I've watched you climb the ranks, Ashburn. I've served over you, with you, and under you, and I've hated it. I don't like you." He faced Lance squarely, stared him dead in the eye. "But I do know you, and I know that if I get you off of this ship, you are going to do everything you can to keep the galaxy safe, and that's what matters."

"You'd get me off the ship?"

"I'd get you off the damn ship," Stone growled.

Lance felt a small flicker of hope, but he balked at the offer all the same. Life as a Star Federation soldier was all he knew. The few years he'd spend away from the organization had left him broken and terrified. Orion had given him the motivation he needed to make his way back to the Star Federation, and he had never wavered from the life since. If he left now, he would be on his own again, and this time, he would not be able to come back. "If I leave," he said, "I will be court-martialed."

"Yes," Stone said simply, "but what would you do if you stayed?"

Spend days, maybe months trying to convince the higher ups that we can't attack the Neo-Andromedans, Lance realized. *And no matter how convincing I am, we'll run out of time.*

He had to go. He had to break from the Star Federation and operate on his own. He might get further than the Star Federation could, might even find Lissa, but then again, he might fail. If he stayed, he would fail.

I have to go.

Lance took a deep breath to steady himself, then committed to the decision. "When the higher ups learn that I'm gone for good, someone is going to get pulled up to fill the void. If it's you, you'd better keep Keraun in check."

"It won't be me," Stone said. He did not seem upset, just certain. "If anyone, it will be R—Eri..." He sighed heavily. "Captain Anderson."

Lance nodded, knowing that Stone was right. Anderson

and Stone were both among the best captains in the Star Federation, but between the two of them, she was the better soldier. Stone was a much better pilot, and was more in-tune with his subordinates, but Anderson was more dedicated to the Star Federation, more levelheaded, and would be more willing to make the necessary sacrifices.

"If she's promoted," Lance said, "you'd better talk to her before Keraun takes complete control. Somebody needs to be there to stop him. If they're not... Well, it's Keraun."

Stone grunted again. "Yeah." He turned and entered something into one of the machines next to the cot. It beeped twice, then spat out a syringe and six stimulators, five full doses and one half. Stone picked up the syringe and tugged Lance's sleeve up. "This is an immunity booster for infection, and a pain killer to help you move easier." The needle pricked into Lance's arm, and the muscle burned as Stone pressed the syringe down. "But don't push yourself too hard or you'll set yourself back at least a day in the healing process."

"Yes, Dr. Stone."

Stone's eyes were two dark fires as he looked at Lance. He reached over, grabbed the half-dose stim, and shot it into Lance's arm in one quick motion. Lance jumped as the hot pain raced up his arm.

"Half-dose today so that you don't kill yourself." He grabbed the other stims and dumped them into Lance's hands. "Careful how you use the others. I don't want to find your body in the middle of a Phanite forest shot up with stims."

Lance slipped the stimulators into his pocket.

"Take the first shuttle," Stone said. "Standard Star Fed security code so you can get in easily enough, but it has an advanced signal scrambler and it's quick enough to get you to Phan before we can catch you. Anderson will know where you're heading, but at least she won't know where you'll land."

"Thanks," Lance said earnestly. "What about the arkins?"

"Across the hall, three rooms down. No stationary guards, but we do have a patrol so move fast. And Ashburn?"

Lance waited, and saw displeasure and resignation work

their ways across the captain's face.

"You'd better make this escape believable."

Lance blinked and half-raised his arm, wincing in pain. "And how do you propose I do that?"

"We're in a medical bay. There's a machine right behind me that will spit out all sorts of drugs at the push of a button. You can figure out the rest."

CHAPTER 30: PROMISE

It turned out that the tranquilizer Lance hit Jason Stone with was one of the better ones, and the captain had dropped almost immediately. The captain hit his head on a machine on the way down, and Lance worried that he might wake up with a concussion, but at the very least, that would add credibility to the story that Lance had attacked the captain and drugged him before escaping. Captain Anderson would pick apart the details, Lance knew, and Stone would have to hold his own against her once he came to. Lance doubted that the story would hold up, but that was out of his hands now.

The pain of the enerpulse wound flared up again shortly after Lance left the medical bay, but the stims and painkillers took the edge away and let him move.

He found the arkins where Stone had said they would be. When Lance opened the door to their room, he found them lying on the ground, Blade curled up in a tight ball with her injured wing stretched out. Orion was pressed up against her back with his head next to hers, but he snapped upright when the door opened. He took one look at Lance and surged to his feet, but Blade needed some coaxing. Even after they managed to get her on her feet, she hung her head and dragged her wing as she trudged out the door. Orion ducked under the injured wing and propped it off the ground, then pushed his shoulder into Blade's and spurred her on. She snapped at him, once and without any real malice, and in response, he nipped her ear and prodded her forward.

The shuttle was not far from that room, and Lance managed to bypass the security and sneak the arkins onboard before the patrol came around. But his head was still foggy, and it took him a little longer than it should have to power up the shuttle and begin the sprint back to Phan.

As the shuttle tore away from the starship, Lance kept an eye on the trackers. The ship was not on high alert, and the shuttle launch would not have signaled an alarm in the control room, but he watched all the same. He half-expected the starship to pivot and come ripping after him, but he snuck away cleanly.

Lance set a direct course for Phan and then tried to busy himself with other tasks, but his mind was still thick and sludgy. He found focusing difficult, but even if he had been clear and alert, he still would have had trouble with the controls.

The arkins had settled just behind his seat. Their breathing sawed at the edges of his mind in a set rhythm, although he had the feeling that Blade's breaths were the main offenders. Her gaze had not left him since they had boarded the shuttle. Lance felt her eyes on the back of his head now, steady and persistent as an unreachable itch.

Finally, Lance could take it no more. Gently, he swiveled in his seat, wincing as less intense pain pricked at him. He slowly lowered himself to the floor, seating himself just in front of the arkins, and met Blade's stare. He expected intensity. Seething rage, boiling frustration, something. There was none of that. Instead, Blade's eyes were wide and empty. She stared blankly at Lance, not quite waiting for something, but not demanding any action, either.

Lance had never seen such sad eyes before.

"We'll find her," he promised. The words came out as a weak whisper.

Blade whimpered in response, then shut her eyes and turned her face away.

Orion lifted his head from the ground. He stretched his neck, sniffed Blade's cheek, and then rested his chin on her shoulder. His eyes curved towards Lance, bright yellow against the slash of dark fur across his gray face. His eyes were not sad, but Blade's depression was affecting him, and he was doing his best to pull her back.

Lance rubbed the back of his hand against Orion's ear, and the arkin sighed contentedly and turned his head into the contact. Lance knew that had he been taken instead of Lissa, Orion would have been just as downcast as Blade. Although, he wasn't so sure that Lissa would have come after him.

Pointless guessing, Lance realized through the druggy fog of his mind. He would never have been taken. Not alive. There would have been nothing to come after.

That hadn't stopped Lissa from saving his life on Ametria, though. At the very least, he owed her that much of a debt.

Lance pulled himself back into his seat at the control panel, wincing a little as his enerpulse wound groaned in protest. He turned back to the controls, but found himself staring at the display the galaxy presented to him. Shuttles were not built like starships, and they came with a thick, sturdy window at their rounded noses. Lance sat riveted as the stars stretched and then dissolved as the shuttle ran up to top speed.

It was a little unnerving, traveling faster than light in a shuttle. Once they broke the light barrier, there was just blackness. He was reminded of the darkness he had floated in before regaining consciousness, and he remembered his desire to sleep and never wake up. He shuddered at the memory, and tried not to think about it again. He was still alive, after all, and there was a lot of work ahead of him.

And yet, the galaxy was a terrifyingly large place to lose someone in.

Aven will know where to look.

Or the brother's mind may have already dissolved.

Lance shook his head, forcing the doubts to scatter

themselves into the drug fog. Aven had to know. And even if he didn't, Lance would not give up. He may have lived most of his life as a solider, and had the Star Federation behind his every step, but somewhere along the way, he had learned how to hunt. He couldn't compare to Alpha Class bounty hunters, but no one ever just disappeared. There would be a trail to follow, and shadows to chase far beyond the last few stars of the galaxy.

Lance glanced over his shoulder at the arkins. Orion watched him steadily, but Blade had opened her eyes again and it was her gaze that Lance met.

The sad, empty void had been filled. There was a question there now, and a spark that begged to be fanned. Lance forced himself to focus on the spark, and in spite of the dull edges of his mind and the pain in his chest that constantly burned at the outskirts of his awareness, he felt very calm, and ready for whatever was coming.

"We'll find her," Lance said again. This time, the words were heavy with determination, and they lent a little of their strength back to Lance. He turned back to the black emptiness of space, and only looked forward. "I swear it."

ABOUT THE AUTHOR

K. N. Salustro is a writer from New Jersey
who loves outer space, dragons, and good stories.
When not at her day job, she runs an Etsy shop as a
plush artist, and makes art for her Society6
and Redbubble shops.

This is her first novel.

For updates, new content, and other news,
you can follow K. N. Salustro on:

Wordpress: https://knsalustro.wordpress.com/

Facebook: https://www.facebook.com/knsalustro/

Twitter: https://twitter.com/knsalustro